7

This book is to be ret
the last date st

THE GREENWOODERS
GANG

THE GREENWOODERS GANG

Geoffrey Palmer and Noel Lloyd

Illustrated by Meg Davies

The Book Guild Ltd
Sussex, England

Published in Great Britain in 2003 by
The Book Guild Ltd
25 High Street
Lewes, East Sussex
BN7 2LU

First published 1963, 1964 by Dobson Books Ltd

Typesetting in Souvenir Light by
Keyboard Services, Luton, Bedfordshire

Printed in Great Britain by
Antony Rowe Ltd, Chippenham, Wiltshire

A catalogue record for this book is
available from the British Library

ISBN 1 85776 706 3

For Pat and Lorna Quorn,
who made the book possible,
and for Meg Davies,
for her inimitable illustrations

CONTENTS

THE BARROW

Stephen Moore tumbled out of his father's car, followed by Beauty, his spaniel. He waved goodbye to his father and Doctor Moore's Jaguar moved off as the boy and the dog ran up to the Vicarage gate.

Upstairs in the attic playroom of the Vicarage at Edwinton the sound of the car drew Tony Brooks to the window. 'Here's Stephen now,' he said. 'That means we're all here.'

Peter Christy put down the comic he was reading and joined Tony at the window. He and his twin sister Pauline, ten years old, were the youngest members of the Greenwooders. Tony and Stephen, with only a few months between them, were nearly thirteen. Felicity Brooks, Tony's sister, was almost twelve, and Sam Peat six months younger.

They had decided to call themselves the Greenwooders after some quite acrimonious discussion. Tony's first suggestion had been the Merry Men, seeing that they lived in the Robin Hood country, but Felicity and Pauline had poured scorn on that. 'We're not men,' Felicity said indignantly, and added, 'and neither are you yet. It would be a silly name.'

'What about the Sherwood Foresters?' Sam had asked. 'That could include both sexes.'

1

'It's a bit too much like a regiment or a football team,' objected Stephen, 'and it sounds as though there are more of us than there really are.'

Then there was a lot of brow furrowing, head scratching and hastily disposed-of offerings. It was Felicity who came up with the Greenwooders, and its acceptance by the others pleased and surprised her. It was not often she said or did anything that gained their approval. Usually it was 'Oh, Felicity!' from Tony or sighs and raised eyebrows from Stephen. (Sam, of course, was her devoted slave, and believed that every word she uttered was a jewel.) So the Greenwooders became the name of the six-strong gang, and Peter's protest that woods weren't always green had met with the scorn it deserved. 'Ever heard of evergreens?' his sister had hissed at him.

Peter sighed at the powerful car driving smoothly off and almost decided there and then to start saving up for a Jaguar. But he had rifled his money-box only the day before to buy a model car and that had taken enough saving up for, so he thought he would postpone starting his Jaguar account until after the holidays. He withdrew his head from the window and said eagerly, 'Can I go down and let Stephen in?'

'All right,' said Tony, 'but don't make Beauty bark. If Prince hears him he'll kick up a rumpus and my father is working in his study.'

Peter opened the door, but before he could get a foot outside Felicity stopped him. 'Don't slide down the banisters,' she said. 'Last time you kicked some varnish off and we got blamed.'

Peter looked shocked. 'As if I would,' he said, and darted out.

2

The attic was the Greenwooders' headquarters and on the first day of the holidays it was their custom to meet and discuss what they would do during the weeks to come. The Vicarage was large and rambling, and some rooms were unused. Tony's father, the Vicar, had given the children a choice of rooms for their own playroom, but the oddly shaped attic, with its sloping roof and the splendid view of Sherwood Forest from its windows, had almost chosen itself. One great advantage, which had not occurred to them until after they had chosen it, was that they could make as much noise as they liked without bothering the grown-ups, and this was quite a consideration during some of their more lively discussions.

Meetings never took place at the houses of the other Greenwooders. There was no spare room at the doctor's house and in any case noise would not have been welcome. Doctor Moore could be decidedly tetchy on occasions, though he was much better than he used to be. Stephen's mother had died when he was a baby and the household was ruled by Old Eva, as she was affectionately known to everybody in the village. (Only the postman, delivering an occasional letter to Miss Frampton, could have divulged her surname.) Old Eva was a stickler for boring things like tidiness and cleanliness but Stephen had his own way of getting round her, and in spite of her sharp tongue she was putty in his hands.

Peter and Pauline Christy's parents kept the Post Office. The living quarters behind the shop were only just big enough for the four of them as it was, and when the new baby arrived in the summer they would be even more cramped. Peter had suggested that he would be

3

happy to move into a tent in the back garden but he had not expected his kind offer to be taken seriously, and he was right.

There would have been room for the Greenwooders at the farmhouse where Sam Peat lived with his mother and father, but it was a long way from the village. Besides, as Sam pointed out, there were so many odd jobs to do on a farm that they could never have been sure of being undisturbed for more than five minutes. Sam's father was one of their great friends but he had a habit of suggesting that they might like to help mucking out the pigs or leading in the cows when they would rather have been playing in the fields.

The Vicarage, then, proved the ideal meeting place, and although Tony and Felicity lived there officially the other Greenwooders felt almost equally at home.

Stephen Moore reached the attic with Peter behind him and a panting dog bringing up the rear. Stephen was tall for his age, red-haired and with an Irish temper which occasionally got the better of him. 'Hi,' he said, taking his accustomed place on the broken-down sofa.

'Hi,' said the others. Beauty snuffled around happily then flopped down with his head on his master's feet and promptly went to sleep.

'Where's Prince?' Stephen asked.

'He's with Dad in the study,' Felicity replied. 'Dad pretends not to spoil him but he does really, like anything, and Prince adores it.' She paused, and her tone grew reminiscent. 'Doesn't it seem ages since Miss Pope-Cunningham gave us Bunty's puppies?'

'I wouldn't be without Chummy for anything. He's marvellous at working the hedges and driving birds from

4

the low coverts. My Dad says there's nothing like a cocker spaniel,' said Sam.

'Except another cocker spaniel,' said Peter. 'Our George is a daft little dog. All he does is chew things. There's hardly a slipper left in the house. Considering that George and Chummy and Prince and Beauty are all brothers it's strange how different they are.'

'Not so strange when you consider how different Tony and Felicity are,' Stephen observed.

'But they're brother and sister...' Peter began.

'Oh, don't be so literal!' said Stephen.

Tony clapped his hands for order. 'Let's get down to business and discuss what we're going to do during the next three weeks. I've got an idea but I'd like to hear what the rest of you think first.'

Felicity wrinkled her brows. 'I suppose we couldn't...' she began. 'No ... that wouldn't do ... I know, what about ... no that wouldn't be possible ... should we ... no...'

The others gazed at her. Stephen shook his head at Tony and raised his eyebrows. 'Isn't she marvellous?' Tony said in a voice of wonder. 'People would pay to see her if we put her in a side-show. Well, Felicity, what is your great scheme?'

'I can't think of one,' Felicity said humbly.

'Well, at least we can relax now. Have you got any ideas, Sam?'

Sam shook his head gloomily. 'I shan't be able to be with you very much, there's so much work to be done on the farm at this time of the year. I might be able to get away sometimes but I can't make any definite arrangements.'

'Stephen?'

'Just messing about, I suppose. If the weather's fine we can spend most of the time in the forest, practising archery, climbing trees, having picnics, bird watching – things like that. And don't forget we've got some holiday homework.'

There was a concerted groan from Tony, Felicity and Sam who, with Stephen, went to the High School at Retfield, twelve miles from Edwinton. 'Why remind us of that?' Felicity demanded. 'I've got some History to do – an essay on the causes and effects of the Hundred Years' War. Why on earth they had to go on fighting all that time, goodness knows. You'd think they'd have got tired long before the end. I wouldn't have minded learning some Shakespeare, but wars ... ugh!'

'We've got some Chemistry experiments to write up, haven't we, Stephen?' said Tony. 'But they shouldn't take too long if we get together over them.'

'I've also got an essay to do,' said Stephen, 'one that I handed in at the end of the term which old Simpkin said he couldn't read.'

Sam sighed. 'I'm the unluckiest. I've got to read a book. A whole book, not just a chapter,' he added disgustedly. 'What's more, I've got to write out the plot, so I can't just pretend that I've read it. I suppose you wouldn't like to read it for me, Felicity?' He tried to put on a soulful expression which did not match his snub nose and general air of independence.

'Sorry.' Felicity shook her head. 'If the Hundred Years' War had only lasted fifty years I might have had the time.'

Tony brought matters to a head by raising his voice. 'This is my plan!'

'This is my plan!'

The noise stopped. Stephen resumed his seat and Felicity draped herself against the bookcase, like a picture of the actress Sarah Bernhardt she had once seen. 'Let's have it, master mind,' she said.

'I've been reading a book about prehistoric Britain, about Neolithic people, the Beaker Folk, the Food Vessel tribes, the Celtic invasions, Stonehenge, and suchlike.' Pauline gazed at him open-mouthed. She had never heard of any of them except Stonehenge and thought Tony wonderfully clever even to remember the names.

'And especially about barrows,' Tony went on.

'Barrows?' Sam cocked an eyebrow. 'Did they have barrows in those days? To wheel stones about, I suppose.'

'Barrows,' said Tony, looking at him severely, 'are graves, sort of mounds. They are houses of earth or stone that prehistoric people used to bury their dead in. Inside there are rooms and all kinds of things have been found inside ... skeletons, for instance...'

'Ugh!' shuddered Pauline.

'...skeletons, pots, tools and weapons, jewellery and ornaments. These barrows are found all over the country. There are long ones, round ones, small ones and big ones. Some are made all of stone, some of earth and covered by grass. You've heard of Sutton Hoo, haven't you?'

'Sutton what? I mean, Sutton who?' Peter looked at the others in a bewildered way.

'I knew you were going to say that,' Tony said resignedly.

Peter grinned.' Well...' he said.

Tony went on. 'Sutton Hoo Barrow was discovered in 1939. Inside it was the impression of a Saxon burial ship and some wonderful jewellery and gold plate – now in the British Museum,' he added like a kindly schoolmaster.

'Seen it,' said Sam, 'when we had our form trip last year.'

'Did you really?' said Tony, his eyes brightening. 'You lucky thing. Well, as I was saying, barrows – all over the place. And if so, why not here, at Edwinton? And if there

8

is, why don't we excavate one and dig up whatever is inside?'

'Sounds easy,' said Stephen, 'but can you do it just like that? Wouldn't you have to get somebody's permission?'

'Pooh,' said Tony, which didn't seem a very satisfactory answer but nobody questioned it.

'But how do we find a thingummy – a barrow?' asked Sam. 'What does it look like?'

'I told you – a grassy mound. Now, think hard, everybody – where is there such a thing around here?'

They took on various attitudes suggesting deep concentration. Only Beauty's heavy breathing broke the silence.

'I don't remember ever seeing anything like that,' said Stephen eventually.

'Nor me,' said Sam.

Felicity, Pauline and Peter continued to look dumb.

'Well, I know where there's one,' Tony said triumphantly, 'and you ought to know it too, Sam, considering it's in one of your fields!'

Sam looked up enquiringly. 'Which one?'

'The one right at the edge of your land, just before you get to Hunter's Copse. Don't you call it Tump Rise?'

'I know where you mean,' Sam said slowly. 'That old bit of pasture that Dad says is no good because the grass is so poor and the soil is worn out. There is a sort of little swelling in it . . .'

'That's right,' Tony said. 'That's what made me start thinking. In my book there's a barrow somewhere in Gloucestershire called Hetty Pegler's Tump. I don't know who Hetty Pegler was but her tump is a barrow. That's probably why your field is called Tump Rise, you see.'

'I don't know about that. I asked my Dad about it once and he said all it meant was "the hump" and must somehow have got changed to "tump",' Sam said.

'All the same, it's worth having a go,' said Tony. 'It'd be easy to get your Dad's permission to dig, wouldn't it?'

Sam grinned. Tony's growing excitement had infected him. 'Especially if we don't ask him first! I'm game to try!'

Stephen got up quickly, dislodging Beauty, who flopped to the floor, opened one eye briefly and went to sleep again. 'What will we need?'

'I'll look in my book again,' said Tony, 'and find out exactly what they do. We'll start first thing tomorrow morning. Picnic lunch, everybody, and boots. Who knows, perhaps we'll make history!'

'Or get blisters,' Felicity whispered to Pauline.

'I hope we don't find that Tump Rise is just a big molehill,' said Sam.

'It would have to be an enormous mole to throw up a hill like that,' Tony replied.

'Moles are blind,' said Peter, for no reason at all except that he thought he was being left out of the conversation.

'Lucky moles, they won't be able to see you,' Tony said. 'Let's go down and have a look in the potting shed and see what we can take.'

The meeting broke up. The three bigger boys clattered down the stairs first, talking in enthusiastic tones of the next day's digging. Peter waited till they had got to the hall before he took a surreptitious trip down the banisters. Felicity and Pauline showed far less enthusiasm and stayed behind for a few minutes.

'Do you know what I think?' Felicity asked.

10

'What?'

'That we're going to have a very dreary time tomorrow – just digging and digging – getting hot and dirty and finding nothing.'

Pauline sighed in sympathy. 'And the boys will order us about, and we'll do everything wrong and get told off. Do we have to go, Felicity?'

'If we don't we'll never hear the end of it. Besides, it's one of the Greenwooders' rules that whatever we do we do together. Remember what a job we had to get the boys to agree to that?'

'Mmm. Oh well, perhaps it won't be too bad. When it's all over we can think of something to do and they'll have to come in with us,' said Pauline.

Felicity's voice sank to a whisper although they were alone. 'I'm worried about one thing, though.'

'What is it?'

'Promise you won't tell?'

'Cross my heart,' said Pauline, making an elaborate gesture.

'I'm frightened of worms! If we find any when we're digging I shall scream!'

'Goodness,' said Miss Pope-Cunningham, 'you look as though you're going to be very busy.'

The children were passing her house on their way to Peat's Farm. She was working in her garden, dressed as usual in a bizarre outfit, which this time consisted of a man's long raincoat, a scarf tied tightly round her head and wellington boots several sizes too large. The Greenwooders were laden with gardening tools of every

11

description – spades, forks, trowels, a pair of shears, a sieve, and a ball of thick twine.

They stopped as Miss Pope-Cunningham spoke to them. Beauty snuffled round the gate. He could smell Bunty, his mother, who was worrying a piece of stick further up the path.

'We're going excavating,' said Tony politely.

'That sounds very exciting. I suppose you wouldn't like to come and excavate my garden? It's an absolute wilderness. I haven't had time to do anything to it since Mr Chesworth went down with a bad back.'

The Greenwooders looked at each other, slightly embarrassed. The same thought occurred to all three of them. Miss Pope-Cunningham lived on her own and they knew how difficult it must be to keep her large garden in order without help. They ought to offer – but they just couldn't. Archaeology was much more important. Stephen stepped into the breach.

'We'd like to help you with the garden, but it's not possible today, I'm afraid,' he said. 'Would you like us to come back later in the week?'

'That's very kind of you, but I didn't really mean it,' Miss Pope-Cunningham smiled. 'You're on holiday and I'm sure you have much more interesting things to do. No, I wield a nifty spade when I get started – and start I must. This convolvulus seems to spring up faster than I can cut it down! Goodbye! Happy excavating!'

Soon the children had left the houses at the edge of the village behind and were in the open country. They walked along the grass track at the side of the main road until they came to Hoggit's Lane, which led to the farm.

The farm lay about a quarter of a mile from the main

road, an untidy straggle of redbrick buildings which looked as though they had ripened in the sunshine of many years. The farmhouse itself was solid and square, with symmetrically placed windows, but in the two hundred years since it had been built there had been so many additions and alterations that the original shape was only just detectable. The outhouses and barns made three sides of a square round the house. Outside the square on one side was the stackyard, and on the other a fenced-in paddock in which hens, ducks and geese roamed, and an aged donkey spent his time flicking away flies with his tail. Fields, both arable and pasture, covered many acres, and beyond the last field, Tump Rise, the first trees of Sherwood Forest rose in a thin array like the vanguard of an advancing army.

Whatever the season of the year, Hoggit's Lane always seemed to be muddy. Halfway along it a gate into one of the fields on the left-hand side led on to a narrow bridle path that followed the course of the River Medding on its way from Retfield through Edwinton to Ollerthorp, the next village, a couple of miles away. The Medding ran shallowly over pebbles, and bushes and trees leaned over it at such an acute angle that it was a wonder they did not fall into the water. Occasionally there was a break in the undergrowth and it was possible to clamber down the bank and fish for minnows in the clear water, or paddle in a small stretch where the pebbles gave way to sand. Tall willowherb grew on the banks, and clusters of golden kingcups. There were bursts of celandines and a riot of pink and white campion. The field through which the path ran was carpeted with cowslips and clover.

Sam led the gang through the gate and along the bridle

path until they came to a wooden bridge only two planks wide which crossed the stream. They stopped for a moment on the bridge, watching the water gurgling over a little weir. A water rat popped an inquisitive head out of its hole in the bank, blinked at them with two bright beads, decided they were up to no good, and disappeared with a twitch of its whiskers. Some yards down the stream a streak of green and blue flashed across the water, hardly there before it was gone.

'A kingfisher!' cried Pauline. 'I'm sure it was!'

'I often see it,' remarked Sam. 'It's got a nest round here.'

'Oh, Sam, and you never told us!'

'You never asked me,' replied Sam. 'Come on, we'd better get moving.'

They crossed the bridge and got into another field, across which a path led diagonally to the opposite corner. After that there was only one more field to cross and then they had by-passed the farm buildings and were behind the stackyard. In single file they passed through an orchard, went through a little gate, crossed two more fields, one with cows in, and at last reached the end of the farm territory, bounded by dark trunks of a small plantation of fir trees known as Hunter's Copse.

'Well, this is Tump Rise,' Sam said. He pointed to a large swelling in the ground about a hundred yards away. 'And I suppose that this is your barrow.'

Tony's eyes had widened with excitement. 'Yes, that's it! Look, it's sort of round. I bet there's a Bronze Age person buried underneath it ...'

* * *

14

About an hour later Stephen leaned on his spade and mopped his brow. 'Phew,' he called across to Tony. 'This is hot work! How are you getting on?'

'Not bad,' Tony called back.

'You've hardly scratched the surface yet,' Sam said jokingly. He was digging upwards towards the centre of the mound.

'You've had more practice at digging than we have,' Stephen said. 'I bet your shoulders don't ache like mine do!'

Peter, who was helping Stephen and Tony in turn, threw down his gardening fork and ran to the top of the mound. 'I'm the king of the castle,' he sang, 'and I say that we should have a drink break.'

'What a good idea,' said Stephen.

They put down their tools, fetched their bags and squatted down on the grass.

'Hey, Peter, have you been eating the soil?' asked Stephen as he noticed the colour of Peter's face. Peter brushed his face with his hand to get rid of some of the dirt but only succeeded in making it worse.

'Can't help it,' Peter shrugged. 'I had an itchy nose and I scratched it, that's all.'

'You'll have to wash in the stream before your mother sees you,' Tony warned, 'or she won't let you come again.'

'I'm allowed to get dirty in the holidays,' said Peter righteously, tilting his drink bottle up to his mouth and letting the gassy liquid gurgle down his throat.

'What about the girls?' said Sam suddenly.

'Gosh,' said Tony, 'I'd quite forgotten about them. I'd better leave some drink for Felicity. I wonder how they're doing, washing our finds at the pond.'

'Do you think there's anything important yet?' asked Stephen.

'I bet there's a huge gold noggit,' said Peter.

'Nugget,' Tony corrected him. 'No,' he went on in answer to Stephen, 'I shouldn't think so – not yet. We'll have to go deeper, but it's as well to check up as we go along.'

'All I've found,' said Sam, 'is half an old iron hinge. Dunno how that got there.'

'Perhaps it's off the door to the burrow,' Peter said.

'Barrow,' said Tony wearily. 'And they didn't have doors – at least, I don't think they did.'

'What time are we going to have our picnic?' Peter asked.

'At lunchtime,' said Tony. 'Why do you ask when we've just had a drink break? Come on, let's get back to work.'

The four of them picked up their tools and set to work again, though not with quite the same enthusiasm they had started off with.

Meanwhile, over by the pond beyond the clump of trees in the far corner of Tump Rise, Felicity and Pauline were sharing a bar of chocolate. On the ground beside them was the sieve, filled with newly washed stones.

'We ought to get back,' said Pauline.

'Soon,' said Felicity, her mouth full of caramel. 'We might as well wait here as by their silly old dig.'

Pauline didn't really think so. Unlike Felicity she was just a bit excited by the whole idea. 'They might find something while we're away,' she said.

16

'Fat chance of that,' said Felicity scornfully, gesturing towards the sieve of cleaned stones. 'A few more dozen of those for us to carry, more likely. I don't fancy having to wash all the stones in Nottinghamshire.'

'Tony said you can never tell what a thing might be until it's been properly washed.'

Felicity snorted. 'Perhaps he can't, but I'm willing to make a good guess.'

'I know!' cried Pauline. 'Let's take some water from the pond over to the dig. It'll save having to bring all the stones here.'

'What in?' asked Felicity. 'The sieve?'

Pauline laughed. 'We might find an old tin can.'

Felicity considered the suggestion. She was rather pleased at being away from the boys – they were being so serious about the whole business – but on the other hand there was just a chance that they might find something interesting, and it would be terrible to miss that.

'There's a tin box we brought our sandwiches in – that might do. I wish Stephen could teach Beauty how to tell a stone from a – whatever it is we're looking for.'

'Bones,' said Pauline.

Felicity grimaced. 'Eeuh!' Then she brightened.

'Hey, Beauty could tell a bone from a stone. All dogs can recognise bones. Let's suggest that when we get back. Whatever they find can be thrown to Beauty and he can scrape the mud off.'

'He might take it away and bury it,' said Pauline.

She sighed, the conversation was getting nowhere. 'Shall we go back and see if your tin will hold water?' she asked.

Felicity jumped up. 'I suppose we'd better. What

17

shall we do with these stones we've washed? Take them back?'

'Yes,' said Pauline. 'I expect Tony will want to see them.'

'And then put them back exactly where he found them!' said Felicity sarcastically. 'Come on. Let's carry them between us.'

If the girls expected any sort of greeting when they got back to the dig, they certainly didn't get one. Each of the four boys was busy with his own digging area and wrapped in his own thoughts. Not even Beauty noticed them. He was completely absorbed in his own private game, which seemed to consist of determination not to let any birds settle in the field for longer than two seconds.

After an indignant silence Felicity spoke to her brother. Tony put his spade down and inspected the stones they had brought back. 'Nothing there,' he said. 'I think we're still too near the surface. There's another pile there waiting to be washed...'

Felicity explained Pauline's idea about bringing the water from the pond.

'You can if you like,' Tony said, 'but I don't see that it will save you energy. The water will soon get dirty.'

'It's easier getting fresh water than carrying huge piles of stones,' said Felicity. The girls put their plan into operation. Time went slowly by. Nothing of interest was discovered. Only Beauty seemed to be enjoying himself. The children went about their work seriously. Even Peter was subdued and Felicity was too bored to say much. Progress was very slow. Under the top layer the earth of Tump Rise was very hard and digging was not made easier by the toughness of couch grass roots. Sam plodded on solidly, apparently unaffected by the back-breaking work. The other boys were visibly tired and often had to stop to mop their brows and flex their muscles.

Felicity and Pauline sat a short distance away, obediently washing every solid object that was unearthed. The pile of stones grew bigger and bigger. 'There'll soon be enough for Mr Peat to build a new barn,' Felicity observed. 'I don't know what Miss Fullalove will say...'

'Who's Miss Fullalove?' asked Pauline, stifling a yawn. Her enthusiasm had evaporated rapidly.

'Oh, you know, my English teacher. When we write an essay on how we spent our holidays I'll have to say that all we did was wash stones and put them in a pile.' Felicity got up. 'It might be more interesting if I could say I'd done some digging too. The boys look tired out. Let's go and see if we can take over for a bit.'

'Don't be daft,' said Tony when he heard Felicity's offer. 'You wouldn't last five minutes. Hey,' he called Stephen, 'they want to relieve us.'

'Me first,' yelled Peter, running up and pushing his trowel into Pauline's hand.

'Well,' Stephen called back, 'I'm certainly ready for a break. What about having our sandwiches now?'

Tony had not liked to be the first to suggest a rest and he was pleased when Stephen did. 'Good idea. We'll have a break now and carry on after lunch.'

'Naturally,' said Stephen, rather haughtily. 'I didn't mean we should stop for good.' He threw down his spade and stretched himself full length on the grass. Leaving Pauline to hold the trowel Peter dashed to their bag and pulled it open. 'We've got sausage rolls,' he called out, 'and cheese and chutney sandwiches, jam tart and two Mars bars.' He shoved his hand into the bag but brought it out quickly. 'Oh – somebody's squashed the jam tart!'

Pauline threw the trowel down and took the picnic bag away from him. 'And who is that someone? Peter, don't lick your fingers – they're filthy.'

Peter wiped his hands on his trousers. 'They're not now,' he grinned.

The others got their food and soon they were all munching hungrily. Suddenly Sam moaned. 'Oh – I must be going barmy!'

'What's up?' Tony asked.

'Last night, when I told Mum that we were having a picnic, she said she'd make us some cakes, and I've forgotten to bring them . . .'

Mrs Peat's cakes were almost legendary. When the children visited the farm they were always given what they thought were the most delicious cakes they had ever tasted. When Peter realised the enormity of Sam's crime he swallowed his sausage roll. In between chokes he said, 'I'll go for them, Sam.'

'Greedy,' said Pauline. 'Be quiet, or you'll choke yourself to death.'

'I'm not greedy,' Peter gasped, gradually regaining his breath. 'It's just that Sam's Mum will be upset if no one eats them. It's not that I want them!'

'Don't you really, Peter?' said Felicity. 'In that case it wouldn't be fair for you to go for them. Shall we go, Pauline? Then Peter needn't feel obliged to eat any when we get back.'

'I might have just one,' said Peter quickly, 'to be polite.' He took another sausage roll.

'I suppose I'd better go for them,' said Sam, making a half-hearted effort to heave himself off the ground.

'No, Sam,' said Felicity, 'I meant it – Pauline and I will go. You have a rest. After all, you've been digging all morning while we've been sitting down.'

'Hey,' said Tony, 'what are you up to?'

'That's gratitude for you. First we offer to dig, and now we go all the way back to the farm, and all you can do is be suspicious.' Felicity gave a virtuous sniff.

Tony looked ashamed of himself. It was decent of them to offer to go. 'All right, I'm sorry. But finish your sandwiches first.'

'No,' Felicity said, 'we can eat when we get back. If we go now we'll probably be back before you start digging again. Come on, Pauline.'

'Here – catch!' Sam threw the girls a couple of apples. 'Eat those on the way.'

'Thanks,' Felicity said. 'We shan't be long.'

When the girls had gone the boys discussed the morning's work. After their rest they felt brighter and eager to start again. Tony told the others some of the things he had learned about different kinds of barrows and their construction.

'This one is too small to be anything but a round barrow,' he said, 'and there are many different kinds of round ones. There should be a sort of stone box in the middle where the body was buried, though the whole thing probably has a ring of stones round it.'

'Do you think the stones we have dug up are part of that?' Stephen asked.

21

'I shouldn't think so,' Tony said. 'I mean, they were just sort of anywhere, not in a specially made ring. I think we'll have to go several feet deeper yet.'

'If we do find a skeleton, do you think we ought to disturb it?' Stephen asked.

Tony thought for a moment. 'It might not be a skeleton, but an urn – a pottery urn with the ashes of a body in it. Late Bronze Age people used to cremate their dead. We can decide what to do when we find something.'

'I hope we don't have to dig too deep,' said Stephen, 'or Mr Peat won't be very pleased with us.'

'He won't mind,' said Sam. 'I thought I'd better tell him last night and he said it won't do a bit of harm to turn soil over in Tump Rise.'

'Good,' said Tony. 'What did he think of the chances of it being a barrow?'

'He didn't let on,' said Sam, 'although he did say to let him know if it was a grave so that he could come and bring some flowers.'

Tony frowned. 'I don't think he takes us seriously,' he said.

When Felicity had offered to collect the cakes from the farm she had forgotten about the field with the cows in, and did not remember until they had reached the gate. They debated whether to take a chance and run quickly round the edge to the gate on the far side. It was a feasible idea until three of the cows ambled pointedly over towards them and stood looking at them with what seemed to be 'We dare you to' expressions.

'They're supposed to be harmless,' said Pauline, hoping that Felicity would not agree with her.

22

'Yes, but do they know that?' Felicity asked. 'I'm not going to risk it. We'd better go through the next field.'

'The ploughed one?' Pauline asked.

'Yes,' said Felicity. 'I know we shouldn't, but there's no other way. No one will see us and we can tread carefully.'

The girls crossed the ploughed field and approached the farm outbuildings. As they turned a corner by a disused barn they came across Sam's dog Chummy, looking very possessive over a small heap of old bones. He looked up at them, gave a small bark and a wag of his tail, and returned to his guard duty.

'I wonder why Sam didn't take Chummy with him,' said Pauline. 'He and Beauty could have played together.'

'Didn't you know?' said Felicity. 'They fight like mad. They both came to the forest one day and Beauty bit Chummy's ear. Now they growl at each other like hungry lions.'

Mr Peat saw them as they passed the stables. 'Hello there, how are the body snatchers getting on?' he called.

'Fine, thanks,' Felicity called back. 'Is Mrs Peat in?'

'You'll find her at the back of the house.'

Mrs Peat was hanging out washing as the girls opened the gate into the back garden. 'So there you are,' she greeted them. 'Thought somebody would be back.'

She fastened the last tea towel on the clothes line and wiped her hands on her apron. Mrs Peat was small, dumpy and rosy-complexioned, and was always busy about something. She looked like a walking advertisement for life in the country with her flowered dress, flowered apron and a flowered scarf round her head.

'Come in for a minute. Oh, that silly lump of a son

23

of mine,' she said with a comfortable chuckle. 'He'd lose his head if it weren't screwed on. Would you like a glass of milk while you're here?'

'Yes, please!' the girls chorused.

They went into the cosy farm kitchen where, even in the middle of the day's work, everything was shining and tidy. There was a friendly fire burning in the large old-fashioned grate, and a big iron kettle was quietly singing on the hob.

'I'll have a cup of tea myself,' Mrs Peat said. 'Here's your milk and a slice of honey cake.'

She bustled about making tea and then poured herself a cup. She chatted away to the girls, asking about their parents, when the Christys' new baby was expected and how they were getting on at Tump Rise. 'I must say that when Mr Peat told me what you were up to I thought you must all be a bit soft in the head. Still, at your age most things are fun, I suppose.'

After a while the girls, feeling slightly guilty at being away from the others for so long, said that they had better be on their way.

'Aye, they'll be wanting their cakes, I shouldn't wonder. I'll have to make Sam tie a bit of string round his finger in future, though bless me, he'll very likely forget what it's there for. Will you be good girls and take this tea to Mr Peat on your way back?'

'Certainly,' Felicity said, handing the bag of cakes to Pauline and taking the flask into which Mrs Peat had poured the tea and added several spoonfuls of sugar. 'Thank you for the milk,' she added.

'And the cake,' said Pauline.

'You're very welcome. Come and see me again soon.'

Mrs Peat showed them out by the back door. The girls waved goodbye. They delivered the tea to Mr Peat in the stables. 'Ah,' he said, 'that's very nice, just what I needed.'

As they crossed the ploughed field on the way back to Tump Rise Felicity noticed something lying in one of the furrows, and picked it up. 'Look what I've found,' she said.

'What is it?' asked Pauline.

'It's a coin but I can't tell what it is with all the dirt on it. I'll clean it later, there's no time now. It must be my lucky day. I'd never have found it if we'd gone through the field with the cows!' She put the coin in the pocket of her skirt.

There were no sarcastic remarks about the time they had taken when they got back to the dig. The arrival of the cakes was too welcome. Felicity put an old ground sheet several yards from the dig and the weary archaeologists sat down thankfully and watched the basket being unpacked.

'Delicious,' Stephen said, biting into his cake.

'We had milk and honey cake at the farm,' Felicity informed them.

'Lucky dogs,' spluttered Tony with his mouth full.

'I don't think I can tackle these at the moment,' Felicity went on. 'I'm full. I'll keep my share for later. What about you, Pauline?'

'I'll keep mine too,' said Pauline, a trifle wistfully.

'I'll have yours if you don't want them,' Peter volunteered, his blue eyes shining with anticipation.

'I do want them,' his sister retorted, 'but later. You'll have the same as everybody else and not a crumb more.'

'Let's go and see how they've been getting on at the barrow,' Felicity said to Pauline, getting up and beginning to stroll away. Pauline followed her, glancing a little apprehensively over her shoulder as they left the main group.

A few minutes later Mrs Peat's cakes were just a glorious distant memory and the boys decided it was time to return to work. 'What are you doing with the spade?' Tony demanded as he reached the barrow.

Felicity started guiltily, 'I just thought I'd have a bit of a dig while you had stopped,' she said.

'Oh, did you? Well, this dig was my idea and your job is washing the finds. There are plenty more stones to wash if you want something to do.'

Felicity handed over the spade reluctantly. 'Washing stones is the most boring job in the whole world.'

'It's just as important as digging,' said Tony, bending and preparing to lift a spadeful of soil. 'So get the tin and fetch some more water from the pond, and let's get back to our routine.'

It was not long before Tony gave a sudden shout.

'Quick! Stephen! Sam! Here!'

Startled by his excitement the boys dropped their tools and went across to him.

'What's the matter?' Stephen asked anxiously. 'Hurt yourself?'

'No – look at this – I've found something!'

Peter came running up. 'What is it? What have you found?'

'I'm not sure yet.' Tony's voice was tense. 'I thought it was just another stone until I realised it was much too big. Careful now . . .'

'It's a bone!'

They scooped the soil away from the object with their hands and Tony pulled it out carefully. 'Felicity, can you bring the water here?' he said.

'It's a bone!' said Stephen as some of the dirt fell away.

'Aye, that's a bone all right,' said Sam.

'Gosh,' said Tony, 'you're right.' He took the tin of water from Felicity. 'I wonder if there are any more. If it's part of a skeleton there are bound to be.' He laid the bone on the grass and they all stood looking at it reverently.

'Will there be a skull?' Peter asked, his voice suddenly quiet.

'Sure to be, I should think,' Tony replied. 'What luck! I was beginning to think we were wasting our time.'

'Do you think it's Bronze Age man?' Stephen asked.

'Why not?' said Tony. 'Come on, let's dig for the rest.' He made a movement to pick up his spade.

Stephen stopped him. 'No, wait a minute, I'm not sure it would be right – to dig up the rest, I mean.'

Tony stared at him. 'Why not?'

'That's what we've come here to do, isn't it?' asked Sam.

Stephen struggled to put his feelings into words. 'But it's – well – someone's grave. I don't think it's right to disturb it.'

'But archaeologists are always doing that,' said Tony. 'They dig up barrows and open mummies' tombs.'

'There was a story in a comic called The Curse of the Mummy's Tomb,' said Peter. 'It was all about some men –'

'Oh, drop it, Peter,' Stephen interrupted impatiently. 'I know that proper archaeologists open tombs and graves, but they're scientists and know how to do it. They don't dig at random, as we're doing. They probably don't like to disturb bodies either.'

'They take them to museums,' said Tony. 'Honestly, Stephen, I don't think it's wrong.'

Felicity had been listening intently. 'I agree with Stephen,' she said. 'It doesn't seem right, and I vote we put the bone back and fill the hole in and then go home.'

'After all the digging we've done?' Tony said witheringly. 'That would be stupid. The whole idea was to find something, wasn't it?'

'Perhaps it was,' Felicity said, 'but none of us really expected to find anything, did we? But now we have, why not let well alone? All this digging might waken his ghost, whoever he is – or was, I mean.'

Tony pulled a face. 'Ghosts! Oh, talk sense, for goodness sake. Is that what you're worrying about, Stephen?'

Stephen felt a flash of temper rising in him. 'Don't talk rubbish,' he said shortly. 'Of course not. I've told you what I think. A grave shouldn't be tampered with, whether it's a Bronze Age one or the newest one in Edwinton churchyard. I should have thought, with your father being the Vicar, that the same thing might have struck you.'

Tony threw up his arms in despair. He had not reckoned on this. Here they were on the verge of what might be an important discovery, one which might make them important, and this had to happen. There was no point in going on with the digging if Stephen and Felicity were so strongly against it. This sort of quarrel right at the beginning of the holidays might well ruin the whole three weeks. Besides, he admitted reluctantly to himself, there was something in what they said...

In the silence that followed they sat on the ground, with the bone in the middle of the circle they formed. Six pairs of eyes gazed at it, thoughtfully, sadly or with antagonism, according to mood. Then Tony, his words admitting defeat, said, 'If we're not going to dig any more, what are we going to do?' he added in a frustrated tone. 'Can somebody talk sense for a change?'

Stephen looked up sharply and was about to make a cutting remark. He stopped himself in time, telling himself that he must make allowances for Tony's disappoint-

29

ment. 'I think we should find out if it really does belong to a Bronze Age man,' he said quietly.

Tony snorted. 'How do we do that? Ask him?'

'By taking it to the Museum in Retfield,' Stephen said, ignoring the sarcasm. 'Then when we know for certain we can ask advice about whether we should continue digging or not.'

Grudgingly Tony said, 'That's not a bad idea. If they say we should, are you willing to help?'

'Yes,' said Stephen without hesitation.

'Right,' said Tony, jumping up. 'Let's go.'

'What, now?' asked Felicity.

'Yes, now,' Tony told her. 'It's three o'clock, and there's a bus into Retfield at half past. We'll catch that if we hurry.'

Sam, pleased that the argument had ended in such a friendly way, said, 'My Dad's going into Retfield this afternoon. If he hasn't already gone he'll give us a lift.'

'Good,' said Tony, 'let's go and see. That means that we can't all go, though.'

'You can count me out,' said Felicity. 'I don't want to go. I think you are all being very silly about the whole thing. You're staying with me, aren't you, Pauline?'

Pauline looked round doubtfully, then caught a meaningful look in Felicity's eye. 'Yes,' she said. 'Er – I don't suppose there'll be room for all of us in your Dad's car, will there, Sam?'

'Oh, no. He'll have to turf out a few pigs as it is,' Sam said with a straight face.

'That settles it,' said Felicity. 'The boys can go and join their friends and we'll take home as much of the equipment as we can carry.'

30

'See you later then,' Tony said. 'Let's wrap the bone up very carefully. I wonder what it'll turn out to be...'

Pauline looked out of the attic window and watched the four boys just turning in at the gate of the Vicarage.

'They're coming,' she announced.

Felicity joined her. 'They're looking grim,' she said with a note of apprehension in her voice. 'Look at Stephen – his face is like a thunder cloud.'

'I wonder what's happened?' Pauline said. Her hands were twisting nervously.

'Now, Pauline,' Felicity warned her, 'control yourself.'

'You've gone a bit pale,' Pauline said with satisfaction.

'I have not!'

'Yes, you have!'

'No, I haven't – look out – I can hear them. Let's be reading or something when they come in.' Felicity flung herself into a chair and picked up a book at random, not noticing that it was the collected sermons of a nineteenth-century clergyman, dumped by her father in the attic many years ago. Pauline looked over her shoulder, pretending to read with her, though the words might have been in Greek for all the sense she could make of them.

There was a stamping on the stairs and the door was flung open. Tony entered first, carrying a brown paper parcel, from one end of which a piece of bone protruded. He put it on the floor, paused for a moment, then suddenly kicked it into the furthest corner. 'So endeth the story of our Bronze Age man,' he said savagely.

Felicity jumped up. 'Why, Tony, whatever do you mean?'

31

'What do you think I mean? That bone is no more Bronze Age man than you are.'

'It doesn't even belong to a human being,' said Stephen disgustedly.

'It's a sheep's bone!' Peter tried not to giggle as he spoke but there was a wobble in his voice.

'A sheep's bone? What part of a sheep?'

Tony glared at his sister. 'What does it matter what part of a sheep? Don't ask such idiotic questions.'

'A shin bone, the man said,' Peter volunteered.

'Oh, dear, what a shame.' Felicity put on an expression of intense sympathy. 'All that journey for nothing.'

'All that work for nothing, you mean,' Tony said. 'And then to go and make fools of ourselves at the Museum...'

'Actually, the man was quite nice about it,' Stephen said. 'He didn't laugh at us or anything.'

'No, he praised us for our energy and – and – what was the word he used?' asked Sam.

'Enterprise,' Tony said. He gave a bitter laugh. 'Energy and enterprise – and the result is the shin bone of a sheep – oh –' Further words failed him and he began to pace up and down, muttering under his breath.

'Never mind,' Felicity said consolingly, 'better luck next time.'

Tony stopped pacing and glowered at her. 'You're taking this rather lightly, aren't you? Aren't you sorry it's ended like this?'

'Of course I am, and so is Pauline. You're sorry too, aren't you, Pauline?'

'Yes,' said Pauline hastily.

'You didn't seem very surprised at our news,' Stephen said, with a swift look at Felicity.

32

She made a dramatic gesture as though she were a queen renouncing a kingdom. 'Of course I was surprised – I was flabbergasted. You were too, weren't you, Pauline?'

'Yes,' Pauline said again, this time a little tremulously.

'What I can't understand,' Stephen went on, 'is how it got there – er – in that barrow. I can imagine a lot of places where you might find an animal's bone, but why there – a couple of feet under a mound in a field right on the edge of the farm?'

Tony turned to him slowly. 'Yes, that is strange, isn't it?'

'One might even say it was suspicious. Wouldn't you say there's something fishy about the whole business, Felicity?'

'Why, whatever do you mean?' Felicity clutched at a chair for support. 'What can he mean, Pauline?'

'I don't know,' Pauline quavered.

'Let's leave Pauline out of it for the moment, shall we?' Stephen began to act like a barrister questioning someone in court. His voice rose and he jabbed the air with his finger. 'Felicity Brooks, did you, or did you not, have anything to do with the bone being found in the grave?'

Felicity began to splutter. 'But – but – how could I? I didn't find it – you found it, Tony–'

Stephen looked at her over invisible spectacles. 'You know very well what I mean. Let me put the question a different way. Did you put it there?'

There was a long silence. All eyes were turned to Felicity, who was sitting bolt upright in her chair. The seconds ticked away. Nobody spoke or moved, until Felicity broke the silence at last and said, in a small quivering voice, 'Yes, I put it there.'

33

'We put it there,' said Pauline bravely, reaching out to touch Felicity's shoulder.

'No,' Felicity said quickly, 'I did it and it was my idea. Don't blame Pauline.'

Stephen said nothing but stretched our his hands towards Tony as if to say, 'Your witness'.

Tony was nonplussed. 'Of all the – but why? Why the dickens did you do something so stupid?'

'It's not much of a joke,' said Peter, serious for once.

'It wasn't meant to be a joke,' Felicity said. Now that she had been exposed there was no point in pretending further. The best thing would be to tell the truth. 'It was meant to help,' she went on. 'I thought that once you'd found the bone you'd give up and we could think of something else to do.'

'That's pretty selfish,' said Tony. 'Just because you were bored you wanted to spoil our fun.'

'It wasn't that,' Felicity said hurriedly.

'Of course it was,' Tony said. 'But what I want to know is why you let us go into Retfield when you knew all the time what would happen?'

Sam, who had kept silent because he hated to see Felicity so much in the wrong, was suddenly reminded of the horrible moment when the man in the Museum had told them what they had found. 'I think you might have told us before we went,' he said, as mildly as he could.

'If I'd done that you'd simply have gone on digging and the whole idea would have been wasted,' Felicity said weakly. She knew that it was not a very good explanation, but it was the truth.

'Where did you get the bone?' Sam asked suddenly.

'It was one of Chummy's. He had a pile of bones by the old barn, and your father called him as we passed. He ran off and left them and that's when I thought what I could do.'

'Coo,' said Peter, 'robbing a dog of its bones!'

'He had plenty more,' Pauline put in.

'And you planted it when we were eating our cakes, I suppose?' Tony asked.

'Yes,' Felicity replied, 'when Pauline and I went to see how you had been getting on with the digging.'

'Hm,' Tony said. 'I thought there was something suspicious when you didn't want to give me my spade.'

'Never trust a girl,' Stephen muttered.

Stephen's remark brought home to Felicity the enormity of the action. She realised how it looked to the boys. They had had an embarrassing time in Retfield after an exhausting time at Tump Rise, and the story of the hoax had come as a final blow. What if Stephen was right and none of them ever trusted her again? What if she was expelled from the Greenwooders? Tony's voice cut into her thoughts,

'It's done now, and nothing can undo it, but I think it was a mean rotten trick. I hope no one ever does anything like that to you, Felicity.'

If only Tony had said that angrily, Felicity thought, it wouldn't somehow be so bad, but he had made her feel worse. Oh, why did things have to turn out like this! She looked miserably at Pauline. Pauline tried to give her a little smile to indicate that she shared the blame, but the smile never came to life. Instead, her lips quivered, two little tears appeared at the corners of her eyes and fell slowly down her cheek. That was the last straw for

35

Felicity, and she knew that at any moment she was going to burst into tears.

'I'm sorry,' she mumbled in a very shaky voice. She gave a huge sniff, dived into her pocket and hurriedly pulled out her handkerchief. In her anxiety to stem the approaching tears she pulled out, not only her handkerchief, but the entire contents of her pocket, and an assortment of objects was scattered on the floor in front of the chair.

'Tears won't do any good,' said Tony harshly. 'All we can do is to try and forget all about it.'

The sight of the girls in tears brought out all Sam's kindness, and he quickly bent down to recover the things Felicity had dropped, and handed them back to her.

'You've missed something,' Stephen said, picking up a small dirty object from a corner.

'I found it in the ploughed field,' Felicity spluttered through tears. 'Give it to Sam – it's probably his, anyway.'

'I don't want it,' Sam said. He took it from Stephen, looked at it briefly and handed it to Felicity. 'Looks like a foreign coin to me.'

'I used to collect them,' said Tony. 'Let's have a look.' Not really interested, but anxious to lighten the tension, he took the coin and scraped off some of the dirt with a penknife. 'It's a funny shape,' he commented. 'Not really round and thicker than any of the coins we have now. I wonder what it's made of.' He rubbed it on his sleeve then took it to the window to get more light. 'There's a sort of head on one side and some writing on the other.'

'Can I see?' Stephen joined him. 'It looks like one of the Georges.'

Peter looked puzzled. 'George who?' he asked.

36

Stephen threw him an exasperated look. 'I mean, one of the King Georges – First, Second, Third or Fourth.'

'The Hanoverians,' added Tony.

'Oh, them.' Stephen's impatience had little effect on Peter. 'I thought you were talking about real people.'

'They were real once –' Stephen began, but Tony checked him with a gesture.

Felicity, whose tears had started signs of drying up, sniffed again, and said in a wobbly voice, 'It was in that field next to the one with the cows in. We came through that one because Pauline is a bit scared of cows.'

This accusation was enough to turn Pauline's mind from her sorrows. 'Me!' she exclaimed indignantly. 'What about you? I didn't notice you trying to persuade me to go through. You were just as eager as me . . .'

'All right, all right,' Tony said hastily. 'Sam, has anything like this been found before?'

'Not that I know of,' Sam said. He thought for a moment. 'Some oyster shells were turned up a year or two ago, which seemed a bit odd, seeing that we're so far from the sea, but I don't suppose they'd have anything to do with a coin like this.'

'I shouldn't think so.' Tony creased his forehead in thought. 'I suppose we ought to go back to the field and look for some more.'

'Oh, not more digging!' Felicity wailed.

'If we do, you're not coming with us,' Tony told her witheringly. Felicity subsided into sniffles.

'Shall we take this to Retfield Museum tomorrow and ask the curator about it?' said Stephen.

Tony and Sam turned on him. 'No!' they said together. 'We've made fools enough of ourselves today.' Tony

37

added. 'Suppose it turns out to be a medallion or something that was given away in a comic.'

'Or just a bottle top,' said Peter.

'With a king's head on it?' Tony said crushingly.

'Well,' Peter cast round in his mind for a likely explanation for his scorn-provoking remark, 'perhaps a king once had a picnic in the field and brought his own drink.'

'Peter,' his sister said gently, 'sometimes I wonder if you really are my twin.'

'Why not show it to Daddy?' Felicity suggested. 'He knows about all sorts of things. In fact, he's jolly clever.'

'That's the most sensible thing I've heard you say for ages.' The friendliness in Tony's tone made Felicity feel that she was on the verge of being forgiven. 'Come on, let's go and ask him.'

The Vicar was in his study putting the finishing touches to his sermon for Sunday. He was surrounded by books, his spectacles were on the end of his nose and his hair had turned into a cockatoo crest. He heard a thundering noise on the stairs, murmured, 'Those noisy children,' smiled tolerantly and turned over a page.

There was a quick tap on the door and before he had time to speak it burst open. Six children poured in and surrounded his desk.

The Vicar was used to their exuberant ways and did not turn a hair. 'What do you want?' he asked. 'The answer is yes as long as it keeps you quiet!'

'Daddy, look at this.' Tony thrust the coin at him. 'Felicity found it in a field at Sam's farm. Stephen thinks it might be a Georgian coin. Can you tell us, please?'

The Vicar took the coin and peered at it short-sightedly. 'Most unlikely, I should think,' he said in an amused tone. He held it nearer his eyes, then gave a sudden exclamation. He adjusted his spectacles.

There was a long pause and a silence broken only by the children's anxious breathing. The Vicar opened a drawer in his desk and took out a magnifying glass. He pored through it for what seemed endless minutes. At last he straightened his back. 'No, it isn't a Georgian coin,' he said, decidedly.

Six faces dropped. 'I suppose it's a medallion then,' Tony said. 'We thought it might be something of the sort.'

'It's not a medallion either,' his father said. He looked at the crestfallen faces and suddenly his own face lit up with excitement. 'Congratulations, Felicity. You've found a Roman coin!'

'A Roman coin!' Felicity caught her breath. 'Then it's – it's hundreds of years old?'

'Probably sixteen or seventeen hundred years old,' the Vicar said. 'I'll have to go through one of my books to identify it exactly. But the head is of a Roman emperor...'

'Good old Felicity!' Tony forgot she was in disgrace and slapped her on the back. 'I say, do you think it's worth anything, Daddy?'

'To another collector, perhaps, but I hope you will consider giving it to the Museum at Retfield. One should share finds such as this.' The Vicar was turning the coin over in his fingers. 'This is a bronze coin, probably of the second century. Later ones were much smaller. The portrait of the emperor is in high relief, you see. It's difficult to tell which emperor until it's been cleaned.'

39

Sam's mind was off on a different tack. 'How do you think it got into the field?' he asked.

The Vicar got up from his chair and began to move thoughtfully about the room. 'That's an interesting question, Sam. It looks as though there might have been a Roman occupation of some kind there. After all, we're not so far from Newark and Lincoln, which were both important centres, and there was a military camp at Bawtry. But this is mere speculation. The only way we can make sure is to explore the field more thoroughly –'

Tony interrupted him. 'Shall we go now? We've got all the things we used this morning when we were excavating the barrow.'

'What's all this? Excavating a barrow? I didn't know there was one around here.'

'There isn't,' Tony said sadly.

'Then –' the Vicar began.

'We'll tell you about it later, Daddy,' Felicity hastily put in. 'Won't we, Tony?' She gave him a pleading look.

'All right, let's go and look for coins now.' Tony started an eager exodus to the door, but his father held up a restraining hand.

'Just a minute, all of you. Surely tomorrow –'

'Oh, Daddy, please –'

'But Mr Brooks –'

'Sir, can't we go now?'

The Vicar put his hands to his ears. 'Stop! You'll deafen me. Dear me, the young are so impatient. Sam, do you think your father could do with a horde of visitors tonight?'

Felicity gave Sam an unobserved tweak. He flinched, but understood what it was intended to convey. 'Oh, yes,

40

I think so, Mr Brooks. You see, tomorrow is market day and he'll be off to Retfield again. He usually goes pretty early and stays for lunch. I think tonight would be a good time to see him. He'll only be reading the *Farmers' Weekly* or watching the telly.'

'You must understand that there can be no question of doing any digging tonight,' the Vicar said. 'It will be dark soon. These things take a lot of preparation, you know.'

Tony's eager mind leaped to the possibility of evening excavations. 'We could light a bonfire – and have torches –'

'No!' said his father, and that was that. Tony and Felicity knew better than to argue with that tone of voice.

'We'll go in the car,' the Vicar went on, 'show the coin to Mr Peat, ask his permission to do some further investigation, and that will have to do for the time being.' He rubbed his hands together with a sudden spurt of enthusiasm. 'I must say I'm looking forward to finding some Roman remains. It would be a great thing for the village. Just think – a Roman villa – perhaps some mosaic pavements – come, all of you, I'll get the car out...'

They found Mr Peat dozing over his accounts in front of the fire. He was a man who took everything in his stride, and he showed no undue astonishment when Mrs Peat led six children and the slightly embarrassed Vicar into the room.

'Well, well, this is a nice surprise,' he declared in a comfortable voice. 'Sit down, all of you. Sam, draw some more chairs up to the fire. Gets chilly these spring evenings, doesn't it, Vicar?'

'Er, yes, it does,' the Vicar said. 'You must be wondering why we've rather burst in on you like this –'

41

Mr Peat chuckled. 'I guess it's something to do with these Greenwooders, or whatever they call themselves. What have they been up to now? Something wicked, I'll be bound.'

'Now, William, you shouldn't say such things,' his wife chided. 'I'm sure Felicity and Tony would never do anything wicked!'

Felicity cast her eyes down in modest agreement. Her father laughed heartily. 'Then you don't know my children, Mrs Peat! But, no, it's nothing wicked this time. The fact is, Felicity found something in one of your fields this afternoon that might turn out to be very exciting.'

'Oh?' Mr Peat settled his bulky figure in his armchair. 'And what's that?'

Felicity burst in before her father had a chance to explain. 'I found a coin!'

'A Roman coin!' added Peter excitedly. 'Not from a comic!'

Mr Peat sat up. 'Eh, what's that?'

'Let me explain,' said the Vicar. 'Felicity found the coin in a field, evidently turned up by the plough. It is possible, therefore, that there are more where that came from. Indeed, there might even be evidence of a Roman settlement near the farm. It is not unlikely, you know. The Romans were in this part of the country. Think of Newark... The point is, Mr Peat, I wonder whether you would give permission for some investigation to be made – under skilled direction, of course. The Museum authorities would no doubt be interested.'

'Oh,' interrupted Tony, 'but we want to do it.'

'Yes,' added Sam, 'to make up for the barrow.'

'That wasn't...' said Stephen softly.

42

The Vicar shushed them and was about to speak again but Mr Peat did not give him a chance. He seemed not to have listened to most of the explanation. His attention had been riveted by the Vicar's first words.

'Did you say a Roman coin?' he asked.

'Yes,' the Vicar replied. 'I haven't had time to date it yet –'

'Can I see it?' The farmer stretched out his hand eagerly.

'Why, certainly.'

Mr Peat took the coin from the Vicar and examined it carefully. He turned to his wife. 'It is!' he exclaimed. 'Look at this, Lottie. It is, isn't it?'

The others watched in puzzled silence as Mrs Peat rubbed at the coin and adjusted her spectacles to give it a thorough examination. She handed it back to her husband. 'Yes,' she said firmly, 'there's no doubt about it. It is!'

'But we know it is, Dad,' Sam said impatiently. 'Mr Brooks has already told you it's a Roman coin.'

'No, no, son, you don't understand. Does he, Lottie?'

'No, you don't understand, Sam.'

'Neither do I!' The Vicar looked from the farmer to his wife and back again. 'May I ask you why you are so sure that the coin is whatever you think it is?'

Mr Peat held the coin up between two sausage-like fingers. His usual composure seemed to have deserted him. He was positively trembling with excitement. Mrs Peat, clasping and unclasping her hands, shared her husband's feelings. 'That coin,' the farmer declared, 'is the very coin I lost in that field nigh on fifteen years ago. Isn't it, Lottie?'

43

'Yes, Vicar, the very same...'

'The very same, William. There's no doubt about it.'

'What?' The Vicar suddenly looked like a deflated bal-loon.

'Yes, Vicar, the very same. That coin was given to me by my father, and his father gave it to him. That coin has been in our family for generations – a sort of good luck talisman, I suppose you'd call it. I would have given it to Sam when he was twenty-one, and he would have handed it to his son.'

'Hey, steady on, Dad,' said Sam, blushing.

'I won't say that losing it brought any special bad luck,' went on Mr Peat, 'but it was a blow all the same, wasn't it, Lottie?'

'It was indeed,' his wife agreed. 'I remember it as though it was yesterday. And don't forget it was the year that Buttercup lost her calf.'

'So it was. Ah, well, that was a long time ago. I must say that I never expected I'd see the old coin again – and here it is!'

'Thanks to Felicity,' said Sam, looking proudly at her.

'Aye, I mustn't forget to say thank you, young lady.' Mr Peat felt in his pocket and fished out a crumpled £5 note. 'Would you allow me to give her this as a reward, Vicar?'

'Virtue should be its own reward,' the Vicar began, but he saw Felicity's face begin to crumple. 'Well – perhaps this once, though you'd better not make a habit of finding things and expecting to be rewarded, Felicity!'

'I won't, Daddy. Oh, thank you Mr Peat! I've never had so much money at once before.'

'And you're not likely to have it very long either,' muttered Tony.

'What do you mean?' Felicity hissed back.

'If you don't share it with the rest of us I'll tell about how you came to be in the field and about the bones.'

Felicity's dream of pounds' worth of chocolates died as quickly as it had been born. 'All right,' she said reluctantly, giving her brother a look that would have reduced

45

him to ashes if he had seen it. She turned back to the grown-ups, who were talking about coincidences, wedding rings found in herrings' stomachs, letters to and from long-lost relatives crossing in the post, and other fascinating happenings. Mrs Peat produced some lemonade and fruit cake for the children and elderberry wine for the Vicar, and the visit turned into an unexpectedly enjoyable party, with Felicity basking in her new-found popularity. Only Tony and Stephen, remembering their disappointment, maintained a certain reserve.

'She'll be awful for days,' Tony said gloomily.

The party broke up when the Vicar glanced at his watch and tut-tutted at the lateness of the hour. 'We must be getting back,' he explained. 'Your mother will be wondering what on earth has happened to us all.'

There were renewed thanks from Mr Peat, and invitations to visit the farm any time from Mrs Peat. Sam led the visitors to the car and waved them goodbye. On the way home Felicity sat in self-satisfied silence. The twins chatted about the bones, barrows and what they would have for supper. Tony and Stephen cheered up slightly at the thought of sharing Felicity's windfall. The Bronze Age sank back into the obscurity from which it had emerged earlier in the day.

Only the Vicar did not share the cosiness. He sighed as he steered the car rather erratically along the main road. 'It's all ended very satisfactorily, I suppose,' he said to himself, 'and especially for Mr Peat, but I do wish there had been a villa to unearth...'

46

THE ACTRESS

All was quiet in the attic playroom. For once Tony and Felicity were sitting in absolute silence. Tony, deep in concentration, was sitting at a table under the window and was outlining a map. Felicity, curled up in a dilapidated armchair, was reading from the collected works of Shakespeare, balanced precariously on the arm. Although they were only a few feet apart neither was aware of the other. Tony was exploring the thickly wooded coast of the imaginary Pacific island he was drawing. Felicity, richly dressed in blue velvet, was about to make her entrance on the stage of one of London's theatres. And the actress and the explorer went their separate ways.

As Tony cautiously made his way through the jungle Felicity prepared to face her audience, her right hand extended and a charming smile on her face. Then – 'Cuckoo! cuckoo! cuckoo!' broke the silence. The bird in the cuckoo clock that Miss Pope-Cunningham had given them for Christmas told them that it was three o'clock. To Tony it was not the little wooden cuckoo, however, but a fierce native covered in feathers and war-paint who had darted from behind a tree and was uttering strange cries. He had a long spear in his hand and his appearance was wild. Tony hoped he was friendly. 'Me Englishman-explorer-friend –' he muttered.

'I'm going to be an actress!'

To Felicity the sound was neither cuckoo nor native, but an actor giving her an entrance cue. 'Then I must be thy lady,' she said loudly, 'but I know when thou hast stol'n away from fairy land...'

'Pipe down,' growled Tony, jerked from the lush undergrowth of his desert island to the dusty attic.

'And in the shape of Corin sat all day,' continued Felicity, heedless of her brother's grumble, 'playing on pipes of corn and versing love to amorous Phillida.' Tony put down his mapping pen and swivelled round to face

48

his sister. 'Will you shut up! How can I concentrate on this while you go on about corny pipes and Philli-what's-it?'

'I won't shut up,' said Felicity, her poetry voice becoming a little sharp. 'Why should I have to suffer just because you don't like beautiful language?'

'And why should I suffer,' asked Tony, 'because you *do*?'

'You're hopeless,' Felicity sighed. 'Don't you know it's from the *Dream*?'

'More likely from a nightmare, the way you're doing it,' said Tony.

Felicity gave him a pitying smile. 'It's beautiful. *A Midsummer Night's Dream* is Shakespeare's loveliest play.'

'How do you *know*?' Tony said. 'You haven't read them all.'

I just *do*,' said Felicity, raising her eyebrows in a superior way. 'Besides, Mr Howe said so when I told him we'd done it at school.'

'So that's it. I might have known.' Tony imitated her voice. 'Mr Howe said so... Then it must be right.'

'Oh, you're impossible. You don't know anything about Mr Howe. Why are you being so rude about him?'

Felicity sighed. It was awful when Tony was in this mood. 'All you're fit for is drawing stupid maps which aren't even of real places. There are more important things in life, but apparently they're above your head.' She rose, closed her book and gave Tony a withering look. 'If you want me I shall be in my room,' she said, and swept out of the attic.

Tony did not bother to reply but returned to his map.

49

He wished Felicity's actressy period would pass. It had been going on for nearly a year, and was so boring. And now that she had got involved with this actor bloke it looked like getting worse. Westwood Howe! The man sounded like a book...

As soon as Felicity reached her room her feeling of annoyance disappeared. Tony wasn't so bad really – it was just that he was a boy and so did not understand. He had not been at home the day before when Westwood Howe and Alice Kelly had been for tea and Mr Howe had said all those nice things about her. Tony did not seem to mind that he had missed meeting the leading man and the leading lady of the Retfield Repertory Company, but Felicity would have died of frustration if she had not been there. If she had been out with the boys she would have missed Westwood Howe's deep voice, smooth dark hair and craggy features, and Alice Kelly's enormous blue eyes, her blonde hair and laugh that tinkled like Chinese bells. She recalled the actor's phrases with a glow of pride. A nice voice, he had said, and very graceful ... expressive eyes ... sensitive. How could Tony – or Stephen or Peter or Sam – understand poetry, Shakespeare, things like that? Why, when they had all gone into Retfield to see that film, *Henry the Somethingth – Fifth, Sixth?* – all that the boys could get excited about were the horses and battles, while she had listened, captivated by the marvellous words.

It was not often that the Vicarage entertained actors and actresses – in fact, as far as Felicity knew, yesterday had been the first time – and it was strange how it had come about. Mr Howe and Miss Kelly had been visiting Sherwood Forest by car on one of the few occasions

50

during the week when they were not rehearsing, and had decided to have a look round Edwinton Church before going back to Retfield. The Vicar, always eager to show off the beauties of the Early English building, had offered to take them round, and during the tour Westwood Howe and he had discovered that they had known each other in the distant past when they were at school! An altogether marvellous coincidence, Felicity thought. As they had not finished exchanging news when they had finished going round the church the Vicar had invited the visitors to tea.

What an occasion it had been. Felicity had listened entranced to the story of Westwood Howe's career – the parts he had played, the companies he had been in, the famous people he called so casually by their Christian names... She had gazed with admiration at the vivacious Miss Kelly, and had wished that she too could have been fair and willowy, instead of dark and – she had to admit – the tiniest bit dumpy. When her shyness had worn off she had joined in the conversation and had ventured to admit that it was her great ambition to be an actress.

'I thought you wanted to be a kennel maid,' her father had said in surprise. 'Or was it something to do with horses?'

'That was last year,' she had replied coldly.

Her mother had come to her aid. 'Really, Charles, you are terribly behind the times. Have you never heard Felicity in her room doing her endless reciting?'

Reciting! Felicity sighed with exasperation. Parents just couldn't understand... But Mr Howe had understood. It was then that he had said all those nice things. Miss Kelly had been sweet too. 'If you have got it in you to be an

51

actress, then you will be one, my dear. Look at me. Once I was a telephone operator, but I was determined to make the stage my career –'

'And now you're the leading lady of the Retfield Repertory Company,' Westwood Howe had interrupted, with a laugh that Felicity could not quite understand and which caused a frown to pass quickly across Miss Kelly's face. But in a moment all was sunshine again, and the actor was telling them of the time when he had been unavoidably late for an audition and the part had been given to Sir Laurence Olivier instead.

Yes, it had been a wonderful afternoon, Felicity thought, standing in front of the mirror in her bedroom. 'The quality of mercy is not strained,' she declaimed, 'it droppeth as the gentle rain from heaven upon the place beneath...' Not being quite sure of the next lines she gave the mirror a dazzling smile and danced gracefully across the room, only tripping slightly over the edge of the carpet. It was easy to see that Mr Howe had been impressed with her. He wouldn't have bothered to pay her compliments if he hadn't thought she would make a good actress.

She sank on to her bed and gave herself up to day-dreaming. Felicity Brooks, the star of the Shakespeare season at the Old Vic ... small and fair as Desdemona, a tall and brown-eyed Portia, white-faced and tragic as Cordelia ... and it was Westwood Howe who was playing opposite her in each role. He would be very good as Henry the Fifth. He had the dignity of a king. Though she would have to do something about her French if she wanted to play Katharine. She wondered if he were married. Of course, he was too old for her – why, he must

52

be as old as her father if they were at school together. In any case, she had decided that she would never marry. She was going to live for her Art...

The shrilling of the telephone in the hall cut short her reverie. She sat up, listening. Her mother and father were both out. Would Tony hear it in the attic and come down? It was probably Stephen who wanted him anyway. The sound seemed to get more urgent. Oh, blow! She would have to answer it.

She scrambled off the bed and hurried down the stairs. She picked up the receiver. 'Edwinton Vicarage,' she said ungraciously.

'Is that Mrs Brooks?' asked a man's deep voice.

If Felicity had been a bird she would have preened her feathers. To be taken for her mother! 'Er – no,' she replied. 'It's me – I mean, I'm not Mrs Brooks – it's Felicity – *Miss* Brooks,' she finished with an attempt at dignity.

'Ah, Felicity,' the voice went on. 'This is Westwood Howe.' It sounded rather like a BBC announcer reporting a national disaster.

Felicity's voice trembled, then shot up an octave. 'Not – not – *the* Westwood Howe – the actor? Oh!' she squeaked.

Westwood Howe chuckled. 'Yes, young lady, *the* Westwood Howe, as you so cleverly guessed. I really wanted to speak to one of your parents.'

'They're out – I mean – neither of them's in –' Felicity began to gabble meaninglessly. She took a deep breath and started again. 'Can I take a message? Are you coming to tea again?'

'Yes, you can, and no, alas, no tea today. I'm busy in

53

the theatre. This is what I wanted to ask. Next Tuesday we're due to start rehearsing our next play, and a young girl is wanted for a small part – a *very* small part – one line, in fact, at the end of Act Three. It would require very little rehearsal. I remembered how keen you were to act, and I wondered whether your parents would allow you to take this part. That is, of course, if you'd like to do it...'

'Like to do it!' Felicity almost let the receiver drop through her nerveless fingers. She found that her mouth had gone so dry that not a word would come out.

'Are you there?' the voice said anxiously.

Felicity managed a little whisper. 'Yes, I'm here. Thank you very much – I'd – I'd love to do it – oh, *thank* you, Mr Howe.'

'With your parents' permission, of course.'

'Oh, yes, of course, I'll tell them as soon as they come in. One of them will ring you – oh, I'm sure it will be all right – it *must* be!'

'Very well, my dear,' said Westwood Howe briskly. 'I'll expect to hear later. There won't be much money in it, of course,' he added hastily. 'Just a small fee and expenses.'

'Money...' Felicity dismissed the whole sordid subject of money in one scornful breath.

'Goodbye, then, I hope to see you next week.'

'Goodbye...' Felicity put the receiver down slowly and stood as though in a trance. Her eyes shone. Her lips moved and a whisper forced itself out of them. 'I'm going to be an actress...'

Suddenly she became alive. 'Yippee!' she yelled and flew up the stairs. 'Tony! Tony! What do you think?

You'll never guess! Tony, who do you think was on the phone?' She reached the attic and burst in. 'Tony!'

'Mad,' Tony remarked casually, his head bent over his map. 'I knew it would happen one day.'

Felicity waltzed up to him, seized his pen and tugged at his hair to make him look up. 'I'm going to be an actress! I'm going to act with the Retfield Rep. That was Westwood Howe – he's asked me to play a part! Yippee!'

Eagerly she gave him a word by word account of the telephone call. 'So now,' she finished, 'it only remains for Mummy and Daddy to agree and, oh, Tony, I'm *sure* they will!'

For one awful moment Felicity feared that her parents were going to refuse...

'Well, I don't know,' her father said. 'It would mean you being out very late each night.' He saw the look of anguish on her face. 'Well –' he said again. Felicity clasped her hands and gazed at him beseechingly. 'Perhaps Mr Howe will see you get home as quickly as possible. I'll telephone him and find out.'

'Now?' Felicity asked.

'Goodness,' Mrs Brooks said, 'let your father have a cup of tea first.'

The Vicar smiled. 'All right, now – while the kettle is boiling.'

Ten minutes later the arrangements had been made. The times she would be needed for rehearsals were fixed. During the week of the play the stage manager would see her to the bus after the show and would make sure she caught it. The journey took little more than half an hour so she would be home soon after ten-thirty. 'And in bed by quarter to eleven,' her mother said firmly. Her salary was to be a pound a day and travelling expenses.

Felicity was in a seventh heaven of delight. She spent that evening trying out different hairstyles and, as Tony put it, making hideous faces in the mirror. 'Your hair looks like rats' tails however much you mess about with it,' was his comment on her various creations.

'I wonder what my line will be,' Felicity said. 'It's sure to be very important. It's at the end of the play.'

'I expect it will be "Mind the steps as you go out",' said Tony.

Felicity ignored him with a toss of the head. Her hair, piled up insecurely, fell into her eyes and made her look like an Old English sheepdog. She brushed it aside with a Lady Macbeth gesture. 'Perhaps they'll give me more to do – build up my part, I think they call it. I might have a long speech...'

'You might even be asked to sweep the stage after each performance,' said Tony. 'Wouldn't that give you a thrill?'

Felicity flounced out of the room. 'I'm going to find Pauline,' she announced. '*She'll* understand.'

The following Tuesday was to be Felicity's first day at rehearsal. Mr Howe had said that it would be a 'read-through', starting at half-past ten. As she did not appear until nearly the end of the play there was no need for her to arrive at the theatre until twelve o'clock. But Felicity had made it clear to her father that she wanted to be there much earlier. She was eager to spend every minute she possibly could inside the theatre. 'I want to know what the play is about,' she explained, 'and it will be interesting to hear the rest of the company reading their parts.' The Vicar gave in with a good grace and decided that she could catch the half-past nine bus into Retfield.

She woke at six o'clock on the Tuesday morning, and half an hour later she was washed and dressed and ready to catch the bus. She was not going to be late on her first day... It was a bit early for the rest of the family, though. She went downstairs and got things ready for breakfast, but that only took fifteen minutes or so. How slowly the time passed when you wanted it to hurry, she mused. She considered waking Tony but changed her mind at the thought of his heavy sarcasm. No, she would read a play to get herself in the mood for acting. She went up to the attic for the volume of Shakespeare and took it down with her to the kitchen. She settled herself down on the comfortable old sofa and opened the book.

'*Twelfth Night*,' she read aloud, 'or, *What You Will*. Scene – a city in Illyria: and the sea-coast near it. Act One – a room in the Duke's Palace. Enter Duke, Curio, Lords, Musicians attending. Duke: If music be the food of love, play on; Give me excess of it, that, surfeiting, the appetite may sicken and so die...'

'Wake up, Felicity, your breakfast is ready and the bus goes soon,' said a voice. Felicity opened her eyes and saw her mother standing over her. 'I wasn't asleep,' she said, and struggled off the sofa.

'No, darling,' said Mrs Brooks, 'I'm sure you weren't. You always lie on the sofa with your eyes closed and your mouth open. Come on, there's a good girl, and eat your cereal.'

Felicity sat at the table and tucked into her breakfast.

57

It doesn't matter if I did doze off, she thought, I was up awfully early.

The Playhouse at Retfield was in the centre of the town, on the opposite side of the market-place from the Town Hall, and flanked by a big department store on the right and some smaller shops on the left. The bus stopped outside the main entrance to the theatre, and as Felicity stepped off she felt that all her confidence had stayed on the seat she had just left. The sight of the facade, with its playbills and glass frames of photographs, seemed to make the butterflies inside her flap their wings wildly. Now that the moment of her arrival was upon her she wished she was miles away – at least twelve miles away, safe in the attic playroom in the Vicarage.

She climbed the steps and stopped outside the swing doors that led to the foyer. This was the moment she had been waiting for, the moment when she would enter a theatre, not as a member of an audience, but as an actress who would soon be actually on a *stage* with people sitting and looking at *her* and listening to her voice. Suddenly she gulped. 'Oh, dear,' she whispered, 'I wonder if I *can!*' She thought of Tony and Stephen, and what they had said to her the day before. They might have been joking, but they had agreed that no one in his or her right senses would pay money to see her, and Tony had said, 'They'll probably ask for their money back afterwards!'

Indignation brought a return of courage. 'Oh, will they! I'll show them – Tony and Stephen and the whole of Edwinton if they'd like to come!' With her face set with determination she pushed open the swing doors and charged across the foyer to the box-office. She gasped as her progress was cut short by contact with a large masculine body which smelled of tobacco and after-shave lotion.

'Well, well, well,' said Westwood Howe, 'Felicity Brooks, and right on time!' They went into the theatre through a door next to the box-office. Felicity had never been in a completely empty theatre before, but she felt immediately that she belonged there, that it was her kind of world. She sighed with pleasure as she looked round and saw the red plush seats and the plaster cherubs round the stage. The curtains were up and the stage was bare of scenery. She could see right to the whitewashed wall at the back. The sides were bare too, apart from one or two stands which carried floodlights. On each side was a door with an illuminated EXIT sign over it. It was all dimly lit, and the impression of drabness was increased by the makeshift furniture arranged round the stage, several ordinary chairs and a couple of ricketty-looking tables.

'Do you like it?' Westwood Howe's voice cut into her thoughts.

She hesitated a moment. 'It's – it's very interesting.'

The actor laughed. 'You mustn't expect glamour, young lady. Not at this stage of the proceedings, anyway. There's a lot of work to be done before anything like that happens. The first rehearsal is only a read-through of the play – we call it plotting. The actors read their parts slowly while the producer tells them when and where to move.'

'Is that the furniture that's used in the play?' Felicity asked.

Westwood Howe laughed again. 'No! Those things are just odds and ends used to represent the actual furniture. In a theatre even the furniture has to act. For instance those three chairs placed together represent a sofa. The tables might be a desk, a cupboard, or even a table!'

'What about those chairs turned with their backs to us?'

'They are marking exits and entrances. Now, I think it's time to start. You had better come on stage and meet the company.' Westwood Howe led her to a door at the side of the stage. 'This is called the pass door. It is the only way to get backstage from the auditorium. The actors are not allowed to use it once the show has started.'

They went through the heavy wooden pass door and up a few narrow stairs. Then Felicity reached the moment she had been longing for. She was actually on a stage . . . It was not at the moment the colourful fairyland she had expected but it was very thrilling and she hoped that Tony would be suitably impressed when she gave him an account of her experiences.

'Gwen, are you there?' Westwood Howe called. 'Come and meet our latest acquisition.'

'Righto, coming,' a deep voice bellowed from the other side of a door in the wings.

'Gwen is our stage manager,' Westwood Howe told Felicity. 'I'll leave you with her while I go and collect my script.' He walked off, an imposing figure, and Felicity looked after him with awe and growing devotion.

Then the door opened and a small, fat woman rushed out with arm outstretched. 'Ah, there you are,' she said briskly. 'How do you do? My name's Gwen Mortiboy. What's yours?'

'My name's Gwen Mortiboy.'

'Felicity Brooks,' she said, wincing as her fingers were squashed. What a strange-looking woman, she thought. Gwen Mortiboy was hardly any taller than Felicity herself and as round as she was high. She wore black jeans and at least three pullovers under a dark grey cardigan. There was a light green scarf round her neck and her head was bound up in a blue handkerchief, leaving only a few straggling dark hairs in the nape of her neck.

61

'Felicity, eh? That's a mouthful! What shall we call you for short? What do your chums call you?'

'Just Felicity, as a rule,' she answered, rather overwhelmed by the stage manager's powerful personality.

'Must have more patience than I have. Never mind, Felicity it shall be. And I'm Gwen Mortiboy – oh, I've already told you, haven't I? It usually doesn't take long for new chums to say, "You're a naughty boy, Mortiboy". I'm used to it, so you can say it now if you like and get it over. Then I'll say, "Felicity electricity," and we can call it quits. How do you like that?' Gwen went into a great cackle of laughter which dissolved into a cough. 'Oh, hark at me,' she added, and scrabbled in her pocket for a tin of throat pastilles. 'Have a cough drop?'

'Thank you,' said Felicity, and took one.

'Have you got a copy of the play?' asked Gwen, sucking furiously.

'No,' Felicity replied.

'Then we'd better find you one, hadn't we? Not much use if you don't know what to say. Now where did I put those spare copies?' Gwen went over to a chair at the front of the stage. 'Ah, there they are. Let's see, you're playing Hilda, aren't you? She's the daughter. Take this copy. There's not much of it, but don't let that worry you.'

'Oh, it doesn't,' said Felicity. 'It's marvellous to be playing a part, no matter what it's like.'

Gwen smiled at her. 'That's the spirit, Felicity. It isn't the size of the part that matters but how well you do it. As my old father used to say – and he carried a spear at the Old Vic for many a year – "There aren't any small parts. There are only small actors..."' She leaned towards Felicity and spoke very confidentially. 'As a matter of fact, the whole play is about Hilda. You might not come on until the end but the rest of them have been talking about you for *hours*. So you'd better be good. Ah, here come the others now. I'll tell you what – would you like to help me with my prop list?'

Felicity looked blank. 'Yes, but I'm afraid I don't know what a prop list is.'

'Properties – you know, things like teacups, wine-glasses, roast turkeys and revolvers. All the things which are used in a play. Part of my job is to make a list of them as they are mentioned during the read-through. Oh, you've got a pencil. Good. An actress without a pencil is like a car without an engine. You take this little book and when I mention something to you, jot it down. Drag up that stool and sit by me here in the prompt corner.'

By the time they had settled in the prompt corner the rest of the company had assembled on the stage.

'All right, everyone,' Westwood Howe called, 'let's start. By the way, the young lady with Gwen is Felicity Brooks. She's going to play Hilda. There's no point in introducing you all now, Alice will see it gets done during the morning. Now, when the curtain rises the stage is empty. There is a pause, then Mrs Murdoch enters from the garden carrying a bunch of roses.'

'Bunch of roses,' Gwen whispered to Felicity, who dutifully wrote it down.

'You come down to the settee,' Westwood Howe went on to Alice Kelly, 'take some newspapers from under the cushions . . .'

'Newspapers under cushions,' said Gwen. Felicity added it to her list.

'Then you put the flowers on the paper, take out a pair of scissors . . .'

'Scissors,' said Gwen. Sissers, wrote Felicity. That doesn't look right, she thought, but there's no time to think about that now.

'. . . and begin to cut the stems. Claude Murdoch enters – that's you, Graham – where is he? – oh, there you are. Graham, you come on carrying a pile of manuscripts . . .'

'Manuscripts,' said Gwen. But Felicity had already started on the word.

'You go straight over to your wife and you say, "Maud, dear, I've finished the last chapter". Is that clear?'

Alice Kelly and the actor named Graham had been writing the directions into their scripts. 'Yes,' said Alice Kelly.

'The usual corny opening,' said Graham, 'but I suppose it's a slight improvement on the butler finding the maid dusting or the telephone announcing that mother-in-law is coming to stay.'

'This play ran for *months* in Shaftesbury Avenue,' said Westwood Howe reprovingly. 'Let's get on with it . . . curtain up!'

Time passed surprisingly quickly for Felicity. Her list got longer and longer and when Gwen saw it she groaned. 'Goodness knows where I'll get half of those things,' she complained. 'Who in Retfield would be willing to lend us a silver Georgian tea service?'

'I know!' Felicity said eagerly. 'Not in Retfield, that is, but in Edwinton. Miss Pope-Cunningham's got one – I've seen her polishing it – and she'd lend it willingly. Shall I ask her tomorrow?'

'That's a good girl,' Gwen grunted approvingly. 'I can see you're going to be a great help. Tell your Miss Whatever-her-name-is that if she'll lend it to us I'll have it fetched and delivered. Now you'd better stand by, you're on in a moment. Give me your list. There won't be anything else to add.'

Felicity walked to the back of the stage near the two chairs marking the door. Westwood Howe, who had been directing the rehearsal from the auditorium, came down to the front of the footlights. 'Now, Felicity, this is where you come on. Have you been following the play?'

'Yes, Mr Howe,' said Felicity. She decided she would never dare to call him 'Westy' as the others did – it would be like calling her father 'Charles!'

'Good. The situation at the moment is that your father and mother think you have run away from boarding school. They'd sent you there because your father was going to America and your mother was to follow soon after. They were to be away for a year and during that time you were to stay at St Audrey's Academy. All clear?'

'Yes, Mr Howe,' Felicity said again.

'At the last moment your mother couldn't bear the thought of leaving you behind and, after a lot of argument, it has been agreed that you should go too. Then they learn that you have run away from school. You have been missing for twenty-four hours, and they are sure that something terrible has happened to you. They are at their wits' end. A policeman has just told them that there is still no news of you. Your mother is crying and your father is trying to comfort her. Suddenly the door bursts open and you come in. At first your mother doesn't see you. You stand in the centre of the stage and you say, 'Mummy, etc.' What's her cue to come on?'

'I give it,' said Gordon Price, the actor who was playing the policeman. 'It's too soon to give up hope, Mrs Murdoch,' he went on, using a north country accent for his part. 'We've dragged the mill pond – there was nothing there –'

Mrs Murdoch moaned. Felicity made a movement with her hand to suggest she was opening a door, and ran to the centre of the stage. There was a pause during which everyone slowly registered that she was there, and all their eyes were upon her. Alice Kelly rose and stretched out her arms to her.

'Right,' called Westwood Howe. 'Now, Felicity, walk slowly down to your mother.'

Felicity did so.

'Hilda, my darling,' said Alice Kelly, 'you're safe. Thank heavens, you're safe...'

Felicity looked at her script. 'Mummy, I'd decided to be a missionary in Africa but I've changed my mind. I'd miss you so much.'

'I'd miss you very much too, darling, so you're coming to America with us. Run upstairs and tell Granny you're back.' Alice Kelly closed her script, gave a little yawn and looked at her watch.

'Curtain,' said Westwood Howe. 'Jolly good, Felicity. That's the end of the play and it all ends happily, which Retfield will enjoy.'

'If anybody comes,' put in Graham gloomily.

'Of course they'll come. Retfield loves a good comedy-drama,' said Westwood Howe firmly. He gave an athletic

66

leap over the footlights and landed with a heavy thump on the stage. There was a strangled snort from Graham and Westwood Howe looked at him severely. 'Half-past ten tomorrow,' he said. 'We shan't need you, Felicity. See you on Friday.'

'Oh, yes!' Felicity breathed happily.

The first thing Mrs Brooks asked Felicity when she got home was whether she had had a proper lunch.

'Of course I did,' Felicity replied, wondering why parents didn't understand that sometimes there were things more important than eating. 'I had a bite with Gwen at a cafe near the theatre after rehearsal.'

'A bite!' repeated Mrs Brooks. 'What sort of a bite, may I ask?'

'Sausages and chips,' Felicity said. She saw a faint look of disapproval on her mother's face and added hastily, 'with peas. Gwen said it was a very good place to eat. Cheap and nasty, which is better than being expensive and nasty.'

'Good because it's nasty? Whatever do you mean?'

'No, good because it's *cheap!*' Felicity put on her long-suffering 'what *can* one expect of parents?' look and drew breath to start a long explanation.

'All right,' her mother said hastily, 'we'll let it pass. Who is Gwen, anyway?'

'The stage manager,' Felicity said. 'She's awfully sweet.' That was what she had heard Alice Kelly saying about *her* and it sounded very grown-up and theatrical.

'Surely someone named Gwen would be a stage manageress, wouldn't she?' asked Mrs Brooks.

Felicity sighed. 'No, Mummy, in the theatre we say manager. Lots of things are different. For instance, left is right, curtains are tabs, and – and even the furniture has to act!'

'Well, at this moment I have to act as President of the Women's Institute at the Church Hall. You can tell us all about it later on. If you want to find Tony and the gang I was to tell you that they've taken the bows and arrows to the field behind the church. Put your heavy shoes on as the grass will be damp after yesterday's rain.'

'I really ought to learn my part,' Felicity said importantly, 'but I did promise to tell Pauline about today.'

'Please yourself, dear, I must be off.' Mrs Brooks picked up her handbag and walked towards the door.

Suddenly Felicity said, 'Mummy, I'd decided to be a missionary in Africa –'

Mrs Brooks turned and stared at her. 'You've decided to be what?'

'Sorry,' Felicity said, wrenching her mind back to the Vicarage kitchen. 'I wasn't talking to you – it was part of the play.'

'I see,' murmured Mrs Brooks, and went out hurriedly so that Felicity should not see the smile on her face.

'I shall be jolly glad when this week and next are over,' said Tony a few days later. He was sitting astride a branch of an oak tree in the forest and gazing through the young green leaves into a sky of mild eggshell blue.

'Why?' asked Pauline, puffing as she scrambled up to join him.

'That sister of mine – she's getting impossible.'

68

'Why, what's she doing?' Pauline heaved a plump leg over the branch, settled herself against the trunk and prepared to listen sympathetically. Picking some young acorns she proceeded to drop them one by one on to Peter, who was scrabbling with a stick in the undergrowth beneath the tree, not looking for anything in particular but just enjoying the look and smell of the turned-up loam.

'She's behaving as though she wrote all Shakespeare's plays herself and has to act all the parts,' Tony said. 'She bounces around muttering and moaning, and every time I speak to her she looks at me as though I'm something the cat brought in. She's never there when there's any work to be done, and I've had to do her share of the washing-up as well as my own for days. Anybody would think there'd never been a play before this thing she's in. If you ask me,' he went on bitterly, 'it sounds a real shocker. All she's got is one line and you'd think she was never off the stage.'

'Ah, well,' Pauline offered philosophically, 'it won't be long before it's all over and then we can forget all about it. But you must admit, it is exciting to think that one of us is an actress, a real actress, getting paid for it.'

Tony brightened up slightly. 'She won't be able to spend any of her earnings, that's one good thing. It'll go straight into her Post Office account.'

'Grown-ups never seem to be sensible about money, do they? It always has to be *saved*.' Pauline said the last word with as much scorn as her good nature could summon up. 'It's a pity there wasn't a part in the play for you, isn't it?'

'Me!' Tony nearly fell out of the tree with indignation.

'Me – act! Why I wouldn't set foot on a stage if they paid me a thousand pounds a week! Putting stuff on your face and pretending to be somebody different, saying a lot of gooey things – no fear!'

'I would – for a thousand pounds a week,' said Pauline dreamily. 'Think of all the lovely things you could buy – a bicycle, new skates – and a box of chocolates every day! Peter,' she called down, 'have you got any of those jelly babies left?'

'No,' Peter called back, 'and considering that you took charge of the bag, that's a pretty silly question.'

'It was just a faint hope,' Pauline sighed. 'But I wouldn't be any good – on the stage, I mean. I should giggle. Felicity won't. She'll be very good. I'm looking forward to going next Monday. I shall wear my new blue.'

'I shall wear sackcloth and ashes,' Tony said. 'I say, can you hear all that crashing? I bet that's Dame Felicity Brooks, straight from her starring role in *Elephant Boy*.'

A series of 'Coo-ees', gradually getting louder, announced Felicity's arrival. She came in sight at last through some silver birch saplings, looking like Ophelia on her way to death by drowning. Gracefully she leaned against the slender trunk of a young tree, her hand to her chest, her breath coming in great gasps. Gracefully the slender trunk bent backwards beneath her weight and she was deposited in an undignified heap on the ground.

'Enter fairies, tripping lightly,' Tony remarked.

Felicity ignored him. 'I came as soon as I got back from rehearsal,' she said loftily. 'Pauline, come down and I'll tell you all about it.'

Pauline began to slither down the tree. Peter stopped his aimless scratching about and sat down on a patch of moss. 'Me too,' he said. 'What did you have to say today?'

'I have to say the same thing every time, silly,' said Felicity. 'But it's the way I say it that's important. Today Mr Howe said that I said it with feeling.'

'Feeling what?' Peter prepared to be sympathetic. 'Were you feeling ill?'

'I was *not* feeling ill. I said my words with *expression*. In fact, Mr Howe thought I put a bit too much expression in them. "Tone it down, Felicity," he said. "This isn't *East Lynne*." I wonder what he meant by that...' Felicity drew herself up regally. 'Still, we actresses can't always be in the right mood. We have to *feel* our way into our part.'

'You have to do an awful lot of feeling,' said Peter. He got up, closed his eyes and began to grope about like a blind man.

'What *are* you doing?' Pauline asked.

'I'm feeling my way into a part,' Peter explained.

Felicity stopped being an actress for a moment. 'Oh, *very* funny – positively hilarious. Come on, Pauline, I'll tell you the rest on the way home, it's nearly tea-time. Peter, you can follow at a respectful distance. Are you coming, Tony?'

'No, I'm waiting for Stephen and Sam. Sam knows where there's a nest of partridge's eggs. We're going to count them.'

'And don't touch them,' Felicity warned him severely. 'You don't want to scare the mother away.'

'We weren't thinking of touching them. Being an actress has made you awfully bossy, I must say.'

Tony heaved several exaggerated sighs of relief as the

71

others went off. He took a comic from his pocket and settled down to a quiet read until Stephen and Sam arrived. It's nice to be on your own, he reflected, and forget about silly sisters who think they're actresses. She used to be all right, not at all bad as girls go. Perhaps, when that soppy play was over, she would return to normal, or as normal as she ever could be. And nobody had better try to get *him* mixed up with such nonsense...

Monday arrived at last, the great day, the first night of the play. Felicity had gone to Retfield early in the afternoon for the dress rehearsal. Before she left to catch the bus she received so many wishes of good luck and little charms and mascots that she felt a prickly feeling at the back of her eyes. Tears did come at the very last moment when her mother said, 'I know you'll do very well, darling. Don't forget, we'll all be there watching you.' She took Felicity's right hand and crossed two of her fingers. 'There,' she said, knowing Felicity's fondness for signs and omens, 'keep them crossed until you enter the theatre and then everything will be all right. Now run along.'

Felicity swallowed a last gulp, dispersed the mist before her eyes with a vigorous rub, and skipped off to the bus stop at the crossroads.

Edwinton was certainly turning out in force. Mr and Mrs Brooks were going on their own, and Doctor Moore was taking Stephen, Tony and Sam. Old Eva was making a whole day of the occasion. She had left for Retfield early in the morning to visit her sister's family, and the whole eight of them were going to the theatre. 'Look out

72

for us, we'll be sitting on the very front row,' she had told Felicity proudly. Peter and Pauline were going with their parents, much to Peter's disgust. He would much rather had been with the other boys in the doctor's Jaguar. Miss Pope-Cunningham was going in her ancient Austin Seven, almost as excited at the thought of seeing her silver tea service on the stage as she was at seeing Felicity. She was surprised that no one had accepted her offer of a lift. 'We want to *get* there' had been the unspoken thought behind every polite refusal.

Lady Blogg, who lived at Edwinton Hall, and who was a great organiser and opener of garden fêtes, had hired a bus to take thirty-five people from the village. 'We'll all clap like mad for the dear girl,' she had told Mrs Brooks, 'all thirty-five of us. It used to be called a claque when I was a girl. People used to go to the opera just to applaud their favourite singer. Didn't matter how badly he sang, the claque would clap. Not,' she added hastily, 'that Felicity will be bad!'

There was an unusual air of excitement in Edwinton. Even Tony forgot his annoyance at Felicity's grand manner when he was stopped by people in the street and congratulated on his sister's behalf. 'You know,' he said to Stephen as they waited for Sam in the doctor's house, 'she must be pretty good to act with the Rep.'

'I suppose she must,' said Stephen. 'What if she stays?'

'What do you mean?'

'Doesn't come back – keeps on with the theatre –'

'I never thought of that,' said Tony, suddenly thinking how dreary things would be without his sister, irritating though she often was. 'She couldn't though,' he added. 'She's only twelve. I think there's a law about it.'

73

'Is there?' said Stephen. 'Anyway, she's got to go back to school after the holidays. Gosh, I wouldn't like it, would you?'

'Acting?'

'Yes – in front of all those people. It's bad enough in a school play.'

'Horrible. At least in the school play it's mostly your parents there and they don't matter. Felicity doesn't seem to mind a bit. Strange.'

At that moment there was a ring at the door.

'That'll be Sam,' said Stephen, leaping up. 'Come on, Tony.'

Stephen hurried to the front door but his father had got there first and opened it to Sam. 'Ah, Sam,' said the Doctor, 'there you are. Now we can go. Round to the garage, boys, and I'll get the car out. I hope there are no sudden illnesses in Edwinton while I'm away – though I don't think anybody would dare to be ill *tonight!*'

As the Jaguar turned into the main Retfield road Dr Moore gave a sigh of annoyance. 'Well, well,' he said, 'isn't that just my luck – we're right at the back of a convoy! The Felicity Brooks Fan Club members have all started out at the same time.'

'Guess who's ahead of us,' said Stephen, who was sitting in front.

The two boys in the back craned their necks to see. There, in the dead centre of the road, creeping along at a steady twenty-five miles an hour, was Miss Pope-Cunningham's Austin Seven.

'Close your eyes,' said Alice Kelly. She took up a

powder puff and powdered down the greasepaint on Felicity's face. 'There now, what do you think of yourself?'

Felicity looked into the large mirror over the dressing-room table. 'Oh, thank you,' she said, 'it's marvellous!' She had not realised just what a difference greasepaint could make. Not only were her eyebrows smooth and dark, her eyes looked larger and bluer, her complexion a milky rose but, marvel of marvels, her slightly snub nose looked perfectly straight.

'It's easy when you know how,' Alice Kelly said, putting the finishing touches to her own make-up. 'You'll be able to do it yourself before the end of the week.' There was a knock at the door and Gwen popped her head round. 'Five minutes, please,' she said.

'Five minutes,' Felicity repeated excitedly.

'Well, it's ten minutes really,' said Gwen. 'Then, in five minutes time, it's "Beginners, please". Don't ask me why. How're you feeling? Not nervous?'

'N-no.' Felicity was a bit dubious but decided she had better put a bold front on. 'Not any more,' she added with a gulp.

'That's the spirit,' said Gwen. 'Come and stand in the wings, or with me in the prompt corner if you want to. Good luck.'

'Thank you,' Felicity whispered.

Then, one by one, the rest of the company came to the door with 'Good luck' and 'All the best'. Gwen came back along the corridor with a call of 'Beginners, please!' Westwood Howe was the last to appear at the dressing-room door. 'This is it,' he announced. 'You've got a long wait, Felicity, but remember, you're every bit as impor-

75

tant as any of the others. A play depends on teamwork and you're part of the team. Good luck, my dear. I know you're going to be splendid.'

Slightly dazed by the tension and excitement in the atmosphere, Felicity went to the prompt corner where Gwen was making her last minute preparations. She looked up at the clock. Two minutes to go...

The theatre was almost full. All the Edwinton people had settled in their seats and the bells that were rung before the curtain went up had sounded. Dr Moore and the boys were sitting in the front row of the circle. They could see Old Eva and her family in the stalls and there had been some furious waving. Tony's father and mother were in the circle too, but further back, and the rest of their friends and acquaintances seemed to be in the stalls.

Peter, in the seventh row of the stalls, was still trying to think of a way of joining Tony, Stephen and Sam. 'I could see ever so much better from up there,' he said, 'and there might be a spare seat.'

'You will see very well from here,' his mother told him, 'and do stop fidgeting.' Reluctantly he gave in and turned again to his programme. 'Mum, it says a play in three acts. What's an act?'

'It means the play is in three parts, and each one is called an act,' said Mrs Christy patiently.

'You are ignorant,' Pauline hissed at him.

'So are you,' he hissed back. 'You can't even spell rhododendron.'

'What's that got to do with knowing what an act is?' said Pauline. 'We haven't come here for a spelling lesson.'

'I bet you can't spell fuchsia either!' Peter challenged her.

76

'I don't *like* fuchsia, so why should I have to spell it? Anyway, I bet you can't spell it either.'

'Oh, yes, I can. It's f-e-w-'

'Children, behave yourselves,' Mrs Christy interrupted. 'Do you want to be taken out before the play begins?'

'No!' cried Pauline. Peter buried his nose in his programme, muttering fiercely to himself about sisters who couldn't stick to the point.

The pianist, who had been regaling the audience with selections from 'Chu Chin Chow', suddenly switched to a series of loud chords which announced the National Anthem. The audience rose to its feet with a loud rumble. Peter began to sing in a loud voice, 'God save our gracious...'

'Sh!' his mother said sharply.

'Well, we do it at school,' he grumbled. 'I didn't know you're not supposed to sing.'

Mrs Christy sighed, looked over at her husband, standing on the other side of the twins, and shook her head helplessly. 'Never again,' she mouthed. Mr Christy grinned and jerked a thumb upwards.

The anthem over, there was another rumble as people sat down again. Gradually the noise subsided and the theatre grew quiet and expectant. The only light came from the footlights shining up at the curtain. Then the curtains moved apart with a swishing sound and the play began.

During the first interval the children met in the coffee bar where they swapped impressions during spoonfuls of ice cream. Peter was unashamedly bored and said so loudly. 'It's all talk,' he said.

'A play *is* talking,' Pauline said. She was not prepared

77

to admit that she had not understood much of the talk. In any case, it didn't matter. It was quite enough to watch the actors at work and listen to their voices.

'Not *all* talk though,' Peter insisted. 'Last Christmas when we went to *Treasure Island* lots of things kept on happening. There were pirates and fights and things. Not like this.' Peter closed his mouth round a large piece of ice cream and made a pirate face at his sister.

'That was for children and this is for grown-ups. I think it's marvellous, don't you, Tony?'

Tony, who secretly agreed with Peter, was non-committal. 'It's all right.'

'When is Felicity coming on?' Peter asked for the umpteenth time.

'Not till the end,' said Stephen. 'She told us at least fifty times.' Stephen was glad that his opinion of the play had not been sought because he would have had to admit that he liked it. It was like watching a real family, with an affectionate, fussy mother, a father too much wrapped up in his work to notice what was going on, and a funny servant who reminded him at times of Old Eva. I wonder if my mother would have been like that, he wondered.

'Did you see the way the stars came out as it got darker?' said Sam, more interested in the technical side than in the problems of human relationships. 'I wonder how that was done. I mean, they just sort of came. Tony, do you think Felicity can get us behind the scenes when it's over?'

'I expect so,' said Tony. 'We'll have to go round to pick her up.'

'Quite a treat,' Dr Moore was saying, drinking coffee with the other parents. 'It's the first time I've been to a

78

play for years. It knocks spots off television, that I must say.'

'We have so little time to spare for theatre-going, alas,' said Mrs Brooks, 'and they are a splendid little company, aren't they, Charles?'

The Vicar puffed at his pipe. 'Yes, my dear, very good, and you can hear every word they say. More than I can say for the chap who came to preach last month – what was his name, dear?'

'You mean Mr Fortescue?'

'That's the chap – muttered into his waistcoat. Made his Amens sound like yawns.' Mr Brooks, deciding that his pipe would not draw, tapped it out into the ash-tray. Then he gave a little chuckle, his thoughts having returned to the play. 'It's been quite a surprise – I would never have thought it of him –'

'What has, dear, and who wouldn't you have thought it of?' Mrs Brooks was used to her husband's odd utterances.

'Fred – he was such a timid lad when we were at school together.'

'Who's Fred, Vicar?' asked the doctor, raising puzzled eyebrows.

The Vicar chuckled again. 'I suppose I ought not to tell you this, but Westwood Howe – Felicity's idol of the moment – isn't Westwood Howe really. That's only a stage name. His real name is Fred Glossop...'

Then the bell rang, summoning them back to their seats for the second act. Back stage the call went round, 'Act Two beginners, please.'

Felicity had stayed with Gwen in the prompt corner, fascinated by the view of the play she had from there.

79

During the first act she had been so interested in watching that she had forgotten she was due to become part of the proceedings before long. The interval had broken the spell and Gwen noticed her hands twisting together and the restless shuffling of her feet. 'Butterflies?' she asked.

'A few,' Felicity admitted.

'It's the worst part, the waiting,' said Gwen. 'It's better to open the play and get it over quickly. Sometimes they make me play a part when they're absolutely stuck and I hate it.'

'Hate acting?' Felicity was astounded that anyone who worked in the theatre could dream of saying such a thing.

'Loathe it. Stage management suits me fine, but if I have to go on that stage I'm quivering like a jelly the whole time, and for hours before and hours after. And there's quite a lot of me to quiver!' Gwen poked her head on to the stage through the square hole used for prompting. 'Everyone there? Right. Stand by. Curtain going ... up.' She pressed a red button which gave a signal to a stage hand in the flies and the dusty velvet curtains swung apart again.

When the third and last act started the air of expectancy among the Edwinton contingent began to reach its peak. Peter, thinking that Felicity might come on and go off without him noticing, sat forward in his seat and breathed so heavily that the lady in front of him turned up the collar of her dress. Sam, in the circle, who now more than ever thought that Felicity was the nicest and cleverest girl he had ever known, stared at the stage fixedly. He must not miss one second of what was happening. The lighting effects must take a back seat. Tony, to his surprise, discovered that he was nervous, as though it was he who was about to make an appearance. He grasped his lucky bun penny tightly. After all, the honour of the Brooks family was at stake. Stephen, realising how Tony was feeling, gave him a nudge. 'Relax,' he whispered with a grin.

Mr and Mrs Brooks were absorbed in the play, but at the same moment turned to each other and smiled. 'I wonder what she is feeling like,' Mrs Brooks said.

'I remember when I preached my first sermon –' the Vicar began, but his wife put her finger to her lips and he stopped.

'I wonder what they're thinking,' said Felicity to herself as she stood outside the door through which she was to make her entrance. 'I wish I was with them, and not here!'

The minutes passed. She muttered her line over and over to herself. She felt her legs gradually getting wobbly. Her mouth suddenly became dry and however much she licked her lips she felt that her tongue was moving around in a cave of ashes. There was nobody near her, nobody to give her a smile of encouragement. She was alone, and the terrible moment was fast approaching. So *this* is what being nervous means, she thought. I wish I could run away. I wish this was only a nightmare. I wish –

She heard, as from a vast distance, the policeman on stage saying comfortingly, 'It's too soon to give up hope, Mrs Murdoch. We've dragged the mill pond – there was nothing there –'

Felicity drew in her breath sharply. It's me – I'm on! was her panic-stricken thought. What do I *say*?

She opened the door and stood in the entrance. The sudden brightness after the darkness of the wings made her blink. The auditorium was a black void, though living and breathing, waiting like a caged animal to spring. They were all out there, family and friends – she mustn't let them down. She lifted her head and walked slowly towards Alice Kelly, who was waiting for her with her arms stretched out.

'Hilda, my darling,' said her 'mother', 'you're safe. Thank heavens, you're safe...'

Felicity's voice came loud and clear. It echoed in every corner of the theatre. 'Mummy, I'd decided to be a missionary in Africa, but I've changed my mind. I'd mush you so mich!'

A great silence fell on the theatre. Felicity saw Alice Kelly's eyes glaze over and mouth drop open. The policeman suddenly turned his back to the audience as though overcome with emotion. She realised what she had said and her hand flew up to cover the surge of redness that threatened to burst through the greasepaint and set her face on fire. She tried again.

'I'd mich you so mush – no, I mean – I'd much you so miss – no – oh, you know what I mean!' she finished desperately.

Alice Kelly gazed wildly into the wings as though searching for help but all she could see was Gwen Mortiboy's round face, creased up with agonised delight. There was a sighing coming over the footlights like steam escaping from a giant valve.

Felicity didn't want the ground to open and swallow her up, as she had read in books. She just wanted not to exist at all. She wanted there never to have been such a person as Felicity Brooks who could have done something so *awful*. Her only thought was to get away from

82

the hissing steam and the accusing glare of Alice Kelly. But she could not move. She felt the redness in her face recede and whiteness take its place.

The final lines of the play belonged to Alice Kelly. She started to say them without any conviction, without any of the warmth that a mother would feel on welcoming back a lost daughter. 'I'd muss you very mich too, darling . . .'

She stopped, aghast. The sighing of the audience turned into a gentle breeze of not very well controlled laughter. She struggled on with her line . . . 'so you're coming to America with us. Run upstairs and tell Granny you're back.'

Thankful to have something to do, Felicity rushed to the door at the centre of the back flat and pushed. Nothing happened. The door would not budge. She pushed harder. Again there was no result. She looked back at Alice Kelly with desperation in her face. 'Pull, not push,' Alice Kelly mouthed. Felicity pushed.

With a creak and a groan the flat sagged backwards and exposed a gaping hole in the line of the wall as though a rather gentle earthquake had decided to demolish the room bit by bit. There was a strangled yelp from behind and Gwen Mortiboy's head and shoulders appeared in the gap, her arms straining to keep the recalcitrant flat from complete collapse.

The laughter from the front swelled into a gale. A picture of Granny, hanging by the side of the door, fell on to the stage. Felicity left the flat to the efforts of the gallant Gwen, picked up the picture, looked round wildly for somewhere to put it, could only see, in her panic, the hands of Alice Kelly quivering in front of her, thrust it

'Look, Mummy, Granny wants to come too!'

into the hands, and blurted out, 'Look, Mummy, Granny wants to come too...'

The curtains suddenly and blessedly came together with a rush. A forest fire of laughter and wild clapping filled the theatre. The sound of the applause was like the cracking of bullets in a Western film. Peter banged his palms together until they hurt. 'Good old Felicity!' he yelled. 'Pauline, wasn't that super?'

In the circle Tony and Stephen looked at each other. 'What –' they both began. Then they looked hastily away and concentrated on making as much noise as possible. The Vicar gave a little sigh and began to pull out his pipe. But Mrs Brooks nudged him. 'Applaud, Charles,' she whispered. 'Suppose Felicity can see you...' Behind the curtain Felicity stood as though turned to stone. Then she felt her hand grabbed by the policeman. 'Come on, into line,' he muttered. She was pulled downstage and joined the others, ready to take their first call. The curtains parted. The applause swelled. The curtains swung together, parted, came together and parted again. Westwood Howe, who for once had only been playing a small part, stepped forward. He raised a hand gracefully and the applause subsided raggedly. He gave a short speech of thanks, announced the play for the following week, bowed and stepped back. The curtains swished together for the last time and the cast started to move off the stage to the dressing-rooms. Nobody looked at Felicity. She burst into tears.

'Why, my dear child, whatever are you crying about?' Westwood Howe turned back and put an arm round her shoulders.

Sobs turned into a howl. 'I spoiled everything. I got my words mixed up, I pulled the scenery down and the play was a flop. I want to go home – I'm a failure...'

Westwood Howe sat on a chair and pulled Felicity towards him. 'Now, that's enough of that nonsense. Of course you weren't a failure. Was she, Alice?' he called to Alice Kelly, who was passing by.

Alice Kelly managed a rather wintry smile. 'Of course not. You – you managed very well, Felicity. You showed great presence of mind.' She patted Felicity vaguely on the head and went off.

'When we were rehearsing the door opened the other way,' Felicity got out through her sobs.

'We were using last week's door, you see.'

'But I should have remembered which way it opened from the dress rehearsal – it was the proper door then,' Felicity said.

'Well, you forgot – and that could happen to any of us. In the circumstances you did very well. Presence of mind – that's what you showed, just as Alice said. Why, I don't know anybody else who could have thought of such a good line when the picture came down. It just *made* that final curtain.'

'Do you – do you think so?' Felicity gazed at him with streaming eyes.

'I should think I do mean it. The audience loved it – didn't you hear the laughter?'

'I – I thought that was because I'd made such a mess of things –'

'They were laughing because it was funny. *You* had made it funny. If you hadn't said what you did it would have been a fiasco. You did rather go to pieces on your words, but we can put that down to first night nerves. It's quite understandable. But the last line – well, do you know what? We're going to put it in every night this week! Gwen will arrange for the picture to fall at that point in the play. Of course we'll try not to bring the set down too . . .'

'Then – then I didn't let the play down so badly?'

The actor gave a booming laugh. 'You gave it a really strong ending. Now, cheer up, my dear, and dry those eyes, or your father will think you've been rehearsing the death of little Willie.'

Felicity gulped and a small smile appeared on her tear-streaked face. 'Thank you, Mr Howe, thank you very much.'

They began to move off stage. 'I'll tell you something else,' Westwood Howe said. 'Your father and I were in a play at school once. We did *The Merchant of Venice*. Do you know what your father, who was playing Portia, did?'

'No, what did he do?'

'He only missed out "The quality of mercy" speech completely!'

Felicity reached the dressing-room feeling decidedly less miserable. But she was very quiet as she removed her make-up and changed into her ordinary clothes. She slipped out of the theatre as unobtrusively as possible and only Gwen Mortiboy saw her go and clapped her on the back with a 'Well done, my hearty! You certainly showed them how farce should be played! Only next time, don't bring me into it . . .'

The family was waiting for her outside the stage door. Felicity had never been so glad to see them. Tony was there too as he was returning in the family car instead of with the Doctor. Mrs Brooks put her arms around her and gave her a kiss. 'Very nice, Felicity, we did enjoy it,' she said.

Her father kissed her too. 'You did very well. Hidden talent in the family coming to the fore! You'll be the toast of Edwinton.'

'You were smashing,' Tony said. 'Your part was jolly funny – but you never told us about that last line. You said –'

'Tony,' his father interrupted, 'you can discuss that

later. Come with me now to fetch the car. Your mother and Felicity can stroll round to the front of the theatre and wait there.'

Sitting in the back of the car on the homeward journey, Felicity decided to tell Tony the truth. 'Tony,' she said quietly, 'you know that line you asked about – the last one?'

'Yes, you're a dark horse not telling us. I'm glad you didn't, though, because it was funny and it wouldn't have been if we'd known about it.'

'Tony, I made it up.'

Tony started. 'You – what?'

'I made it up,' said Felicity, 'on the spur of the moment.'

'What!'

'It's true. I felt such a fool for making a mess of the first speech, and then when the door wouldn't open I didn't know what to do. I felt like crying but – well, you can't cry on the stage, not when you're not supposed to, if you see what I mean.'

'Go on,' said Tony.

'Well, the picture fell down, and as I picked it up I thought – the horse.'

'What horse?'

'Daddy's horse. Oh, Tony, you remember – when Daddy was moving his study last year and we were helping him.'

'You mean that picture – by someone called Stubbs or something? What about it?'

'It fell down, just like the picture in the play, as we were folding the curtains.'

'I remember now. It just missed bonking Dad on the head.' Tony smiled as he remembered.

88

'Yes. Then Daddy picked it up and said to it, "So you want to change your stable too." That is what came into my head tonight. So I said, "Granny wants to come too".'

'Come where too?'

'To America, soppy, didn't you follow the play?' said Felicity, exasperated.

'Of course I did. Wasn't old Howe annoyed at you putting in a line that wasn't in the play?'

'Certainly not,' said Felicity with dignity. 'Westy,' she went on, greatly daring, 'said that I must keep the line in every night and Gwen is going to make the picture fall down specially.'

'Well, well, well,' said Tony, 'fancy you writing your own lines. Wonders will never cease.'

'You know, Tony, I might write a play – I think I could. You can help me if you like.'

Tony burst into incredulous laughter. 'You – write a play! You'd give yourself all the lines!'

'I would *not!*' Felicity said sharply.

Mrs Brooks turned round to them from the front seat. 'Don't get too excited, you two. You've had a tiring day, Felicity, and there are five more days ahead. Perhaps they'll ask you to do a play during your next holidays. Would you like that?'

Suddenly the whole scene flashed before Felicity's eyes. She shuddered as she heard her voice saying the dreadfully mixed-up lines, and she remembered vividly the terrible feeling when she wanted to disappear. 'Er – no, I don't think I would. Not yet, anyway.'

In the darkness Mrs Brooks smiled.

'Tony,' Felicity said after a pause, 'how do you learn to be a kennel maid?'

89

SPRING FLOOD

It started to rain in Edwinton on the first day of spring, and a fortnight later it was still raining. The sodden sky smothered the village like an old grey blanket. The rain beat on roofs and filled the guttering to overflowing. Gardens were drowned and spring flowers dashed ruthlessly to the ground. The few people who ventured out, huddled under umbrellas, squelched miserably from puddle to puddle, and were spattered by great spurts of dirty water sent up by passing cars. Fields were quagmires and Sherwood Forest was deserted and forlorn.

Never, so everybody declared, had they known anything like it. 'It's the end of the world, I'm sure,' quavered little Miss Plumb, who was afraid of her own shadow. ''Tweren't like this when we had Fahrenheit,' said Old Eva.

Day after day, relentlessly, the rain continued. Farmers shook their heads and prophesied ruin. The Vicar said prayers in church for fine weather, but the rain, like steel rods, hit the ground and broke into a thousand hissing drops. People's tempers became frayed, and children, bored and fretful at having to stay indoors, were subject to unaccustomed nagging and snapped commands to keep quiet.

The Greenwooders saw little of each other during the fortnight. Tony and Felicity, Stephen and Sam returned home from Retfield High by bus each afternoon and parted hurriedly to go their separate ways. After tea there was homework. Tony and Felicity retired to the attic play-room, and in between writing essays and doing algebra squabbled half-heartedly over nothing at all. Sam went about his jobs on the farm, which normally he enjoyed, his head and shoulders hunched under a piece of sacking, wishing his father had chosen some other way of making a living. Stephen, with only Old Eva for company, banged his way about the house and sulked. His father, who had never been busier, was seldom available for a game of chess. Peter and Pauline, who went to the school in the village, saw nothing of their friends. Peter drove his parents to distraction by his attempts to build an ark in the sitting-room, and Pauline seemed to spend most of her time wringing her hands and saying, 'Peter, there isn't room for that in here!'

At the lower end of the village there was alarm. The River Medding, which flowed behind the houses and gardens of Mill Lane, and which was usually a gentle, ambling stream, was rising rapidly. Its placid waters were swirling angrily, and more than a dozen houses were threatened with engulfment. The anxious inhabitants were making preparations to move out. They shifted furniture and carpets to upstairs rooms and tried to stop up every cavity that might let in the impending floods. 'Another two days before it comes,' said the wiseacres. 'The water's not quite up to the top of the river bank.'

Mrs Haddock, the oldest inhabitant of Edwinton, sniffed unbelievingly. 'That river'll never flood,' she said. 'You mark my words. It never has in all the years I've been living here, and never won't.'

91

'Don't be so sure,' Mrs Gedge, her next door neighbour, said. 'There's a first time for everything.'

'No.' Mrs Haddock was adamant. 'Here I am and here I stay.'

Catastrophe broke on the fourteenth day of the rain, a day before it was expected. During a night of torrential downpour the river burst its banks and roared over the gardens of Mill Lane. It swept everything aside that blocked its path and battered against the stone cottages as though it were possessed of a fierce hatred for them. In a few hours it had risen to the level of the windows. The muddy water seeped under the doors and filled the downstairs rooms. It rose inch by inch, lapping against the walls, staining the wallpaper, stealthily taking possession of kitchen, living-room and larder. It seemed that the whole row would be submerged in no time at all.

Rescue efforts were quickly organised. The village firemen turned out to fight water instead of fire. They tried to wade through the flood to the houses but found the water too deep. They got long ladders and set them up as near to the houses as possible and most of the people were able to climb out of their bedroom windows and clamber down the sloping rungs to safety. Wet and shivering, they either went to relatives or friends in the village or to the Church Hall, which Mrs Brooks had hurriedly opened and warmed by electric fires. There, with mattresses and blankets the Vicar had scurried round the village to collect, and with tea and sandwiches provided by Miss Pope-Cunningham, they spent the rest of the night reliving their experiences and declaring that never did they think the likes of what had happened would ever happen to them. 'It's just like being in a book,' said Mrs Gedge, her shock giving way to a thrilled excitement.

Mrs Haddock's cottage had received the full brunt of the force of the flood, and the water had reached almost to the level of the bedroom window. The rescuers soon realised that it would be impossible to fix up a ladder for the old lady to climb down. Sergeant Burrows, the village policeman, and Mr Mottershead, the chief of the voluntary fire brigade, stood in Mill Lane, up to their knees in water, conferring anxiously.

'Don't suppose the old girl can swim,' Mr Mottershead said, his vast frame beginning to shake with laughter.

'If she'd got a broomstick with her she could fly to dry land,' said the policeman, not to be outdone.

'Help!' came the thin voice of Mrs Haddock. 'Get me out of here.' She could just make out the forms of the two men in the darkness. 'Don't stand there, you two. Help an old woman!'

'Is there a boat in the village?' asked Mr Mottershead.

Sergeant Burrows thought hard. 'Don't think there is –' he began. Then he brightened. 'Come to think of it, Len Cottam at Mill Lane Corner – he's got one. Keeps it in his garden shed, goodness knows why. I think he was set on being a sailor when he was a lad, but never managed to get farther afield than Ollerthorp. I don't suppose it's seaworthy, but we can try. Hold on, ma,' he called to Mrs Haddock. 'We'll be along with a boat in a couple of minutes.'

'You'd better hurry,' Mrs Haddock called back. 'Minnie's getting cold. She don't like the water. And no more do I,' she grumbled to herself, watching the two men disappear. 'Nasty wet stuff.'

93

The policeman and Mr Mottershead returned in a few minutes, carrying between them an ancient and wrinkled boat which looked the reverse of seaworthy, and they stood at the edge of the water, gazing doubtfully across to the half submerged cottage.

'Do you think it's safe?' said Mr Mottershead. 'I do weigh sixteen stone, you know.'

'And me thirteen,' sighed the sergeant. 'That's twenty-nine altogether. There's one thing – the old lady won't add much to the total!' He surveyed the decrepit craft with dismay. 'I suppose we'll have to risk it. Can't leave Mrs Haddock there – it'll be days before the water goes down. If it ever does,' he added pessimistically. 'If only it would stop raining...' He shook himself like an out-size sheep dog and the drops flew off his helmet and cape. 'Come on, Bert. You get in and I'll shove off and nip in after you.'

The greengrocer pushed the boat into the water and gingerly lowered himself into it. There was a creak of protesting wood and the boat sank to within a few inches of the gunwales, rocking wildly. Mr Mottershead clutched the sides. 'Hurry up, Jim,' he called, 'this isn't going to last long.'

The sergeant pushed the boat and it began to glide slowly over the expanse of water. He splashed after it and heaved himself over the side. The boat sank a little more and began to ship water. 'Do you think we'll do it?' he asked with alarm in his voice.

Mr Mottershead grunted. 'Dunno, but here goes, any-way.' He took the pair of warped oars and started to row as steadily as he could.

The boat wobbled onwards. The rain beating on the

94

wooden slats was like an explosion of soft bullets. The two men, water dripping from every part of them, grimly bent their energies to getting through the turgid flood and reaching the end cottage without capsizing their elderly craft.

They reached it after some anxious minutes and the boat bumped gently against the wall under the bedroom window. Sergeant Burrows looked up at old Mrs Haddock and wondered whether her extra weight would mean disaster. 'Now, ma,' he said, 'we've come to get you.' He stood up cautiously and the boat gave a violent lurch. 'See if you can get over the ledge and I'll take you in my arms.'

Mrs Haddock drew back from the window. 'Get in that thing?' she said. 'Not likely. Gallivanting about in boats at my age, it's not decent. Isn't there any other way of getting me down?'

The policeman sighed. 'No, ma, there isn't. And if you stay there arguing, there won't be no boat either. It'll have sunk beneath us. Now, now, now,' he said in his best policeman voice, 'be sensible, Mrs Haddock. We've had a job to get here, and we're none too safe. You can't be left here alone, that's certain. No one knows how much higher the water will get, nor how long it'll stay. Try to get out of the window, there's a good girl, and let's be off.'

'Girl!' Mrs Haddock gave a harsh cackle. 'It's a long time since I've been called a girl, young man! All right, turn your eyes away, the both of you, and you'll see what a girl of ninety-six can do!'

The two men averted their eyes as Mrs Haddock drew a chair up to the window, climbed on to it, and stiffly pulled herself up till she was sitting on the window ledge. 'Thought I couldn't do it, didn't you?' she chuckled. 'Now,

95

'Hey, Minnie, what are you doing?'

Minnie, you stay on my shoulder while these lads lift me down.'

Sergeant Burrows, swaying slightly, held out his arms and Mrs Haddock slowly slid into them, then down his chest and finished up straight-backed and dignified in the bottom of the boat. 'You see?' she declared. 'Easy! Wish I'd got me umbrella, though. Don't fancy getting wet in me nightdress. Hey, Minnie, what are you doing?'

The black cat had jumped down from her mistress' shoulder and was perched on the edge of the boat, looking wildly round her. Her tail was waving ominously and her claws scratched on the wood. Mr Mottershead put out a hand to grab her and Minnie arched her back and spat. He quickly withdrew and the boat rocked. Minnie glared at him. 'Careful!' Mrs Haddock cried. 'Don't let her fall into the water.'

Mr Mottershead lunged again, and Minnie leaped. 'Ouch!' he yelled, glaring at the red scratch all along the back of his hand. 'Why, you little –' Forgetting where he was, he stood up to make another grab at the hissing cat, overbalanced and fell out of the boat and backwards into the water. There was a great splash. Minnie seemed to take wings and fly as the water hit her. With a single bound she reached the window ledge and disappeared into the darkness of the bedroom beyond.

'Bert!' the sergeant yelled. 'Are you all right?' He leaned over the side as best he could and groped feverishly in the murky depths.

'Minnie!' Mrs Haddock called. 'You naughty cat! Come back this minute, d'you hear?'

There was a gurgling in the water and Mr Mottershead's head appeared. His hair was plastered down to his skull and water streamed down his face. 'Glug – glug,' he bubbled and went under again.

The next time he appeared he had struggled to the cottage wall and was clinging to a drain pipe. 'That – that – cat –' he gasped.

'Minnie!' Mrs Haddock called again. 'Drat you – wait till I get my hands on you, my lady.' For the first time she noticed Mr Mottershead clinging to the pipe. 'What are you doing there, lad?' she asked, puzzled.

The policeman manoeuvred the boat back to the wall and held it as steady as possible while the greengrocer, spluttering and panting, crawled over the side and fell floundering like a stranded porpoise in the alarmingly large pool of water which had gathered in the bottom. Sergeant Burrows grabbed the oars and swung the boat round for the return journey.

'Stop!' Mrs Haddock cried. 'We can't go without Minnie!'

'Ma,' the sergeant replied grimly, 'we're going without Minnie unless we all want to finish up swimming to land.'

'But – but I can't go and leave her.' The old lady turned a distressed face to him. 'Me and Minnie's always together. She wouldn't know what to do without me, nor me without her – and not a fish head in the house. Please, young Jim,' she pleaded. 'Just go back and try once more.'

Mr Mottershead gave an almighty sneeze. 'Don't you dare,' he said to the policeman. 'I'll catch my death if I don't get home to a mustard bath. Who's more important, I'd have you know, a mangy old cat or me?'

'She's not mangy,' Mrs Haddock retorted with spirit. 'Her fur's lovely. She gets the best liver every Friday when I get me pension, and I comb her regular. I won't go without my cat, I tell you!' She folded her arms and sat upright, the light of battle in her eyes.

'Sorry, ma.' Sergeant Burrows was pulling strongly towards dry land. 'Bert's soaked to the skin, and it can't be good for you either, sitting there in those thin clothes. No, it's back to a warm fire and some hot soup for all of us.'

Mrs Haddock seemed to crumple suddenly, and her fighting spirit evaporated. A few tears trickled down her wrinkled old face. She sniffed once or twice, then fell silent. She turned her head once to look behind her at the open window of the cottage as they rowed away from it, then, with a hard, set expression on her face, she allowed herself to be handed out of the boat, wrapped in a large blanket, put into a car and taken to the Vicarage, where Mrs Brooks had put hot water bottles in a bed in one of the spare rooms.

Felicity and Tony, called from their beds in the middle of the night to help with the rescue work, thought they had never had a more thrilling time. Felicity cut sandwiches, heated up tins of soup hurriedly fetched from the grocer's – and difficult it had been to wake him up – and scuttled about between the Vicarage and the Church Hall, feeling like a cross between Florence Nightingale, Elizabeth Fry and Grace Darling. None of the homeless people sitting around the hall was free from her ministrations. It was a secret disappointment that none of them needed bandaging or their temperatures taken. Apart from being wet, tired, anxious about their homes and property, the old ones excited and resigned, the young ones excited and frightened, they seemed to be all right. In any case, Doctor Moore was moving around among them, and Felicity had to be content with trotting round after him, proud to be his assistant.

When Mrs Haddock arrived at the Vicarage the main part of the excitement was over. The refugees in the hall had settled down to uneasy sleep, the Vicar and his wife had returned home and, with Tony and Felicity, were yawning over a last cup of tea. They all hurried out to the front door when the car drew up, and Felicity dashed out to give the old lady her arm.

But Mrs Haddock waved it aside, and with a stiff dignity climbed the steps and reached the hall. She saw the reception committee, but apart from bobbing her head at the Vicar, gave no sign of recognition. 'I'm an old woman and I'm tired,' she announced. 'I want to go to my bed.'

'So you shall,' said Mrs Brooks soothingly. 'Everything is ready. The room is warm and there are hot water bottles in the bed. Come with me, my dear, and when you've settled down Felicity will bring you some hot milk.'

'Thank 'ee,' Mrs Haddock said gruffly. Then the mention of milk seemed to pierce her indifference, and she gave a little moan. 'Minnie – my poor Minnie. I shall never sleep without I know where she is and what she's doing. Mean, heartless men – they wouldn't go back for her, you know. She's all I've got, and now she's gone – drownded, as like as not, and lying in a watery grave. She couldn't stomach water.' Her rheumy old eyes filled, and she blinked the tears away savagely. 'Won't somebody help to find my Minnie?'

An embarrassed Sergeant Burrows, hovering in the background, explained briefly what had happened, and there were sympathetic exclamations from his listeners. 'Oh, what a shame,' Felicity said, her tender heart wrung with pity.

'I'm sure she'll be all right,' said Mrs Brooks. 'The sergeant and Mr Mottershead would have been endangering their own lives and yours if they had not got you away when they did. People must come before animals, you know.'

100

'*Some* people, perhaps! I know Minnie's only a cat,' Mrs Haddock said as she began to mount the stairs, 'but she's as much as a person to me. I'm ninety-six, and she's not much younger in cat age. She'll be lost without me, poor Min. She'll be a corpse before I see her again, I know she will.'

Mrs Brooks was helping the old lady across the landing to the room prepared for her. 'Don't forget that cats have nine lives,' she said with an attempt at humour.

'Not my Minnie, she hasn't. She's only got one left. The other eight went long ago. There was the time the bus hit her, and when she was savaged by that nasty dog of the Gedges, and when some dratted boys tied a can to her tail and threw her into the river, and...' The last the listeners downstairs heard was a recital of how Minnie had lost the rest of her eight lives, followed by, 'And I don't want no hot milk, thank you. I couldn't bear to drink it with Minnie starving and fretting in an empty house...'

Though it was four o'clock by the time everybody had got to bed, the Brooks family were up at the usual time the next morning. Mrs Brooks had a worried look as she got breakfast ready for Felicity and Tony. 'It's Mrs Haddock,' she explained. 'She's still pining for her cat. I'm sure she never slept during the night, and this morning she would not even have a cup of tea. I shall have to call the doctor in if she's going to be like this.'

'Poor old lady,' said Felicity, and Tony glumly surveyed his cornflakes and wondered how he would feel if he were separated from Prince, his cocker spaniel, now nestling contentedly at his feet.

Mrs Brooks sighed. 'I must go up again and see if she's

all right. Hurry up with your breakfasts, children, and don't miss the bus. I hope you'll explain to your teachers if they see you falling asleep at odd times during the day!'

On the bus to Retfield Felicity, Tony, Stephen and Sam occupied the back seats. Usually Tony compared homework notes with Stephen, as they were in the same form, and Felicity with Sam, who were in parallel forms and had the same teachers, but for once school matters were forgotten. Stephen and Sam were suitably impressed by the account of the previous night's experiences which Felicity dramatically, and Tony matter-of-factly, related, and regretted that they had not been there to share the excitement.

'I can't get Mrs Haddock's face out of my mind,' Felicity said in a troubled voice.

'It must be awful to be old and have nothing but a cat to care for,' said Tony. There was a heavy silence. The bus rumbled into the outskirts of Retfield and the children gathered together their belongings. 'Felicity, don't stick your umbrella in my leg,' Tony said irritably.

'Sorry,' Felicity said, without any of her usual spirit.

Tony looked at her curiously, but said nothing. The bus jerked to a stop in the market-place, and the four children alighted so soberly that the conductor looked at them in amazement. 'All going to get the cane?' he asked.

Felicity stuck her nose in the air, and Sam pulled his face into a tolerable imitation of Popeye. Tony said, as they walked along the slippery pavement, dodging between people with shopping bags and workers striding to their offices, 'We'd better have a meeting tonight, rain or no rain. The attic at six o'clock – all right?'

102

'We've got to rescue Mrs Haddock's cat!' Tony came straight to the point with the minimum of words when the Greenwooders met in the attic that evening. Peter and Pauline had not arrived, but Felicity had telephoned them and they were expected any moment.

'How?' asked Stephen, equally bluntly.

'Yes, how?' said Sam. 'Her cottage is surrounded by water. I had a look earlier on.'

'So did I,' said Tony, 'and it looked pretty hopeless. The water's still nearly up to the window ledge and there's no way of getting near the house.'

'Unless we borrow Mr Cottam's boat. But it's a funny thing,' Sam said, 'I didn't see any sign of it.'

'I'm not surprised,' said Stephen. 'I can tell you where it is.'

'Where?' asked Sam.

'At the bottom of the water.'

'Do you mean it's *sunk*?' said Felicity.

'Went down like a ton of bricks. Len Cottam told me. I thought our only chance of getting the cat was by borrowing the boat so I cycled down to see Len Cottam after school.'

'Why didn't you tell us?' Tony said.

'I'm telling you now,' Stephen said. 'I only had the idea after I left you at the bus stop. Len Cottam told me what had happened. When Sergeant Burrows and Mr Mottershead got Mrs Haddock to dry land Mr Mottershead went off home to change, leaving the sergeant to tie up the boat. He didn't do it very well, that's all. When Len Cottam went to see that everything was all right, there

103

was his boat, fifty yards out and sinking rapidly. He thinks she's sprung a leak.'

A general depression settled over the Greenwooders. Felicity dropped down on the rocking-chair. 'Well, that's that,' she said. 'It's a pity Sergeant Burrows wasn't a scout and got his knotting badge.'

'Oh, you can't blame him,' said Tony. 'It was a pretty brave thing he and Mr Mottershead did.'

'Even Len Cottam didn't blame anybody,' said Stephen. 'He got all sentimental and said he was glad his boat had saved a life before she died herself.'

'Cor, did he?' said Sam. 'I bet he was relieved that the captain didn't have to go down with the ship.'

'This is hardly the time for jokes,' said Felicity severely. 'Can't we think of some way to get that cat?'

At that moment the door burst open and Peter and Pauline entered. Peter was full of high spirits, in marked contrast to the rest of them. 'The front door was open,' he said, 'so we came in. Billy Catchpole said he saw fishes swimming in the telephone box at the end of Mill Lane. I don't believe him, do you, because how did they get in when the door was shut?' He became aware of his friends' disapproving looks. 'What's up? What's happened?'

'Felicity has just told us that this is no time for silly jokes,' said Sam.

'It's not a joke. Billy Catchpole said –'

'Peter, we are having a serious discussion about rescuing Mrs Haddock's cat, and if you have any suggestions – which I doubt – we should be glad to hear them,' said Tony. 'As you weren't here when we began I'll tell you what has happened so far...'

104

Peter listened intently and grew serious for once. 'We can help, can't we, Pauline?' he said.

'Can we?' Pauline asked quaveringly.

'Of course.' He turned to the others. 'I've got a boat!' He saw that no one believed him and his expression became hurt. 'Really,' he insisted, 'I mean it.'

'You've got a *boat?*' Tony asked incredulously.

'Well, *I* haven't exactly, and it isn't actually a boat, but I think I could get the loan of a jolly good rubber dinghy.'

Fresh hope flooded into the Greenwooders, and they waited for Peter to enlarge on his statement.

'It belongs to my Uncle Gordon.'

'The one in the Merchant Navy?' said Felicity.

'Yes, he's an engineer. The last time he stayed with us he left a lot of things behind and this dinghy was one of them. He hadn't had it very long and didn't want to take it with him on his next trip. He told Pauline and me that we could use it if we wanted to, and Dad said we could take it on holiday if we go to the seaside this year.'

'What's it like?' Tony asked, an edge of excitement in his voice.

'Smashing!' said Peter.

They waited for him to continue, but he sat smiling with pleasure at the thought of sailing the dinghy at the seaside.

'Tell us some more,' Stephen said impatiently. 'How big is it?'

'It's quite big,' said Peter.

Stephen groaned. 'How long? Six feet?'

Peter wrinkled his brow, trying to imagine how long six feet was. 'A bit more than that because it's taller than

105

Uncle Gordon when it's standing on end, and it's about that wide.' He stretched his arms about three feet apart. 'It's meant to hold one, but I think two of us could get in.'

'This sounds interesting,' said Tony. 'Cheer up, Minnie, all is not lost!'

'But,' said Pauline, 'it's made of rubber. What if it should have a puncture?'

'Yes,' Felicity added, 'Mr Cottam's boat sank and it was made of *wood*!' She did not want to save Minnie at the expense of a couple of Greenwooders.

'It won't sink,' said Peter. 'Uncle Gordon explained that. The tubes that you blow up are divided into two. If one gets a puncture, the other keeps you afloat.'

'But what if they both have punctures?'

'Don't be so negative,' said Stephen with a laugh. 'Why should they have any punctures at all? The flood water isn't full of swordfish. The point is, Peter, do you think your Mum and Dad will let us use the dinghy?'

The fact that his parents might prevent their rescue attempt had not occurred to Peter, but it was a hurdle that could be jumped when they came to it. 'I don't see why not,' he said, a little hesitantly. 'We can but ask, anyway.'

'Let's get our plan cut and dried before we do,' Tony suggested. 'It will probably be all right if we can say definitely who's going and what we're going to do. Only two of us can use the dinghy. What's a fair way of choosing?'

'Whoever goes must be good swimmers,' said Felicity. 'Whatever you say about not having punctures, anything might happen.'

'That's sensible,' said Tony, and Felicity glowed. 'Where does that leave us?'

'It leaves me out in the cold,' Sam said ruefully. 'I can't swim at all – never could get the hang of it.'

'Bad luck,' said Tony. 'What about you, Peter? It is your dinghy – in a way.'

'I'm the best swimmer in the school,' Peter declared proudly. 'Uncle Gordon taught me when I was three.'

'I can only do a length or two,' said Pauline, 'which probably isn't good enough.'

Felicity proudly said, 'I swam ten lengths the other day, but I know Tony can swim more than me.'

'Then it's between Stephen and me for the other place,' said Tony. 'I can do twelve lengths of the pool and I've got a life-saving certificate.'

Stephen sighed. 'I can't beat that, I'm afraid. I'd like to go, but it's your job, Tony.'

'That seems to settle it then.' Tony turned to Peter. 'You and I have to rescue the cat. By the way, what about oars? Do dinghies have oars?'

'This one has,' said Peter. 'Two, and they collapse in the middle. There's a kind of blow thing with it too.'

'You mean bellows,' said Tony.

'Do I? Anyway, there is one. Uncle Gordon did show me how to get the dinghy ready for sailing, but there's a book of instructions if we go wrong.'

'Jolly good,' said Tony. 'Let's start as early as we can tomorrow morning. Thank goodness it's Saturday and there's no school.'

'Tony, will you come and see my Mum and Dad so that I can ask to borrow the dinghy when you're there?' said Peter. 'They'll think it'll be all right if

107

you're going too. They think you're safe!'

'Little do they know,' Felicity whispered to Pauline.

'Of course I'll come,' Tony agreed willingly. 'We'd better go straightaway, then if they say we can have the dinghy we can bring it round here tonight. Is it heavy?'

'Well, it's not light,' Peter answered. 'I can carry it by myself, but it's easier with two.'

Tony got up. 'On our way then. We shan't be long,' he said to the others.

All the Greenwooders' parents shared the belief that children must learn by experience, and they rarely stopped the children from doing things they had set their hearts on. There were limits beyond which the children could not go, and they recognised such limits. Tony and Peter were careful to get permission to use the dinghy because they knew there was a certain amount of danger involved in their enterprise, but, as Tony pointed out to Mr and Mrs Christy, they were both good swimmers and the dinghy was practically unsinkable. At first Mrs Christy put on her most harassed expression and was doubtful, but Mr Christy soon talked her round. After the boys had returned to the Vicarage, proudly carrying the kitbag containing the dinghy, he said to her, 'You can't keep them wrapped in cotton wool, you know. They've got to learn to take risks.'

'But Peter is such a madcap,' Mrs Christy sighed. 'However, if they manage to find Mrs Haddock's cat I suppose it'll be worth the risk. I must admit I feel easier in my mind knowing that Tony will be in charge.'

'That's the spirit,' said Mr Christy, his nut-brown face

108

creasing into a smile, 'and you never know – they might win the George Medal!'

Miraculously, the rain stopped during the night and the next morning Tony awoke to glorious spring sunshine. He shot out of bed and drew back the curtains. Everything glistened in the sunlight, and as he gazed past the church to the forest he marvelled at the clean freshness of the sky, the trees still sparkling with raindrops, and the road beneath like a shining ribbon. It was almost impossible to believe that there had been so many days of rain-soaked gloom. Won't it be awful, he thought suddenly, if the flood has gone down and there'll be no need to use the dinghy after all! Then he caught sight of two refugees from Mill Lane leaving their temporary residence, the Church Hall, and immediately felt ashamed of his selfish thought. 'They'd like to see things back to normal, I bet,' he muttered.

He was about to turn away from the window when his attention was alerted by a piercing whistle. He looked down. Peter was standing at the gate, dressed in an anorak, jeans and wellingtons, signalling to be let in. The church clock struck seven as Tony put on his dressing-gown and hurried down the stairs.

'You said you were going to start early,' Peter said when Tony opened the front door and expressed surprise at seeing him.

'But not this early,' Tony said. 'No one will be up here till eight o'clock. You'd better come up to my room.'

'I thought it would be better if we got there before there were too many people about,' Peter explained. 'Then nobody will try to stop us.'

'Who'd stop us, anyway?'

Peter shrugged. 'I don't know,' he said vaguely. 'Just people.'

'What you really mean is that you can't wait to get started – isn't that it?'

'Every minute we delay, Minnie's life is in greater peril,' said Peter.

Tony grinned. 'Greater what?'

'You know – peril. Like those in peril on the sea. Don't forget your swimming trunks, Tony. I've got mine on and we might have to swim for it.'

Tony opened a drawer. 'I hadn't thought of that.' He was soon dressed and ready and they went downstairs for an apple and a banana and some cornflakes, deciding that there was no time for a cooked breakfast. Then they went back to the attic to pick up the dinghy.

'Going *already?*' asked Felicity, coming face to face with them on the landing. 'I thought I heard somebody moving about – why the hurry?'

Tony explained. 'We didn't think you'd want to bother coming with us,' he finished, in case she should think they were trying to avoid her.

'I would have done,' Felicity said, 'but Pauline and I are going to the Church Hall to help get breakfast ready.'

'Will you tell Stephen and Sam we've gone?' Tony asked.

'Yes, but I don't think they'll be here until quite late. Stephen made arrangements to give a hand at the farm. Mr Peat's had quite a bit of flooding too. Good luck. I hope everything goes well and that you return safe and sound – with Minnie.'

The boys were halfway down the stairs when Felicity

110

called after them. 'Oh, wait a minute – I nearly forgot –' She darted back to her room and returned a moment later with a small brown paper bag. 'Cat food – in case you need something to entice Minnie. She'll probably be scared stiff at the sight of you.'

'Thanks, that's a good idea,' said Tony. 'Where did you get it?'

'From Mrs Haddock. She brought some in her hand-bag so I borrowed it last night when I went in with her Ovaltine. I'll replace it today as soon as the shops open.'

Tony grinned at Peter, who was dancing with impatience. 'Now we really must be off. Don't say anything to Mrs Haddock about what we're doing, will you?'

'No?' said Felicity, in disappointed tones. 'I thought it would cheer her up.'

'It probably would, but think what would happen if we *didn't* bring Minnie back, or if the cat was dead...'

'Don't even *say* that!' said Felicity. 'I see what you mean.' She watched the boys depart, keeping her fingers crossed on their behalf, then went to the kitchen to put the kettle on. The family would be up soon, and this was going to be a heavy day.

Tony and Peter paused as they crossed the bridge over the River Medding, a little way before the turning into Mill Lane. Peter looked down into the dark brown frothy water. 'It's almost up to the arch. If there'd been another day of rain the whole of the High Street would have been flooded,' he said.

'And the village cut off from this direction,' said Tony, 'with no way to Nottingham except all the way round

111

Retfield. It's a good job the rest of Edwinton is on higher ground. Goodness knows what would have happened to us all, with only one battered boat.'

'And a dinghy,' added Peter, which remark brought them back to earth and to their immediate purpose.

They turned into Mill Lane and walked to the edge of the flood. The valley was a picture of quiet desolation. In the far distance the chequered fields, patterned with trees and hedges, presented a contrast of brilliant, sunlit green to the bowl of dark, muddy flood water round which they formed a semi-circle. Mill Lane was marked with a straggly row of roofs, chimney pots and TV aerials. Some of the taller houses revealed bedroom windows, but the general impression was of a lot of low bungalows. Here and there were the tops of trees, looking weird and unreal with no trunks visible. The water was dotted with various floating objects which had come from the flooded houses, some of whose windows had been broken. The boys stood for a moment in silence, suddenly aware that their task was going to be more difficult than they had anticipated.

'I don't see how Minnie could have survived that,' Tony said glumly. 'Let's get the dinghy blown up.'

They took the dinghy from the kitbag and laid it out flat on the ground. Peter joined the parts of the oars together while Tony attached the bellows to the valve of the first main tube, then to the other, and soon the dinghy was inflated. When Peter had fitted in the floorboards they were ready to take to the water. They carried the dinghy to the edge of the water and gingerly lifted it until it was afloat. Peter held on to the rope. 'You get in, Tony,' he said. 'I'll get in last because I'm lighter.'

Tony carefully climbed in over the bow and crawled astern. Peter threw in the rope and as the dinghy slowly moved away he scrambled in himself. 'It's all right,' Peter said as Tony clung to the sides. 'It won't overturn.'

'You might be more careful,' Tony grumbled. 'Who's going to row?'

'We can both take an oar,' said Peter, 'though there isn't much room.' They fitted the oars into the rowlocks, Peter taking the starboard oar and Tony the port. As Tony had to sit well astern of Peter it meant that he had to lean forward uncomfortably to work his oar. They tried shouting the stroke to each other, but when they found themselves going round in circles it became clear that having an oar each wasn't going to work.

'Let me take them both,' said Tony. 'At this rate we shall get nowhere fast.' Peter moved further into the bows and Tony took a position amidships. They waited until the dinghy had steadied itself, then began to move slowly but surely in the direction of the almost submerged houses.

'Keep still, Peter!' Tony cried. He was finding it hard work trying to keep the light craft steady in the water. There was no keel to help it to keep stable and it had a tendency to bob about like a cork. Tony felt that Peter, leaning over and dangling his hand in the water, was not assisting him.

They passed the first house, standing bare and forlorn, its windows like eyes looking hopelessly for its missing occupants, and sailed on till they reached the end house of the last row. As they drew near Peter concentrated his gaze on the open bedroom window, hoping for a glimpse of Minnie. Suddenly the boat took a buffeting that almost made Tony drop the oars. 'What's that?' he asked in alarm.

Peter steadied himself and peered over the side. 'It's only the top of a bush,' he said casually, as though sailing over bushes was the most natural thing in the world.

'We'll have to watch for obstacles like that,' said Tony. 'If we have to go round to the back of the house there'll probably be clothes line posts still standing. Pauline wasn't so far out when she talked about punctures.'

'The other tube will keep us afloat – I *told* you,' said Peter.

'That,' said Tony with a shudder, 'is no comfort at all.'

They drew alongside Mrs Haddock's house after a lot of manoeuvring. As soon as Tony stopped rowing the dinghy floated away. 'You'll have to grab the window-sill to keep us alongside,' Tony said. The window-sill was about three feet above the dinghy. 'Stand up, grab the window and then climb in. Can you take the rope with you?'

'I think so, if you pass it to me,' said Peter.

Tony drew up his knees to steady the oars while he found the end of the rope, and passed it to Peter. 'Be careful when you stand up. Leave it till the last moment, then it won't be so risky.'

Tony tried to row in reverse, but it didn't work. The only thing to do was to go round in a complete circle and make the approach again. They came up to the window. 'Now!' he said. Peter stood up, and in spite of some fierce rocking managed to remain upright as the dinghy edged to the window. He grabbed at the sill and held on for dear life as the dinghy bumped away, and only just missed kicking Tony's head.

'Pull the rope!' Tony yelled, and tried to dip the oars to halt the dinghy's progress.

'I can't,' Peter called back. 'I'm hanging on the window-sill.'

The boat was almost stationary now, but it had travelled the full distance which the length of the rope allowed. Peter gave a yelp as the rope, clutched in his left hand, nearly pulled him off the ledge, but Tony was able to reverse slightly, the rope slackened and the danger subsided. 'Can you climb in?' Tony said.

'I'll try,' said Peter, out of breath and a bit giddy. He heaved with all his might and hauled himself through the window, and landed in a sprawling heap on the bedroom floor.

'Are you all right in there?' Tony called, hearing the thud.

Peter's face appeared, grinning with relief. 'Yes, thank you. I'll find somewhere to tie up the rope.' A minute later he was back again. 'I've tied it to the bed,' he said. 'It ought to be safe enough, it's made of iron.'

'Any sign of the cat?'

'Just a sec – I'll see.' Peter disappeared again. Tony waited, drumming his fingers anxiously on the side of the dinghy. Then he saw Peter at the window again. 'Coo,' Peter said, 'there isn't half a mess in here. I had a look through the door and the water comes to the top of the stairs and on to the landing. There's all sorts of things floating about – boxes and papers and things and a big spider's web – everything will be ruined –'

'What about Minnie?' Tony interrupted him.

'I didn't see any – oh, Minnie! I forgot to look. Wait a minute.' Peter withdrew his head, and Tony bobbed impatiently in the dinghy.

115

'Tony!' came Peter's voice.

'Yes,' Tony shouted back, eager for news.

'It wasn't a spider's web, it was a hair net...'

Tony did not bother to reply, but wondered whether to risk climbing in himself. If Peter was in one of his scatter-brained moods they would accomplish nothing. He had just decided against the attempt when Peter poked his head out. 'There's no sign of any cat,' he said. 'I've looked everywhere – under the bed, up the chimney and in the cupboards, and I've called her too. She isn't there. There's a huge box in the wardrobe though. I thought they were sweets inside and I just popped one in my mouth because I thought Mrs Haddock wouldn't mind as we are looking for Minnie, but they were mothballs. Eeugh!'

Tony laughed. 'Serves you right for looting. Listen, can you get into the back room? Minnie might be there. If she isn't she probably fell out of the window and got drowned.'

Peter picked his way through the water on the landing to the door at the far end. It led to a very small room containing only a bed, a cane chair and a cupboard, and nowhere for a cat to hide. He opened the cupboard and saw a big metal trunk. I wonder, he thought, if Minnie got in there somehow. He lifted the lid and found that the trunk was full of clothes, on the top of which were heaps of faded old photographs. He picked one up. It showed a stately lady, dressed in a long frock with a tight waist and an enormous hat with feathers round it. She was holding the arm of a short, stocky man in soldier's uniform who sported a long waxed moustache. At the bottom, in copperplate writing, were the words: Emily and Albert,

116

1916. 'Albert Haddock,' he said aloud, and giggled. He would like to have examined more of the photographs, but thought of Tony's wrath and closed the lid hurriedly.

He went to the window and looked out. It was as though he was in the middle of a great lake. To the right the rest of Edwinton lay dry and secure, but the water in front of him stretched far beyond the Medding flowing past the end of the garden. A movement in one of the two apple trees in Mrs Haddock's garden suddenly caught his eye. It couldn't be! How could she have got there? He looked again. There was no doubt at all – there was a cat in the tree!

'Minnie! Minnie!' he called urgently. The cat stopped licking her paws and turned her head languidly. She looked Peter up and down and returned to her toilet. 'Oh, what a time to *wash!*' Peter muttered. He closed the window with a bang and hurried back to the front room window. 'I've found her,' he announced.

'Good,' said Tony happily. 'You've been long enough. Bring her out and we'll get back.'

Peter explained that the cat was not in the house but in a tree. 'I can't understand how she got out,' he finished. 'The window wasn't open at the back. She'd have to get out of this window.'

'Oh, cats can get anywhere when they want to,' said Tony. 'We'd better row round to the back and catch her. Tie a slip knot in the rope before you jump down, then we can pull it loose.'

Peter lowered himself into the dinghy without mishap, but when they came to pull the slip knot free it only seemed to tighten. They managed to pull the bed towards the window but decided that it might collapse altogether if they hauled too hard on the rope, so Peter, with much puffing and blowing, had to climb in again and release the rope. He looped it through the handle on the lower edge of the top frame and, holding one end, dropped back into the dinghy. He released his end of the rope and pulled it through the handle. 'Why didn't you think of that the first time?' Tony said scathingly.

'Why didn't you?'

'Oh, don't let's argue. Ready?'

Beyond Mrs Haddock's cottage was open country. Tony rowed the dinghy steadily along the side of the house, keeping as near to the wall as possible, until the back garden came into view,

'Which tree is Minnie in?' Tony asked.

'The second one – look, there she is.' Peter waved at the cat as though expecting her to wave back.

'She would be in the one furthest away,' said Tony. 'Hold tight while I try to row over to the right.'

'Starboard,' Peter corrected him smugly.

Tony lifted the right oar out of the water and turned the dinghy with the left oar. Suddenly there was a jolt and it came to a standstill. Peter fell backwards into the stern. 'Grab the oar,' Tony shouted to him.

'I can't,' Peter gasped, struggling to get himself upright. 'We seem to be caught on something.'

The oar, which had been jerked out of Tony's hand, floated slowly away. 'Peter,' he yelled, 'try to get it – we'll get nowhere without it!'

Peter leaned as far as he dared over the dinghy's side and stretched his arm out as far as it would go, but the oar was inches away. 'Hold on to my legs and then I might be able to reach it,' he said.

The other oar was fast in its rowlock, and Tony risked leaving it unattended while he turned round and held on to Peter's sturdy legs. 'Be careful,' he warned. Peter, his body almost halfway over the side, making the dinghy lean over dangerously, gave a cry of triumph as his fingers closed round the oar. 'Pull me back – I can't move,' he said.

Tony grabbed the seat of his trousers and managed to pull both Peter and the oar to safety. 'Phew,' he whistled. 'That was tricky.'

'Yes,' said Peter, 'and I'm all wet. What made us stop, I wonder?'

They peered over the side, and saw that the obstacle was the wall which separated the garden from the field on the other side. The top of it was just under the water, and the dinghy had got caught between two uneven stones.

'We'll have to push ourselves off somehow,' said Tony.

'But how?' asked Peter. 'We can only push ourselves off it this side, and we want to be the other.'

'That's true,' Tony said. 'I wonder if there's a lower bit we can get over further along.'

'Can't we row along this side of the wall and get into the garden from the river end?' Peter said. 'I know. If we both crowd into the bows we can joggle ourselves off the wall and over the other side.'

'And we'll jolly well joggle ourselves into the water!' said Tony.

'I don't see why,' Peter objected. 'These dinghies are supposed to keep afloat whatever you do. It might work. Let's try.'

Tony was not very keen on the idea, but neither was he keen on the alternative, which would involve much more rowing. 'All right,' he agreed, 'but be very careful.'

He removed the oars, placed them carefully in the bottom and then slowly pushed himself into the bows. Peter crawled over to him. Now that all the weight was concentrated at the front the dinghy's stern rose perilously out of the water, and the boys felt themselves leaning equally perilously into it.

'Now – joggle!' said Peter, and began to shake himself up and down. There was no need for Tony to joggle, because Peter's efforts did the trick. The dinghy slipped off the wall over on to the garden side, and off they floated again.

Soon they arrived at the tree in whose branches the cat sat. She looked down at them curiously. 'We'd better try calling her first,' Tony said, with little hope that the rescue would be as easy as that. He was right. All their calling only succeeded in making the cat turn her back on them with dignified superiority. They considered poking one of the oars up into the tree, but apart from the fact that it would not reach the cat, they did not want to frighten her. Then Tony remembered the paper bag that Felicity had given him. 'The cat food – let's try bribery!' He fished in the bag and produced a small tin.

'Jolly good,' said Peter. 'She'll love that.'

'That is something we'll never know,' Tony said bitterly. 'My clever sister has forgotten the tin-opener...'

Peter groaned. 'And I haven't got my all-purpose knife either. Perhaps she could smell it through the tin.'

Tony made a noise that sounded like 'Arrrgh,' and threw the tin into the bottom of the dinghy, from which it bounced up and over the side, falling into the water with a plop. 'Well, that's that,' he said.

The only thing to do, they decided, was to climb the

tree and carry the cat down. Tony hung on to the low-est branch and kept the dinghy steady while Peter pulled himself up into the tree. 'It's like being on dry land again,' Peter called happily as he threaded his way through the branches. He was in his element. Tree climbing had always been one of his favourite pastimes, and to climb one with a purpose other than merely getting as high as possible was a great pleasure. The cat was almost within reach – one more branch and the job would be done. He wedged his foot in a fork, reached up to the next branch and pulled himself up level with the cat. When he was safely lodged he let go of his branch and reached out towards the animal. The cat, who clearly had not expected a mere human to beat her at her own game, dodged Peter's outstretched arms, arched her back, spat, and darted up to a higher branch.

'Stupid animal,' said Peter, withdrawing his hand quickly. 'We're only doing this for your sake. Come on and don't be so silly!' But his words fell on deaf ears. The cat looked down from her new position as if daring the foolhardy boy to follow her. He followed. Tony watched with his heart in his mouth. The higher the branches, the slenderer they became, and although Peter was not heavy, he doubted whether the branches would bear his weight. 'Chase her down if you can,' he shouted, 'and I'll take over.'

'I'll try,' Peter called back. He continued to climb, talk-ing to the cat as he went, explaining, imploring and criti-cising to the full extent of his vocabulary. The cat waited for him to get within reach once more, then at the last moment she spat again and scuttled down the other fork, leaving Peter stranded at the top.

'I'm coming up,' said Tony. The cat was now halfway up the tree. If he mounted the tree she would be trapped, and between them they could catch her. He took the rope and tied it to the lowest of the overhanging branches and eased himself into them. He used kinder words than Peter had done to the now bewildered cat, who seemed convinced that the two humans were her deadly enemies, and kept up a constant hissing and spitting. Tony climbed higher and Peter lower.

'Careful, Peter,' Tony said breathlessly. 'We've got her trapped.' He stood with his feet firmly planted on a thick branch, his back against the trunk. Peter was immediately above him, and the cat was on a branch level with his shoulder. 'Can you manage to get on the branch that the cat's on?' he asked.

'I'll try,' Peter said. He eased himself along until he felt the branch beginning to bend. He gripped it firmly and let himself down until his feet touched the one below. He straddled it, released the upper branch and grabbed the lower. They were now all on the same branch, the cat between the two boys.

'Good,' said Tony, 'now come towards me.' Peter began to move towards him inch by inch. The cat seemed to sense that the game was up. As Peter approached her she moved towards Tony. Neither boy dared speak. In a strange sort of way they were all hypnotised – the boys by the cat and the cat by the boys. Nearer to the cat Peter sidled. Nearer to Tony edged the cat. The atmosphere was tense. They were only inches away from each other. Soon they would have to act...

'Grab!' yelled Tony.

'Got her!' yelled Peter.

Both boys grabbed. The cat let out an ear-splitting yowl and leaped off the branch, and the boys began to sway alarmingly.

'Help!' Peter yelled. 'I'm falling!'

Tony had the trunk at his back and used it for support while he hung on to a wildly wobbling Peter. 'No, you're all right. Steady now.'

Gradually Peter regained his balance. 'Cor,' he said, in a shaky voice, 'I thought I really would fall. What happened to Minnie?'

Tony did not really care, but thought he had better not say so. 'She jumped, the stupid cat. I hope she can swim –'

'Look – in the dinghy,' Peter interrupted. Tony looked down. Sitting in the dinghy, and apparently quite unconcerned, was the cat, meticulously washing herself.

'She does nothing but wash!' said Peter in disgust. 'Why couldn't she have come into the dinghy in the first place. Causing us all this trouble – well, at least the worst is over.'

'We hope,' said Tony. 'We'd better get back into the dinghy before she decides to nip back into the tree. You go first.'

Peter lowered himself on to the next branch down. 'I feel like a monkey...'

'You look like one too,' said Tony, good humour returning after the fright they had had.

'No, I think I'll be Tarzan.' Peter gave a trumpeting call and swung down still lower, to the branch to which the dinghy was tied. In his enthusiasm for jungle acrobatics he landed with more force than he had intended. To his horror the branch broke from the tree with an ominous crack and fell gracefully into the water. The dinghy began to dance away, carrying with it the broken branch and the rope.

'Now look what you've done,' Tony cried, his voice cracking in sudden panic. 'We're stranded!'

Peter was hanging from the branch, his legs thrashing about in the air. 'How can I look? What about me?'

'Stop swinging,' Tony ordered. 'The branch you're hanging on will give way soon. Edge along it with your hands to that short branch near the trunk.' Peter looked down at the water, shuddered, and obeyed Tony's instructions. He reached safety just before he thought his arms would come out of their sockets.

'Did you say the worst was over?' said Tony. 'At the rate we're going Minnie will have to get a rescue party to save us!' He began to unbutton his shirt, took it off and hung it over his branch.

'What are you doing?' Peter asked, aware that it was not the most sensible question he had ever asked.

Tony's trousers and shoes followed his shirt. 'There's only one thing to do,' he said. 'Swim out to the dinghy and bring it back.'

'Hadn't I better go?'

'No.' Tony crouched on the branch dressed only in swimming trunks and socks. 'I'm glad I took your advice about trunks.' He stood as upright as the tree would allow, counted three to himself and jumped into the dark water.

Peter watched him disappear, and as the ripples grew wider and wider waited anxiously for a sign of his reappearance.

*   *   *

124

'I'm glad I took your advice about trunks.'

In the small kitchen attached to the Church Hall Felicity and Pauline were surrounded by pots and pans, packets of cereal, mounds of eggs, jars of marmalade and piles of sliced bread. Felicity stood at the sink with her arms deep in foamy water while Pauline dried cups and plates, knives and forks and stacked them away neatly in the cupboard. Miss Pope-Cunningham, with face flushed and hair escaping from its usual disciplined waves, was at the gas cooker, frying egg after egg with magnificent abandon; and little Miss Plumb darted to and fro between kitchen and hall with pots of tea and plates of eggs on toast. Mrs Brooks and other ladies were busy serving, and the sound of voices, the wailing of babies, the clatter of crockery and an unattended radio filled the hall with a discordant medley of sound.

125

Felicity looked up at the battered old alarm clock standing on a shelf and gave a start. 'Pauline, just look at the time – it's well after nine. The boys should be back by now. They've had time to rescue twenty cats.'

Pauline screwed her neck round to see the clock. 'I'd no idea it was so late – time does fly when you're busy.'

Felicity took her hands out of the water and dried them. 'That'll do for the time being, there's enough plates and things to be going on with. I *am* worried, Pauline.'

'I'm sure everything's all right,' said Pauline. 'I expect they're having a marvellous time pretending they're at the seaside.'

But Felicity could not shake off a feeling of unease. 'We'd better go down to Mill Lane. I'll tell Mother we're off and pop in home first to see if Mrs Haddock is all right. I'm afraid we must be going now,' she said to Miss Pope-Cunningham. 'We have some – er – some rather important business to attend to.'

'You've been splendid, girls!' Miss Pope-Cunningham cried.

Felicity and Pauline squeezed their way out of the kitchen, hastily explained to Mrs Brooks what they were going to do, and returned to the Vicarage. Felicity disappeared up the stairs and Pauline could hear her calling out, 'Is there anything you would like, Mrs Haddock?'

A thin old voice crackled from the bedroom like a bad telephone connection. 'My Minnie – that's all I want...'

Felicity rejoined Pauline in the hall, shaking her head in a worried way. 'I only hope that Tony and Peter manage to find the wretched creature.'

They set off down High Street to the bridge over the Medding and then to where Mill Lane turned off. Felicity

126

shaded her eyes with her hand. 'No sign of the boys,' she said. 'Oh, Pauline, I do hope nothing's happened to them.'

Pauline caught some of Felicity's anxiety. 'Of course it hasn't,' she declared, but her words lacked conviction. 'I can't see Mrs Haddock's cottage from here.'

'It's the last one in the end row,' Felicity said, pointing into the distance. 'It looks as deserted as everywhere else. Let's get nearer – we can go as far as the water's edge.'

'There'll be an awful lot of clearing up to do when the water has gone down,' Pauline said as they walked along. 'Think what it will be like in the houses, with mud all over everything and the furniture bashed about and carpets ruined.'

'My father was talking about organising a cleaning squad, especially for Mrs Haddock and the people who can't manage for themselves. I said that the Greenwooders would help.'

'Oh, good,' said Pauline happily. 'I shall look forward to that. I like to get things clean. Ugh, doesn't this water look nasty? I wouldn't like to wade very far in it, even with wellingtons on.'

They gazed at the scene in awe. The absence of familiar landmarks made it seem as though they were in a dream in which they knew where they were supposed to be but could not recognise the ordinary things of everyday life. The water, now still, holding in its menace, looked as though it was sucking away from beneath at the foundations of the narrow road. Debris was floating about aimlessly – a henhouse, a small table upside down, some dead chickens, branches of trees, uprooted

127

bushes – as if they had been hurled ruthlessly into the water by an angry giant. Tears came to Pauline's eyes. 'Oh, those poor chickens,' she exclaimed. 'Felicity, isn't it terrible?'

'Yes,' Felicity answered absentmindedly. Pauline looked at her curiously. It wasn't like Felicity not to show sympathy towards birds and animals. Then she saw that Felicity was not looking at the bedraggled bodies of the dead chickens but at the upturned table which was swirling slowly in the direction of the bridge. 'What's the matter?' Pauline asked.

'Look at that table!' Felicity grabbed her arm and began to pull her back from the water. 'We must get back to the bridge! Can't you see what's on the table?'

Tony came up gasping, spat out water with an expression of distaste, and struck out for the dinghy. With a few long strokes he reached it and grasped the side. For a moment he hung on, then twisted his body round and prepared to haul it back to the tree. Before he could get started, however, the cat, perverse as ever, quietly stretched out a paw and drew her claws lovingly down his arm.

Tony yelled and let go. Off went the dinghy again.

'What's the matter?' Peter called. 'You've let it go.'

'So would you,' Tony said from between clenched teeth, 'if a bad-tempered beast had nearly clawed you to bits.' He swam after the dinghy, leaving a thin trail of blood in the water. 'This is the last time, my girl, that I'm going to bother. If you get up to any funny tricks this time, I shall leave you to sink or swim on your own.'

But the cat seemed suddenly to have exhausted her violence. She allowed Tony to pull the dinghy behind him as he slowly regained the tree.

With one arm round the trunk, Tony held the dinghy firm while Peter carefully lowered himself into it. Then he climbed aboard himself after rolling up his clothes into a bundle and dumping them in the bottom. The dinghy lurched and the cat wailed horribly, staring at the water with huge, green frightened eyes. Tony slumped down and looked at the scratch on his arm. 'Hope it doesn't turn septic. Peter, you'd better row, I'm exhausted.'

The dinghy steered an uncertain course back to its starting point. Peter, sitting amidships with the oars wavering clumsily out of rhythm, started to sing, happily and tunelessly. 'Pull for the shore, sailors, pull for the shore; we've found the cat we're looking for, and we don't want any more...'

'Any more what?' Tony growled.

'Adventures,' said Peter, catching a crab.

The dinghy slid to a halt. The boys got out. Tony felt in the pocket of his trousers and found a rather grubby handkerchief with which he started to dry himself. Then 'Yoo-hoo!' they heard.

They turned round. Felicity and Pauline were running towards them, and Felicity was carrying something black and furry in her arms.

'What on earth has Felicity got?' said Tony. He looked down into the dinghy, where the cat that had caused them so much trouble was peacefully asleep, curled into an innocent-looking ball. 'I thought for a moment –'

'Thank goodness you're safe! Where on earth have you been? We've been so worried,' Felicity panted.

129

'Oh, Peter, you are dirty,' said Pauline. 'But it's nice to see you.'

'We've got Minnie!' Felicity said triumphantly, lifting up her burden.

'You've got what?' Tony's head jerked from one cat to the other. 'But – but you can't have. We've got Minnie!'

Felicity peered into the dinghy, then looked doubtfully at the cat in her arms. 'No, this is Minnie – I'm sure it is – we found her floating on a table. It reached the bridge and couldn't go under because the water was too high, so all we had to do was lean over and lift her off.'

'But we found Minnie in an apple tree in Mrs Haddock's garden,' Tony insisted. 'Didn't we, Peter?'

Peter nodded. 'And we didn't half have a job to capture her. We fell out of trees, and nearly got drowned, and got clawed, and – oh, *everything* happened.'

Tony had given up the attempt to dry himself with his inadequate towel, and was putting on shirt and trousers over his still wet body and trunks. 'This must be Minnie – it simply must. If we've gone to all that trouble for the wrong cat, I'll – I'll –' Words failed him and he gestured wildly.

'I know,' said Pauline. 'Let's call them by their name – I mean, call them by her name – er – call her by her name, and see which one answers, and then we'll know which one is Minnie.'

'It might work.' Tony lifted the cat from the dinghy, keeping a sharp eye on her claws. The cat opened her eyes sleepily. Tony chucked her under the chin. 'Min, Min, Minnie,' he called seductively. The cat closed her eyes and gave the cat's equivalent of a snore.

'You see!' cried Felicity.

130

'Well, you try,' Tony said.

Felicity tickled her cat between the ears. 'Minnie, Minnie, there's a good girl. Who's a lovely pussy-cat, Minnie?'

The cat stared haughtily into the distance and twitched her nose as if to say, '*That's* not my name...'

'You see!' cried Tony.

Peter danced between Tony and Felicity, darting to first one cat and then the other. 'Minnie, Minnie, Minnie.' His voice got louder and more despairing. With a last disgusted '*Minnie!*' he gave up. 'It's no good. I bet neither of them is Minnie. I'm going to deflate the dinghy.' He set to work to open the valves and roll the tube fabric towards them, squeezing out the air.

'Wouldn't it be awful if neither of them was?' said Felicity.

'There's only one way to find out,' said Pauline. 'We'll have to take them both to Mrs Haddock...'

Mrs Haddock was sitting up in bed with Mrs Brooks' fluffy bed-jacket round her shoulders. Her thin white hair was neatly brushed and her knotted old hands rested on the eiderdown. She would have been the picture of a sweet old lady if her eyes had not been so mournful and her mouth not twitching with distress. Mrs Brooks was standing over her with a bowl of chicken broth, vainly trying to persuade her to take nourishment.

Four Greenwooders filed into the bedroom and stood awkwardly in a line before the bed. Felicity was holding one black cat and Tony the other, both animals supremely uninterested in their surroundings.

'Whatever are you doing?' Mrs Brooks began. 'Felicity – your dress!'

131

'Which, Mrs Haddock?'

Felicity and Tony held up their cats. Mrs Haddock peered shortsightedly at them. 'Which, Mrs Haddock?' Felicity said in a small voice, and Tony shifted nervously.

'Minnie!' said Mrs Haddock sharply. 'Come here at once, you naughty girl!' Minnie leaped from Felicity's clutch and sprang on to the bed. Mrs Haddock gathered her up and began to croon over her, tears trickling down her wrinkled cheeks. 'There, there,' she murmured. 'Are you back with your old mother, then – oh, you've given me such a fright, you bad thing.'

Felicity turned a look of triumph on the boys, but seeing their crestfallen expressions she turned away hastily. Tony regarded the animal in his arms with aversion. 'To think,' he said, 'we went through all that for the wrong cat! I've a jolly good mind to put her back where we found her.'

Peter sniffed. 'Then you'll have to do it yourself. I'm fed up with cats for good and all.'

Mrs Haddock raised her head and looked at the children severely. 'What have you brought that nasty creature here for? That's Minnie's eldest daughter, and a bad-tempered madam she is too. Belongs to Mrs Gedge next door, she does, and she's allus after Minnie's fish. Take her away. Go away, you. Shoo! I think I'll have that broth now, Mrs Brooks, if you'd be so kind. I find I've got quite an appetite all of a sudden...'

When the children were back in the hall, the boys sheepish and the girls trying not to look embarrassed for the boys' sakes, Mrs Brooks came downstairs and followed them to the front door. They gave her a sketchy outline of their adventures.

'I think you've been splendid, all of you,' she said, 'especially Peter and Tony. You've made Mrs Haddock very happy, and the fact that you came back with two cats, and one of them was the wrong one, doesn't matter at all. I'm very proud of you!'

Tony and Peter began to brighten up. 'At least,' Tony said, 'we've rescued Mrs Gedge's cat, and she'll be just as pleased as Mrs Haddock was with hers. We'd better take it to her at the Church Hall. I'm tired of carrying this lump. Peter, there's an old cat basket in the cupboard under the stairs. Will you get it out, please?'

Mrs Brooks went towards the kitchen, and Minnie's daughter was put in the basket, where she curled up and went to sleep again. 'You can leave the dinghy in the garden shed,' Tony said to Peter, 'and we'll take it to your place when we get back. Ready?'

Felicity was looking through the open door. 'Oh, no!' she suddenly moaned softly.

'What's the matter?' Tony asked.

'Look!'

They followed her gaze. Coming up the path, swaggering with satisfaction, their faces wreathed in smiles, were Stephen and Sam, and in his arms Sam was carrying a big black cat...

Felicity stood poised on the top step like a tragedy queen and pointed an accusing finger at the two boys. 'That's not Minnie!'

'I know – it's Timmy.' Sam looked at Stephen in a puzzled way and then at the others, now grouped in the doorway as though ready to defend the Vicarage from a horde of invaders. 'Timmy – from the farm,' he explained.

'But – but –' Felicity dropped her arm. 'I didn't know he was lost.'

Sam sighed patiently. 'He isn't. We've brought him for Mrs Haddock in case Minnie got drowned. We thought he might do as a substitute –'

'Does your mother know?' Felicity demanded.

'She suggested it,' said Sam. 'She said, 'Why not lend Timmy to keep Mrs Haddock company till she's up and about again?'

134

Tony gave a short laugh. 'That's good, that is. You try substituting anything for the precious Minnie!' He indicated the basket. 'We tried – with this!'

Stephen frowned. 'I don't get this. Did you find Minnie, or didn't you?'

Tony laughed again. 'We did – at least, the girls did. We found Gertie Gedge, or whatever her silly name is, and we're taking her back to her owner. It was nice of you to think of lending Timmy, but your generosity is not necessary.'

Sam ruffled the big cat's fur. 'Sorry, Timmy,' he said. 'Here, why don't you go for a little run before we take you back?'

He put the huge tom cat on the path. Timmy, tail erect, began to weave in and out of Sam's legs, purring like the engine of a very expensive car.

'I wonder how he'd get on with this one,' said Tony, taking Mrs Gedge's cat out of the basket and setting her down by Timmy's side. But there was no opportunity of finding out. The Brooks' spaniel, Prince, chose that moment to wander round to the front of the house from the kitchen garden. His melting brown eyes fixed themselves on the cats. For a second nothing happened while the three animals weighed each other up. Then there was a frenzied bark from Prince, unearthly wailing from the cats, and they all exploded into action. The cats darted and scuttled this way and that, and Prince tried to chase them both at once, doubling back on his tracks when one cat streaked ahead, then wheeling round to search for the other. Round and round the garden they went, through the bushes and over the flower beds, in confused patterns and a medley of yelps and cries.

135

It had begun and ended so quickly that the children had no time to intervene. They stood, open-mouthed and helpless, as Prince, his tail wagging like a metronome gone mad, ambled back to them. His tongue hung from his mouth, his eyes sparkled, and he seemed to pant with satisfaction. 'There you are – no cats now!' his expression clearly said.

It was true. There were no cats to be seen. Timmy had disappeared behind the house, and the Gedge cat somewhere in the direction of the church.

'That's done it,' said Sam. 'I'm off to find Timmy. Funny, isn't it? This all started off with a cat hunt.'

'And is finishing with one too,' said Tony. 'We'd better find ours, Peter, after all the trouble we've had rescuing her!'

THE RUNAWAY

There were lights ahead, red, green and yellow, shining like tropical fruit in the dusk of early evening. Raucous shouts, cracks of rifle fire and pings of balls hitting metal targets splintered the air, and the broken-hearted cries of a jilted lover singing a barrel-organ dirge thickened the atmosphere like the relentless spread of spilt treacle. The organ's blare, the dip and swing and sway of machines and the dull redness of the sky above brought tingling expectancy to the feet of the Greenwooders as they hurried up Church Street to the corner of Sherwood Forest.

The annual Easter fair had started. It had been held, for as long as anybody in the village could remember, in a field belonging to Peat's Farm near the cricket ground. The older people in the village shook their heads every year and declared that the Easter fair was not what it was when they were young, when it had been one of the few excitements they could look forward to during the year. Indeed, compared with larger and flashier travelling fairs, it did, especially in daylight, look a rather tired and shabby affair. But when the naphtha flares were hissing, the wooden horses of the roundabout were sailing round with their arrogant heads high, when the stalls were filled with gaudy ornaments and over-sized dolls, when pennies rolled and coconuts fell and coloured balls danced in a glittering fountain, then magic was created. The lack of paint, the muddy ground and the shoddiness of the trinkets were lost in the tinsel net of glamour which ensnared the whole scene.

'Come on,' said Peter urgently, and the Greenwooders began to quicken their pace as the music changed to a swirling walk that gave them a cheery welcome.

On the edge of the fairground the caravans of the fair people stood in darkness. The moon, well over in the sky as though retreating from the unequal competition of the glare below, was a honey-coloured stranger. Ahead of them was a promise – of excitement, mystery, perhaps of danger. They seemed to be entering another world suspended in time, unreal but full of meaning.

Peter gave a gasp of satisfaction as they entered the fairground and looked round him eagerly. 'What first?' he demanded.

'Hey, steady on,' protested Stephen good-humouredly. 'We'd better make a plan of campaign.'

'The swinging-boats?' suggested Tony.

'Not for me,' said Felicity with a shudder. 'They make me feel sick. I think I'd like some candy-floss.'

'I suppose that *won't* make you feel sick,' Tony said scornfully. 'I'd like to start with the rifle-range.'

'A good idea,' said Sam.

'Oh, no, not shooting,' Felicity wailed. 'Why must you be such barbarians? Pauline, wouldn't you like to start with the roundabouts?'

Pauline was looking round her with starry eyes. 'Look, there's a stall where you can win a doll,' she said. 'Let's go and see what you have to do.'

138

Stephen made an impatient movement. 'This is getting us nowhere. We'll be here arguing all night.'

'Suppose we split up,' suggested Sam. 'It's too crowded for us all to keep together.'

'I know,' said Tony, 'let's arrange to meet here in, say, half an hour and have some lemonade and hot dogs. Felicity and Pauline can go and win dolls and things, and Stephen, Sam and I will start with the rifle range. How's that?'

The others agreed. 'Peter, who'll you go with?' said Pauline. 'The boys or us?' There was no reply.

'*Peter*,' said his sister severely. She looked round to where he had been standing. There was no Peter there. She gave a great sigh. 'Now where's he got to?' she said.

'He must have wandered off,' said Stephen. 'Oh, well, it's no use trying to find him in this crowd. One of us will be sure to spot him somewhere. Whoever does will tell him about our arrangements. OK?'

'OK,' said Felicity. 'Pauline, let's go and get some candy-floss and then try for a doll.'

Pauline looked a bit anxious. 'I suppose he'll be all right. Mother doesn't like us not to be together and she did ask me to see that he didn't do anything silly.'

'Of course he'll be all right,' declared Felicity confidently. 'He'll come looking for *us* as soon as his money begins to give out.'

'Yes, that's true,' said Pauline, brightening. 'I've got some of his. He asked me to save it for when he'd spent up, then he'd have a pleasant surprise to find he'd got some more. Though I can't see how it would be a surprise when he knows I've got it.'

'I can believe anything of your twin,' said Felicity. 'Oh,

139

look, there's somebody with some candy-floss. Come on, let's go and find the stall. I haven't had any since last year and I'm just beginning to realise how much I've missed it!'

Peter, tired of indecision, had just walked away from his friends and lost himself among the crowds. He wandered about, happy for the moment to let the sounds and colours swirl around him, not conscious of anything in particular. The smell of fish and chips drifted into his nostrils and he registered a desire to have some later on. But not now – he was content to let the twinkling lights and mechanical music soak into him. He felt as though he were part of it all, as though he had never had another existence. He could not remember a time when he was not caught up in the magic...

He found himself watching some hefty youths swinging a heavy mallet and making a bell clang with the success of their efforts. I wonder if I could do that, he thought. I bet I'm as strong as they are even though I'm little. He approached the man in charge of the machine. 'How much?' he asked.

The man looked at him and laughed. 'Ten pence to you, sonny,' he said, 'but be careful. Little 'uns like you don't often know their own strength. Don't break my machine or I'll be out of work.'

Peter handed over a ten pence piece and picked up the mallet. He swung it over his head and brought it down with all his might. The indicator rose a couple of feet and sighed down to the bottom again. He flung the mallet down and walked away, good-natured laughter pursuing him.

A voice behind him called 'Hi!'

140

Peter turned round, wondering whether the call was meant for him. A freckle-faced boy in faded jeans, about his own age, was standing in front of the coconut shy, a look of recognition on his face. 'Don't you remember me?' he asked. 'I'm Lenny Ball.'

Peter had to think hard for a moment. Then 'Hallo,' he said. 'Yes, I remember you. We met last year, didn't we?'

'Yes, you showed me round the forest. I was wondering whether you'd be here tonight.'

Peter cast his mind back to the previous year's fair. He remembered that he had been standing outside the fairground on the afternoon before it opened in the evening, and had got talking to the boy whose father kept the coconut shy. Peter had found it fascinating to hear about a way of life so very different from his own. He had asked numerous questions and Lenny had told him of his travels, of the villages where the fair stayed for a few days at a time, and of their winter quarters on the outskirts of Nottingham. Lenny only went to school during those months and Peter was suitably envious. Altogether, it was a strange, restless existence, full of variety and interest, but decidedly hard at times. Peter had not been able to make up his mind whether or not to give up all home comforts in favour of becoming a vagabond or letting the fair move on without him, but when the rain poured down in the evening and the fair was washed out the decision was made for him. But it had been touch and go ...

He grinned at Lenny. 'So you're still with the fair. Have you been to school recently?'

Lenny shook his head. 'Not for a few weeks now. Shan't see any more of that until the winter. Not half

141

glad about that – can't understand fractions and adjectives, and things like that.' Peter felt a great sympathy. 'Nor can I, and I have to go all the time.' Then he noticed that the other boy's arm was in plaster, nearly hidden by his shabby lumber jacket. 'What have you done to your arm?'

'Broke it,' said Lenny. 'Yesterday. Fell over a rope. My Dad wasn't half mad.' He added, with a touch of gloomy pride. 'Had to go to hospital and have this put on, and I've got to keep it on for three weeks.'

'Does it hurt?' Peter asked.

'Not so much now but it aches like anything. Doctor says I've got to rest it as much as possible for the time being. Dad's mad about that as well. I shan't be able to help him at the stall for a few days. My big brother's at the rifle range and my Ma's doing the Hoopla. He's carrying on something awful. Would you like to autograph the plaster?' He extracted a pen from the back pocket of his trousers and held it out to Peter. 'Everybody's doing it.'

Peter absentmindedly scrawled his name on the already grimy cast. A thought was forming in his mind. 'What do you have to do – when you help your father, I mean?' he asked.

'Oh, pick up all the balls and put 'em back in the box, fix the nuts on when they're knocked off, give out the prizes – that sort of thing,' replied Lenny.

'Do you – do you have to shout?' Peter said eagerly.

'Of course. You can't expect people to stop if you don't let 'em know you're there.'

Peter's next words came out in a rush. 'Lenny – do you think your father would let me help – just for tonight? I could do all those things you said, and I could shout –

'Hey, Dad, this is – this is – er –'

I've got a very strong voice. Oh, do ask him! Will you?'
He started to jump up and down.

Lenny put on a look of extreme pain and led Peter up
to the shy where Lenny's father, temporarily having a
quiet time, was taking a long drink from a bottle of beer.
Peter looked at him in admiration. Mr Ball was big and
burly. His face was burned a reddish-brown. His bare
arms bulged with muscles. He wore corduroy trousers, a
blue shirt and a red muffler round his neck. I bet he could
make that bell ring, thought Peter. The top would fly off
and go whizzing up in the air. And I bet he could knock
his own coconuts down ten times out of ten.

'Hey, Dad,' said Lenny, 'this is – this is – er –'

'Peter Christy,' Peter said humbly.

'Peter – him and me's pals from last year,' Lenny went on. 'He wants to help you tonight. Can he?'

'I'm very quick at learning things,' said Peter quickly, 'and my voice carries like anything.'

Mr Ball lowered his bottle and looked at Peter. He seemed amused at what he saw. 'So you want to join us?' he asked.

'Only for tonight,' Peter said. 'To give Lenny's arm a rest.'

'Well, I could do with somebody,' Mr Ball said, rubbing his chin. 'A nice nippy little chap might be a great help. Of course I could only pay you Union rates –'

'Oh, I don't want *paying!*' Peter protested. 'I only want to *help!*'

'Bless me, you're an oddity – it isn't often we come across your sort. All right, then, you can start as soon as you like. Lenny'll tell you what to do, and when you've got the hang of it he can go and rest that arm of his.' He suddenly started bawling. ' 'ere you are, 'ere you are, ladies and gentlemen. Four balls for twenty pence. Win a coconut – every one of them full of milk! Luverly coconuts! Knock one down and it's yours! Four balls for twenty pence! Who wants a go?'

Peter listened, fascinated. A group of lads had approached the coconut shy and were beginning to fish in their pockets for money. Mr Ball handed out the wooden balls. Clang! The first ball hit the metal sheet at the back. So did the second. Plop! The third ball thudded against a nut balanced on its cup and it wobbled and toppled over. The last throw was a failure.

'Go on, give him a nut,' Lenny said.

Peter, almost bursting with happiness, darted to the

144

heap of coconuts lying by the side of the stall, picked one out at random and presented it to the youth. He had started! He was at work!

An hour later he was hot, sweaty and dirty. His voice was hoarse with shouting and his back ached with bending. Mr Ball had kindly retired to his seat and left everything to Peter except taking the money. Peter would have offered to take over completely but there just wasn't time to do *everything*. He was quite agreeable to letting the owner of the coconut shy remain nominally in charge. His skinny treble did not have the power of Mr Ball's voice but it was more penetrating, and had caused quite a few onlookers to clap their hands to their ears. The customers, many of whom recognised him, were amused at the ferocious energy he brought to the job, and someone had even given him twenty pence for himself . . . Once he had looked up from his labours to find the rest of the Greenwooders gazing at him open-mouthed.

'Peter!' Pauline had said in a shocked voice.

'Roll up, roll up!' was his answer. 'Four balls for twenty pence! Come on now, now's your chance to win a lovely coconut!'

Tony, Stephen, Sam, Pauline and Felicity each had, in turn, had twenty penceworth, but not one of them was successful.

'What will Mother say?' Pauline groaned. 'Peter, do you think you *ought*?'

'Who wants a lovely coconut?' Peter shouted. Then, in a lower tone, 'Why don't you go away? You're holding up the business!'

145

With a resigned shrug Pauline turned away. She took Felicity by the arm and as they moved off Peter heard her say something about 'What will he get up to next? All the same, I bet it's fun...'

At ten o'clock the fair was at its height. It seemed to Peter that this new life had been going on as long as he could remember, and that it would never end. It was not until he saw his father approaching the stall that he was jerked back to reality. He suddenly realised how tired he was. He straightened his back, put a handful of wooden balls in their box and felt that his legs were made of lead and that somebody had banged him over the head with one of the coconuts. He smiled at his father, rather uncertainly.

'Well, young man,' Mr Christy said.

'Hello, Dad,' Peter answered. He leaned against the side of the stall and breathed heavily.

Mr Christy was a small man, with a face as brown and wrinkled as a nut. Peter was very proud of him because he had been a great sportsman, and even now turned out regularly for Edwinton cricket team, for whom he was an opening bat and a useful spin bowler. Another point in his favour was that he took the twins' goings-on with complete equanimity and, as Mrs Christy sometimes complained, regarded them more as mischievous young puppies than as human beings. He seemed to expect them to be naughty occasionally and do ungrown-up-like things, and his favourite expression was 'You can't put old heads on young shoulders.' Peter and Pauline approved of their father wholeheartedly. They loved their mother too, but she was inclined to be too fussy about cleanliness behind the ears, the state of the kitchen floor and the loss of handkerchiefs.

146

'Enjoying yourself?' Mr Christy asked.

'Oh, *yes!*' said Peter. 'But I'm a bit tired now,' he added.

'Then I think it's time you came along home. The others are waiting at the gate. Say goodnight to the boss. I've got some news for you.'

Peter thankfully relinquished his job. He went up to Mr Ball and said, 'I'm afraid I've got to go now. My father's come for me. Do you think you can manage on your own?'

'Manage?' Mr Ball roared. 'Aye, just about, I should think. So you're off, are you? You stuck it well, little 'un. You'll make a good barker one of these days. You're a sight nippier than that Lenny o' mine. I'd give you a job any day! Here, pick yourself the biggest nut you can find. Goodnight, young 'un, and many thanks. You've got a right good worker there,' he called to Mr Christy.

Peter swaggered off with his father, clutching his wages. His head was swimming with tiredness but his heart was full of pride. A 'right good worker', was he? It was the first time he had been called that, he admitted to himself, but at last somebody had recognised his true worth. And he knew where he could get a job any time. I bet there aren't many kids in Edwinton who've had that said to them . . .

'Did you say you'd got some news for me, Dad?' he asked.

'I did,' Mr Christy replied. 'See if you can guess what it is. I'll give you a clue – we've got a visitor coming to stay for a week or two.'

'A visitor?' Peter repeated, wrinkling up his nose in thought. Then he exclaimed excitedly, 'I know – it's Uncle

Gordon! Hooray!' Mr Christy's brother Gordon was by far and away Peter's favourite uncle. He was a merchant seaman, the chief engineer on a tanker, and during his rare visits Peter and Pauline would listen enthralled for hours to the tales of his adventures.

Mr Christy said nothing for a moment, and his silence sowed the seeds of doubt in Peter's mind. 'It *is* Uncle Gordon, Dad, isn't it?'

'No, I'm afraid it isn't,' said his father, well aware that Peter would be disappointed. 'It's Aunt Edna.'

On hearing that name Peter stopped dead in his tracks, looked up at his father and groaned, 'Oh, *no!*'

'Now, that's no way to talk,' Mr Christy admonished. 'Don't be rude.' But his rebuke was half-hearted.

'Well...' Peter said protestingly, and then fell silent.

Mr Christy looked down at Peter, who seemed to have lost all his bounce, and put his arm round his son's shoulder. 'Never mind, Peter, it won't be for long. Anyway, you'll be out with the Greenwooders for most of the day.' Secretly Mr Christy sympathised with Peter and had himself groaned inwardly when the telegram announcing the arrival of Aunt Edna had come. She was really Peter's great-aunt and a very difficult lady indeed to get on with. Her visits usually meant a round of grouses, complaints and criticisms, and during them everybody was on tenterhooks. But the most disagreeable aspect of Aunt Edna was her conviction that little girls were all angels and incapable of the slightest wrongdoing, while little boys were agents of the devil and spent every waking minute planning and executing evil. In other words, Pauline was the apple of her eye and Peter was the worm in the apple.

'Come on, cheer up, Peter,' said Mr Christy. 'You don't want the others to see that long face, do you?'

Peter sighed. 'No, I suppose not.' Then he added cryptically, 'No jam tarts for a week if she – er – Aunt Edna gets at them!'

The rest of the gang met them at the gate of the fairground and they began the walk home, chatting about the evening's activities and comparing winnings. Stephen was self-consciously carrying a goldfish in a plastic bag full of water; Tony had a plaster Alsatian dog he had decided to present to his mother, knowing full well she would hate it; Sam had an ashtray and Felicity a violently coloured ball that made her feel bilious just to look at it.

Peter and Pauline hung back and walked a little way behind the others. 'You know, Peter, don't you? I can tell by your face,' Pauline said softly.

'Yes,' he said, 'I know all right – just when I was feeling happy. Oh, why does she have to spoil the holidays?'

'I know,' Pauline said suddenly, 'let's pretend that whatever I do you do really but whatever you do you don't but I do.'

'I beg your pardon!'

'I said – oh, never mind, it's too complicated.' Pauline kicked gloomily at a stone. 'It seems as if we'll just have to put up with things till she goes.'

Peter agreed wearily. 'I suppose so – and get used to there being no jam tarts . . .'

'What *is* all this about jam tarts?' Their father's voice recalled the twins to their whereabouts. They had reached the crossroads, and Tony and Felicity were about to leave them.

'What's the matter with you two?' asked Tony. 'You

149

look as though you'd just discovered that the holidays are over.'

'Huh,' said Peter. 'They are – for us, anyway.'

'What do you mean?' said Felicity.

Mr Christy interrupted quickly. 'Don't take any notice of him, he's just being silly. Come along, children.'

'Good night,' Peter and Pauline said, in unusually subdued tones.

'See you tomorrow,' Tony called as he and Felicity turned right along the road that led to the Vicarage.

'You might – and you mightn't,' Peter muttered under his breath darkly.

Sam left at the same time to go in the opposite direction, and a few minutes later Stephen said 'Goodnight' at his gate. The twins and their father walked on to the Post Office in silence. Mr Christy put his key in the lock, paused, looked over his shoulder and said, 'Now, children, I want you to forget your sulks. I won't have your mother upset. You're both tired, so you'd better have a glass of milk and some biscuits and go straight to bed. All right?'

Peter gave a huge yawn. 'Yes, Dad,' he said. That suited him. He was eager for once to go to bed. In the privacy of his own room he could work out the details of a plan that had started to sprout in his mind during the walk from the forest corner...

Peter lay in bed, staring at the ceiling, deep in concentration. He must not risk dropping off to sleep before everything was worked out thoroughly. What was that saying? Until all the t's are crossed and the i's dotted.

150

He wondered why it should only be the i's – j's are dotted too, and the f's are crossed. Until all the f's are crossed and the j's dotted... Dotty j. J is dotty, like Aunt Edna. Edna – even her name was silly. Edna ... ed on a ... Edna shoulders ... head on her shoulders ... old head on young shoulders... Granny Green's head on Pauline's shoulders... Peter laughed at the vision he had conjured up and jerked himself back into wakefulness. Gosh, he thought, that was a near thing, I nearly dozed off! I must work things out, cross the t's and dot – oh, no, not *that* again! What was it that Mr Ball had said? 'I'll give you a job any day.' That was it, the answer to everything. He would go away and get a job and miss the whole of Aunt Edna's visit.

He saw the scene in his mind. 'Please can I have that job you promised me, Mr Ball? You said that I was nippier than Lenny and I don't want any wages.' No, that was being too generous. He amended his speech. 'And I don't want much wages.' That would have to do. 'Why, it's Peter Christy,' Mr Ball would say. 'The boy who did so well in Edwinton. You'll be as good a –' What was the word he had used? Something to do with a dog – wagger, howler, barker – that was it, barker! 'You'll be as good a barker as me one of these days. Of course you can have a job with pleasure. I will pay you good wages – five pounds a week and as much coconut as you can eat.'

'That's settled,' said Peter out loud, 'I shall accept.' He began to plan his morning. There were certain things that had to be done before starting his new life. He must take care not to arouse suspicion. Everything must be done exactly as usual. There was Timmy, his rabbit, to

151

see to. The chickens had to be fed. His room had to be tidied – he wondered whether it would be a good idea to put a dummy in his bed as someone had done in a prisoner-of-war story he had once read, but he remembered in time that no one would expect him to be in bed during the day.

Lastly, there was the note. Everyone who ran away left a note. I'll leave it in the hollow oak in the forest near where we play with bows and arrows, he decided. One of the gang was sure to find it there, and it wouldn't be as soon as if he left it in his bedroom.

Well, that seemed to be all – now he could go to sleep. He turned over and closed his eyes tightly. Five seconds later he opened them again and said, 'Gosh, *George!*' He had forgotten the dog! He knew he would miss George very much, and for a moment wondered about taking him with him. No, I can't, he thought, he's half Pauline's and that would be like stealing half a dog. He would have to make time to take George for a little walk before he embarked on his adventure – perhaps the last walk they would ever have together.

The thought saddened him. He screwed his eyes up tightly in case he should be tempted to cry, then gave a huge yawn. Now he must go to sleep. Tomorrow was going to be a very heavy day.

Peter stood at the entrance of the field at the edge of the forest where, the night before, the fair had been held. He gaped unbelievingly at the sight that met his eyes. The field was quite empty. It had been full of colour, noise and excitement. Now it was deserted and forlorn.

'They can't have gone!' he said aloud. But nothing could alter the evidence of his eyes. For one crazy moment he wondered if he had come to the wrong field, but no, although the stalls, lorries and caravans had gone, the litter remained, and he could see the patches of bare ground where the grass had been worn away, and the tread marks of the huge double-wheeled wagons. Nothing was left of the glitter and enchantment, not even the pink-sweet smell of candy-floss or the all-permeating odour of hot-dogs and hamburgers dripping with fried onions. As he looked at the drab scene disappointment welled up in him.

Where were they all, his friends of last night? Lenny with his broken arm and his father, from whom he expected so much? Though he knew the fair was only due to stay at Edwinton for one evening he had not imagined it would leave so soon. He was sure that he would arrive in time to go with it, perhaps to help with the packing up. They must have started at the crack of dawn. Perhaps that was what woke them up. 'Listen, Lenny,' he heard Mr Ball say, 'that was the crack of dawn – it's time to pack up!'

He wished his jobs had not taken so long and that he had not had to wait until his mother and father had gone into Nottingham for the day to do some shopping before meeting Aunt Edna, leaving the Post Office in charge of their assistant, Amy Mottershead, the greengrocer's daughter. Then he would have been in time. Pauline too had been a nuisance. She had hung around for ages before going to meet Felicity. They were going to make cakes in the Vicarage kitchen. Peter had been relieved that there had been no suggestion of him joining them.

Even George had not been helpful. He had slipped his lead while they were on the way to the forest to put the note in the hollow tree and had gone after a cat, and Peter had wasted precious time in getting him back.

He wandered away from the field, vaguely trying to formulate new plans, and found himself outside the two small stone cottages tucked away behind overgrown hedges, the last houses in the village before the start of the forest. He decided to make his way into the forest where he would weigh up the situation and come to a decision. He hoped he would not see any of the Greenwooders there, but it was a chance he would have to take. As he set out along the broad sandy path a harsh, croaking voice brought him to a stop.

'Hey there, boy!'

Hobbling down the path of the first cottage was a tiny stooping figure dressed all in black. It was old Mrs Haddock who, at ninety-six, was Edwinton's oldest inhabitant. Peter knew her from her weekly visits to the Post Office to collect her pension. Besides, he and Tony had rescued her cat from the flood. In thunder, lightning, rain or snow she made the journey and every time she saw Peter or Pauline she produced a paper bag from her massive black handbag and gave them a clove ball.

'Hello, Mrs Haddock,' said Peter, walking back to the cottage gate, wondering vaguely if she had called him back to offer him a sweet.

'Are y'looking for the fair?' Mrs Haddock asked. 'I saw you from t'front room winder.'

'Yes, I was,' Peter answered.

'Ah thowt so,' said the old lady. 'Well, they've gone. Went this morning at first light. A good job too, noisy

154

lot.' She nodded knowingly. 'Weren't like that when I were a girl, none o' them noisy wireless things going full blast.' She gave a little shudder of disgust and turned to go back to her cottage.

'Excuse me, Mrs Haddock,' he called after her, 'do you know where they've gone?'

Mrs Haddock stopped in her tracks. 'Aye, that I do,' she said. 'They've gone to Welham. They allus go there after Edwinton. Except –' she paused and gazed up at the sky as if in deep thought – 'except in 1885. Then they didn't because of the floods. Couldn't get there. Lost two horses and one o' them sea-lions. Drownded. But they 'ave ever since. After Edwinton, Welham.'

'Thank you very much,' Peter shouted. Mrs Haddock nodded again and returned to her front door, muttering about 'them noisy wireless contraptions'. Well, that was something to go on, Peter thought with relief. Welham was only about eight miles away. You had to go through Ollerthorp, cross the common, turn left by the dam, reach the main road and go along it for about three miles, skirt Welham Woods, and there you were, on the green. Welham was a small out-of-the-way village that civilisation seemed to have by-passed. No road ran through it, and though television aerials sprouted from almost every roof many houses still had no proper water supply. Peter set out determinedly to walk...

More than three hours later he was still walking, or rather limping. He had developed a blister on one heel, the afternoon sun struck harshly on the back of his neck, he was thirsty, sticky and thoroughly miserable. Several times he had nearly decided to turn back and call it a day, but the thought of Aunt Edna had spurred him on.

155

Besides, what would the gang say if they knew he couldn't even walk a few miles in order to join the fair people?

He wished that the other Greenwooders were with him, that they had all decided to run away together, but he chided himself. He had better not start thinking like that, that wasn't the way to raise drooping spirits. He plunged his hands further into his pockets and started to whistle, a plaintive sound that soon petered out.

At last he rounded a bend in the road and the village of Welham came into sight. Peter quickened his step. It wouldn't be long now. Soon there would be friendliness, food and drink and a job to do . . .

The stalls had been erected on the village green and the fair had started. As it was only late afternoon there were only a few children present. The crowds would not gather until the evening. There was a half-hearted look about everything. Nobody was shouting, the lights were not on, the music seemed muted. Peter hesitated. Where was the magic? What had gone wrong?

He crossed the road, got on to the green and started to look for Lenny Ball or his father. He found the coconut shy but it was deserted. He wandered round, looking with lacklustre eye on the things which had enchanted him the night before. The horses of the roundabouts needed painting. The brass rails were tarnished. The children who were standing around all seemed to have foolish faces and gaping mouths. The people in charge of stalls and entertainments looked ill-dressed and villainous. Peter longed for a friendly, familiar face.

Then he saw Mr Ball. The burly stallholder had just emerged from one of the caravans parked behind a large and smelly traction engine. He was dressed as he had been the previous evening, but there was something different about him. The flushed good nature was missing. He looked grumpy and out-of-sorts. He shouted back to somebody in the caravan and started off towards the coconut shy.

Peter went towards him eagerly. Mr Ball sat on a stool, pulled out a packet of cigarettes, lit one, and regarded the scene gloomily.

'Hello,' said Peter.

Mr Ball transferred his gaze to the rather bedraggled figure in front of him. 'What do you want?' he enquired.

'Mr Ball – it's me – Peter –'

'Uh – Peter who? I don't know no Peter.'

'But – but – you must remember me. I helped you last night when Lenny couldn't.' Peter felt as though somebody had slapped his face. He stared at the showman. It *was* the man who had joked with him, given him a coconut, promised him a job. What had happened to him?

Mr Ball puffed at his cigarette and stared over Peter's head. He seemed to have forgotten his existence.

Peter thought he would try another approach. 'Where's Lenny?' he said.

'Gone to the 'ospital,' was the brief reply.

There was a silence. Peter looked at the ground, at the sky, at a group of children passing by. Mr Ball continued to smoke, his face creased in a scowl.

'You promised me a job,' Peter said at last. 'You said I was a great help last night, and that you'd give me a job any time I needed one. Well, I need one now...' His voice trailed away miserably.

157

The showman brought his gaze down and seemed at last to enter Peter's world, but casually, with little real interest. 'Oh, yes. You're the kid from Edwinton, aren't you? Pal o' Lenny's. What's this about a job?'

Peter explained humbly. He skirted over the fact of having run away, gave the impression that he had his parents' full consent to leave home, dwelt on his good health and capacity for hard work, and finished up with a rosy picture of the increased prosperity that would come to the coconut shy under its new manager, Peter Christy.

Mr Ball's indifference melted a little under the impassioned harangue. He looked at Peter as though he recognised him at last, and gave what might have passed for a little chuckle. 'Oh, aye, I can place you now. Fact is, last night I was a bit – well, not quite myself, in a manner o' speaking. You understand?'

Peter, remembering the pile of beer bottles in a corner of the stall, nodded. Mr Ball, not quite sober, was a nice man. Sober, he was apparently quite different.

'And,' Mr Ball went on confidentially, 'I'm not too sure how last night finished up. It's the noises in me head, you see. I have to take a drop to stop the noises. Last night the noises was very bad, see?'

'I see,' Peter replied, as one man to another.

There was another pause. Then Peter ventured tentatively, 'The job...?'

'Oh, that. No, I'm afraid that must have been a bit of a joke. Haven't got a vacancy at the moment. I'll put your name down and let you know, if you like.' Mr Ball cocked his head on one side, expecting Peter to appreciate his humour. He did not get the expected response

158

but went on, 'Y'get a lot of chaps after jobs like this, y'know. Needs somebody strong –'

Suddenly Peter gave up. He realised that it was no use. There was nothing to expect from Mr Ball, either now or in the future. Another grown-up who had broken his promise. The world was full of them. It was a rotten life. 'That's all right,' he said shortly. 'I expect I'll manage. Tell Lenny I called.' He blinked suddenly to stop the smarting in his eyes, turned on his heel and left the showman elaborating on the labour situation in the world of the fairground.

Now what was he going to do? He thrust down the feeling of panic that threatened to engulf him. He knew nobody in Welham. He must get back to Edwinton. Running away would have to be postponed, Aunt Edna or no Aunt Edna. It would be better to suffer her constant nagging than have to sleep in a ditch and live on turnips. Peter's imagination began to get out of hand. He could see himself, ragged and starving, staggering up to a cottage and falling unconscious on the doorstep. He could see himself, white and withered in a hospital bed, whispering his last dying request to see his family. Or, with memory gone, wandering from place to place, looking in vain for a familiar face...

He gave a great sigh. No, it would have to be Aunt Edna.

But how was he going to get back to Edwinton without any money? He couldn't walk the eight miles back, that was certain. His blistered foot was really hurting. Besides, it would take hours and it would be dark long before he was home. There was no direct bus between the two villages, even if he could have afforded the fare.

159

There was a train service, however. Welham was on a funny little branch line from Nottingham to Retfield that passed through Edwinton. The trains were very infrequent but there might be one that night, and his penniless state might somehow be surmounted. It was worth trying. He hitched up his trousers, wiped a grimy hand across his eyes and left the fair without a backward look.

The station was half a mile from the village, approached by a narrow road between tall hedges starred with blossom. Peter trudged along it, heedless of its beauty. He stood in the dingy booking-office of Welham Station and studied the timetables carefully. At first they made no sense at all – he couldn't even find the route he wanted. At last, in the left-hand corner of the large sheet, he found 'Nottingham – Welham – Edwinton – Retfield.' This was it. Even then he got lost among the asterisks, the NSs and SOs. In the end he decided that there would be a train in fifteen minutes.

The station seemed to be quite deserted. It might be possible to slip on to the platform, hide in the waiting-room until the train came in and then dart into the first carriage. He tried the glass-panelled door leading from the booking-hall to the platform. It was firmly locked. He sighed, turned and began to wander back up the station approach, deep in thought.

The minutes ticked by. Still no one appeared. Perhaps nobody is coming for the train, he thought. That would ruin his latest idea which was vaguely connected with hiding behind someone as he or she went past the ticket-collector.

The passengers started arriving at last. There was a telephone kiosk immediately outside the entrance to the

160

booking-hall, so Peter was not conspicuous as he stood in its shadow. The first person to arrive was a tall, thin, elderly man in black, carrying a brief-case. He walked so quickly that there was no chance of hiding behind him. Others arrived soon afterwards, singly or in twos or threes, but there was no one who suited Peter's plan. He left the protection of the telephone box and went to the fencing which separated the station approach from the platform and pressed his face to a gap. His heart missed a beat. The signal was down. The train was due at any moment and he was no nearer to getting on to the platform. Then the miracle happened. He had returned to his hiding-place when several things happened at once. The piercing whistle of the train broke into the silence as a taxi turned into the station-yard. The door opened and a very fat lady stepped out, followed by a small dog and a boy of about his own age. There was a flurry of activity as the taxi-driver came round to the door of the cab and began to unload parcel after parcel. The fat lady kept up a running commentary, hardly pausing to take breath.

'Now, Olliphant,' she said to the boy, 'you take Pixie and wait for me in there. How much do I owe you, Mr Grabworthy?'

The taxi-driver muttered something. The fat lady went on, 'Now, my purse ... yes, here we are ... two, four, six pounds ... and fifty pence for yourself ... thank you, I can manage. Oh, there should be another parcel ... that's right, just pile it on top of the others. Olliphant,' she called to the boy, 'I gave you the tickets, didn't I?'

'Yes, mother,' the boy answered. Peter, fascinated by the goings-on, left his hiding-place and stared at the new arrivals. The boy named Olliphant gave him a very

161

'Quick, Mother, the train's in!'

haughty look and solemnly put out his tongue. Peter wanted to grin, but realising the other boy was being rude, he merely muttered 'Elephant!'

Olliphant and his mother entered the booking-hall as the train pulled into the station. Peter followed boldly – perhaps there would be a last-minute chance to put his plan into operation.

'Quick, mother!' yelled Olliphant, brandishing the tickets and pulling the dog on its lead. 'The train's in – we're going to miss it!' He rushed past the ticket-collector on to the platform, leaving his mother behind. She, still talking, did not hear him. 'Oh, dear, we *have* left it late,' she was saying. 'I knew we ought not to have stayed for tea but that coffee cake looked so delicious. Olliphant, give me your hand, I can't see where I am with all these parcels. Have you got the tickets ready? Olliphant, you naughty boy, do you hear what I say?' The fat lady managed to steady the parcels with her right hand and began waving the other one about frantically. 'Give me your hand this minute, Olliphant, or I shall be very cross!'

Peter could see that Olliphant was safely inside a carriage and was blissfully unaware of his mother's distress. The fat lady's voice grew petulant. 'Give me your hand, Olliphant, *this minute!*' There was only one thing to do, so Peter did it. As he took hold of Olliphant's mother's hand her tone immediately changed. 'Good boy,' she said sweetly, 'now come along.'

'Tickets, please,' said the ticket-collector as they went through the door.

'My little boy has the tickets,' the fat lady said. The ticket-collector peered at them through thick pebble glasses. 'Oh, yes, the young man who's just got on the train. That's all right, madam.'

But the fat lady was too preoccupied to hear his words and dragged Peter through the door and towards the waiting train. Peter's heart leapt for joy. He was on! The first ordeal was over. In his gratitude he nearly thanked the fat lady for helping him, but realised at the last moment that he must now make himself scarce. He released her hand and darted down the platform and into the first carriage which had its door open. As he left the fat lady he heard Olliphant say, 'Who was that boy you were talking to, mother?'

'It was you, Olliphant darling, who else do you think it was?'

Peter grinned. Let them sort it out. By the time they found out that the other boy had been him the train would be steaming on its way to Edwinton. He closed the carriage door. The carriage was empty and snug. He sat down in a corner and a great wave of tiredness washed over him. Usually he loved trains and used every minute to explore every inch of the compartment, to study the old-fashioned pictures and dart from side to side trying to see out of both windows at once. But now all he wanted to do was rest. The chuff of the engine told him that the train was moving. Slowly Welham Station slipped away and the train moved out into the open countryside. Peter closed his heavy eyes and his head dropped forward on to his chest.

Pauline looked at her empty plate and wondered if she dared take a potato crisp from the full plate of salad opposite her. She hesitated, then decided that it would not be fair. After all, she had eaten her share. On the other hand, if Peter was so late for his lunch he jolly well deserved to lose a crisp. She looked at the clock on the wall. Half past one.

Where can he be? she asked herself as she took her plate out to the kitchen. He was never late as a rule. He was much too fond of his food. He knew their parents had gone into Nottingham to do some shopping before meeting Aunt Edna, and that she, Pauline, would be making the salad and would give him plenty of spring onions, which he loved, and no tomato, which he hated. She had waited until one o'clock but when there had been no sign of him she had decided to eat alone. She had not been worried then, but now it was different. What could have happened? An accident was unlikely. She would have heard within a few minutes. She covered his plate with another plate and decided to make herself a cup of cocoa. He was probably wrapped up in some fascinating game somewhere and had lost track of the time. Very soon, she tried to assure herself, she would hear his piercing ''Lo, Pauline,' and in he would roll, looking a bit sheepish over his lateness.

Two o'clock, said the clock. Pauline wished it would go backwards for once, back to one o'clock. But it really was two, and there was no Peter. Something was wrong, definitely, and Pauline decided she must go into action.

She poked her head round the door leading into the Post Office. Amy Mottershead was placidly knitting. 'Hello, love,' she said.

'Amy,' said Pauline, looking worried, 'I'm a bit anxious about Peter. He hasn't been home for his lunch yet.'

'Bless you,' Amy answered, 'that's nothing to worry about. Like as not he's up a tree somewhere or fishing for tiddlers in the river.'

'It's not like him to miss a meal,' Pauline insisted.

Amy counted up the stitches on her needles before replying. Her bland, moon-like face remained unruffled by Pauline's concern. 'Well, what's to do about it? He'll come home in his own good time.'

'I'm going to find the Greenwooders,' Pauline said.

'They'll help me. If Peter comes in tell him where I've gone, will you? Tell him to come straight over to the Vicarage – without having his meal first,' she added severely.

'Righto, love, I'll tell him. Off you go. I must get this sleeve finished, I want to wear my new cardigan on Saturday.'

Pauline sighed. She wished she could be as calm as Amy, whom nothing seemed to upset, not even a discrepancy in the stamp book. She left the house and hurried to the Vicarage.

The Vicarage door was open and Pauline ran up the stairs to the attic. The Greenwooders had arranged to meet that afternoon and although she was early she knew that no one would mind.

Felicity greeted her as she opened the door. 'Hello, Pauline, glad you're early. We're going tracking in the forest this afternoon. We're going with Sam and the others will be following in a quarter of an hour –' She saw Pauline's face. 'Why, whatever's the matter?'

'It's Peter,' Pauline said. 'He's missing.'

Tony and Sam looked up from the large map of Edwinton and district they were studying.

'How do you mean – missing?' Tony asked.

Pauline told them the whole story, from the time she had last seen Peter in the morning until the moment she had looked at the clock and decided to take action. When she had finished the others bombarded her with questions.

'Perhaps he went with your mother and father?'

'Didn't he say anything about where he was going?'

'Was he behaving peculiarly at all?'

'No,' Pauline answered to all of them. 'But he did take

166

George out for longer than usual and he did seem a bit impatient just before I came round here this morning to make cakes. But there was nothing else.'

'It's a sort of mystery,' Felicity began gaily. Then she remembered that it might be serious and added glumly, 'which we could well do without.'

'Shall we go to the police?' asked Sam, practical as ever.

Pauline hesitated. 'Oh, I don't think we ought to do that. If he turned up five minutes after we'd reported him missing we would look really silly, wouldn't we?'

'Besides,' said Tony, 'I think the police can only take action when somebody's been missing a certain number of hours – more than two, at any rate.' He jumped up. 'We'll organise a search. We'd better try the forest first.'

'But that's so *big*,' Pauline protested. 'It'd take *hours*.'

'I don't mean all of it,' Tony said impatiently. 'Our special parts, beginning with the clearing with the hollow oak. He may have twisted his foot in a rabbit hole and can't walk or –'

'Or a tree might have fallen on him and killed him!' Pauline wailed. 'Oh, come *on!*'

On the way to the forest corner they met Stephen and told him the news. Stephen refused to consider the possibility of an accident. 'If I know Peter he's just wandered off the beaten track and found himself at Budcombe on the other side of the forest,' he said cheerfully. 'I expect he's playing with some of the boys who come to Edwinton School from there.'

Pauline began to look a little less woeful. 'Do you think so?' she asked. 'Shall we go there first?'

'No, we'd better go the clearing,' said Stephen. 'But

167

first, why not nip home and see if he's returned while you've been at the Vicarage?'

'What a good idea,' said Pauline gratefully, and was off like a flash. She was back in a few minutes, shaking a mournful head. 'He's not there. Amy says nobody's been, not even a customer. I wish she looked as though she cared. She'll be knitting when the world comes to an end...'

The clearing in the forest that was the special haunt of the Greenwooders was approached by a number of paths, one branching from the other and each one getting narrower and more overgrown. It was guarded by a tangle of gorse bushes but there was a prickly passage between them through which the children could twist. At one end of the clearing was an oak tree, gnarled and ancient, its hollow interior hidden from any casual onlooker, and gained by climbing the branches which formed convenient steps.

They reached the clearing after a rather silent trek through the forest and stood in the middle, looking round them. Peter was obviously not there. At the edge of the grassy expanse young shoots of bracken were unfurling their fronds, and behind them silver birch trees thrust their slender trunks into a froth of green leaves. A few birds whirled in the sky like scraps of burned paper blown by the wind. Signs of budding, growing life were everywhere, but there was no sign of a human boy.

Pauline's face began to crumple. 'Oh, *where* can he be?'

Sam looked towards the oak. 'I suppose he couldn't be in the tree?' he suggested. 'Peter! Are you in there?'

'Peter!' they all called, but there was no reply.

There was a movement away from the tree, but Tony halted. 'I know he would have heard us calling,' he said, 'but I think we'd better make quite sure...'

'I'll go,' Sam said. He made towards the tree. Pauline put her hand up to her mouth. 'He might be in there – unconscious,' she breathed.

'Pauline, don't be such an ass,' Stephen said. 'Why do you always go around imagining the worst?'

Sam's head, body, then his feet disappeared among the oak leaves. There was an anxious moment before he spoke. Then they heard him call out, 'No, he's not here.'

'What did I tell you?' said Stephen.

'Then where is he?' Pauline's face began to look agonised again. 'Come on, we'd better go to Budcombe.'

Sam reappeared, climbing down the tree. He dropped to the ground, looking triumphant. 'Peter's not there, but he's left something there,' he announced.

'What?' Pauline rushed forward to him. 'What have you found?'

Sam held out a crumpled piece of paper. 'He's left a note saying that he's run away!'

The children crowded round him and he held out the paper so that they could all see. Peter's writing was unmistakable. The note was short. It said, 'I have gon forever untill Aunt Edna gose.'

'What on earth –' Tony began.

Pauline interrupted him and told them of the imminence of Aunt Edna's arrival, described her character in a few terse words and then burst into tears. 'I'll never see him again...'

'But,' Tony objected, 'he says until your aunt goes.'

'Yes, but he also says it's forever. Oh...'

'Well, you can't have it both ways,' said Stephen. 'I wonder where he's gone to.'

'It wouldn't be much help in running away to tell anybody where he was running to, would it?' Sam said. 'I wonder why he suddenly decided to do it. When did you hear about your Aunt Edna coming, Pauline?'

'My Dad told us when he fetched us home from the fair,' she replied. 'I know Peter was very upset about it.'

'What a pity,' Felicity sighed. 'He'd had such a good time at the fair, hadn't he? Knowing about your aunt must have taken all the enjoyment away. I suppose he wished he could have stayed with the coconut shy, the man who ran it looked a good laugh.'

'Yes, he was still talking about it this morning. I say –' Pauline suddenly got excited. 'Do you think – do you think he's gone off with the fair people?'

'Oh, he wouldn't,' Felicity began. 'Or would he?' she added doubtfully.

'I wouldn't be surprised at anything Peter did,' Stephen said.

'But where have they gone?' asked Pauline.

'Welham,' said Sam. 'At least, I think it's Welham, though it might be Tuxbridge or Normanford.'

'But they're all miles away,' said Pauline. 'How do we get there? We can't walk.'

'I'd ask Daddy to take us in the car,' said Felicity, 'but it's his sick visiting day.'

'His what?' said Stephen, goggling at her.

'It's his day for visiting people who are ill,' Felicity explained.

170

'Oh. My father couldn't take us either. He's visiting sick people, too.'

'I wonder if they ever meet on the same doorstep,' Felicity said.

Pauline butted in. 'Sam, what about your father?'

'Retfield market,' Sam said simply.

'We could go by train,' Tony suggested.

'Not at this time of the afternoon, if we're going to try Welham first. There's only two or three trains a day from here, mornings and evenings,' Sam said. 'No, the only thing we can do is to take a bus to Ollerthorp and walk from there. Perhaps we might get a lift.'

'Five of us?' asked Felicity.

'Can you suggest anything better?' her brother asked.

'No.'

'Then that's what we'll do.' Tony began to lead the way out of the clearing.

'Hold on a minute,' said Stephen. 'We're only guessing that Peter's gone with the fair. What if he's at Budcombe?'

Pauline began to quiver with impatience. 'He must have gone somewhere. Do hurry, everybody. At least, let's get out of the forest. He's not here and we're only wasting time talking.'

They retraced their steps and hurried back to the village. As they approached the field where the fair had been held they saw the bent black figure of Mrs Haddock. She was standing at the gate of her cottage calling her cat, which was as bent and black as she was. 'Minnie, Minnie, come in this instant. D'you hear me, Minnie? Come here, you bad cat.'

171

She looked up as the children drew near. 'Drat that cat. Catch her for me, one of you,' she demanded. 'Trouble is, she knows it's not fish day today, and she's got the sulks.'

Sam picked Minnie up from the grass verge and delivered her to her mistress.

'Thank you, boy,' said Mrs Haddock. She peered at the Greenwooders. 'There's usually six of you,' she said sharply. 'Where's the other one? Him I saw this morning?'

'We don't know,' Pauline said unhappily. 'It's my brother, we're looking for him. Did you really see him?'

The old lady pulled her handbag from her arm and opened it. She took out a paper bag. 'Have a clove ball,' she said, offering the bag to each in turn. 'Yes, I saw him earlier on. Asked me where the fair people had gone to, 'e did, nasty noisy lot.'

'Then we were right!' Pauline cried. 'Did you tell him?'

'Course I did. Why shouldn't I? Gone to Welham, I said. Allus Welham after Edwinton – except in 1885 when it rained and they couldn't get there 'cos of the floods. Lost two horses and one o' them sea-lions, they did. Drownded, they was –'

'Come on, let's go!' said Felicity.

'We'll get the bus by the war memorial,' Tony said. 'Goodbye, Mrs Haddock.'

Mrs Haddock watched the children hurrying down Church Street. 'Allus in a hurry,' she grumbled. 'Everybody's in a hurry these days. Never any time to stop and talk to an old woman.' She turned back to her cottage door. 'Now, Minnie, my girl, you'll have scraps and like it...'

As soon as they were out of Mrs Haddock's sight

172

Felicity took the clove ball out of her mouth and flung it away. 'Ugh!' She screwed up her face in disgust. 'I *hate* clove balls!'

At Ollerthorp they got off the bus and faced the long walk to Welham. They looked longingly at the few cars which passed them, but nobody seemed inclined to pick up a bunch of assorted children. Their usual high spirits had deserted them and they plodded along in single file because of the narrowness of the road and the many blind corners, and spoke little.

The afternoon drew on, the sunshine waned and the air grew chilly, depressing their spirits still further. At last they reached the outskirts of Welham. The sound of raucous music floated out to them. Pauline strained her eyes into the growing dusk. 'I do hope we find him,' she said anxiously.

The fairground was fairly full when they reached the green. 'Let's separate and meet here in ten minutes,' Tony suggested, 'and let's hope that one of us brings Peter back...'

When they met again there was no Peter, but Stephen had Lenny Ball in tow. 'You remember Lenny?' he asked. 'Peter was helping at his father's stall last night.'

Lenny acknowledged their greetings with a wave of his hand. 'Just got back from 'ospital,' he said. ''E says you've lost Peter.'

'Yes,' said Pauline. 'Have you seen him? Oh, I hope you have.'

'No, I haven't seen him,' Lenny said, 'but I haven't been back more'n a few minutes. In an ambulance,' he added proudly. 'But he's been here. You can write your names on my plaster if you like. Peter did last night.'

173

'He has?' They pressed round him eagerly, ignoring his invitation. 'How do you know?'

'My Dad's seen him. He said Peter said to tell me he'd been.'

'But – but why did he come all this way?' said Stephen.

'To get a job with my Dad.'

'So that's it!' Stephen threw a look at the others. 'He's run away and tried to get a job with the fair.'

'Did your Dad give him one?' asked Pauline, scanning the fairground as though expecting to see Peter, sleeves rolled up, in charge of the roundabouts or rifle range.

'No, he told him there was nothing doing. I think he was in one of his moods, my old man, I mean. You usually can't talk to him till the evening, when he's got plenty of beer in him.'

'Then what's happened to Peter? Where's he gone?' Felicity said. Lenny looked blank. 'Dunno.'

'Didn't he say where he was going?' Felicity pressed him.

'Dunno. Don't think so. He just went.'

Pauline could hold back her tears no longer. 'What shall we do now?' she howled. 'Oh, poor Peter – something awful's happened to him – I know it has!' She took out her handkerchief and buried her face in it, her plump shoulders heaving.

'Pauline, don't cry.' Felicity put an arm round her. 'We'll find him. Stephen will think of something, won't you, Stephen?'

Stephen frowned. 'The best thing we can do is to get back to Edwinton immediately. What time are you expecting your mother and father back from Nottingham, Pauline?'

'Not till late,' she managed to get out between sobs. 'They've got to wait for Aunt Edna's train from Sheffield. Oh, whatever will they say when they find Peter's gone?'

'We'll go to the station and see if there's a train.' Stephen led the way out of the fairground, leaving Lenny looking after them in puzzled sympathy. Pauline's hiccoughs and Felicity's comforting murmurs were the last things he heard as he watched them go.

'Aren't you going to write on my plaster?' he called, but there was no reply from the preoccupied Greenwooders.

The steam organ blared out a popular tune as the crowds shifted about the field like the pieces of a kaleidoscope, and the bright lights lit up the scene as if it were daylight. Noise, gaiety and hilarity were everywhere. Peter picked up the great hammer, swung it high over his head and brought it down with a deafening clang. The indicator shot up to the top where it not only rang the bell but smashed it to smithereens.

'See,' Peter yelled. 'I'm the strongest man in the world!'

The crowd applauded. 'Marvellous!' 'Well done!' 'Never seen the like!' they cried. A man stepped forward from the throng of admirers. 'Excuse me, Mr Peter,' he said, 'you have just won my coconut shy as first prize. Please may I come and work for you?'

Peter looked sternly down on Mr Ball, who had sunk to his knees in supplication. 'Well,' he said, 'I'm not so sure. Are you a good worker?'

'Yes, I promise you I am,' said Mr Ball.

'You won't eat too many of the coconuts yourself?'

'No, Mr Peter, I won't eat one unless you say I can, and I will only ask for five shillings a week. Please!'

Peter deliberated for a moment. 'I'll give you a few days' trial,' he said at last. 'Then if my chief assistant Lenny agrees you may keep the job.'

Mr Ball danced with joy. 'Hurray for Peter!' he cried. 'The strongest and best boy in the world! I'll never touch another bottle of beer as long as I live!'

Peter rolled a pound coin down the wooden chute. The stallholder gasped. 'A million pounds! Oh, sir, I'll have to give you the stall instead of the money!'

'Thank you,' Peter said as he picked up a coconut and hurled it at the row of little white balls. 'I can afford it,' he said disdainfully as Mr Ball ran over to tell him he was doing things the wrong way round. Mr Ball's voice had grown rather distant. How strange, Peter thought. 'Come on, laddie,' Mr Ball was saying as he put an arm on Peter's shoulder. 'Come on, or you'll be locked in the sheds. It's lucky I found you.'

Mr Ball faded, and so did the fair. Slowly Peter opened his eyes and focused them on the face that was bent over him. 'That's better,' said the voice. 'Now up you get. Fast asleep you were. Are you all right now?'

Peter found that he was lying full length on the seat of the carriage. He swung himself up and stared at the uniformed man who had been shaking him. He smiled sheepishly. 'Is this Edwinton?' he asked.

The man laughed. 'Edwinton? Ee, you 'ave been in a deep sleep, 'aven't you? No, lad, it's Retfield.'

Suddenly Peter was wide awake. 'Retfield?' he gasped. 'It can't be!'

176

'It certainly is, or I'm asleep meself,' said the man.

'But I wanted to get off at Edwinton,' Peter said.

'That's as may be.'

'That's as *is*,' Peter put in quickly and a feeling of panic swept over him.

'Calm down, laddie,' the man continued soothingly. 'It's not the first time somebody's fallen asleep in a train. Don't you worry. I suppose you're scared because your ticket only takes you as far as Edwinton.'

'It doesn't,' Peter blurted out. 'It doesn't take me anywhere.'

'What's that?' asked the man.

'I haven't got a ticket,' said Peter.

The railwayman's attitude changed. The look of good-natured amusement vanished and annoyance took its place. 'Is that so? Well, that meks things a bit different. Pinching rides, eh? Thought you wouldn't get caught, eh?'

'I didn't mean any harm,' Peter began but the man cut him short.

'That's enough. I've 'eard it all before. You'd better come wi' me.' He took Peter's arm and dragged him out of the carriage. They walked the length of the platform to where the ticket-collector sat in his sentry-box, reading the evening paper.

'Just found this boy, Fred,' said Peter's captor. 'No ticket nor nowt. You'd better deal with 'im, I'm off for me supper. Night, Fred.' He added, with a malevolent look at Peter, 'You'll cop it, you little perisher.'

' 'Night, Alec,' said the ticket-collector. He turned to Peter. 'Now then, what have you been up to?'

Peter felt that everything was unreal. Standing on a deserted Retfield railway platform talking to a perfect

177

stranger who was so obviously unfriendly was not part of his plan. Things had turned out just as badly as they could do. He thought he had better be as polite as possible to begin with. 'Well, it's like this, Mr Fred,' he began.

The ticket-collector cut him short. 'Askew,' he said.

Peter was taken aback. 'Ask me what?'

The ticket-collector clicked his teeth with annoyance. 'Now then, none of your lip. That's my name – Mr Askew.'

Peter felt himself going red. 'I'm sorry,' he said. He made a mental note to tell the gang about the man's funny name if, that was, he ever saw the gang again when he got out of prison. He gulped. 'I didn't mean any harm, Mr Askew, really I didn't. I'll get the fare from my money-box when Pauline gives me the key.'

'Oh, you will, will you?' said Mr Askew, bewildered. 'That's very interesting, but suppose you start from the beginning.'

'All right,' said Peter. 'The trouble is, I could only get tenpence out without them finding out.' He realised that he was not making sense and hurried on with his tale. 'You see, I went to Welham to work but there was no job so I came home by pretending I was the elephant to his mother.'

'I must be going barmy,' Mr Askew said quietly to himself.

'At least I meant to come home.'

'To Retfield,' said Mr Askew in an attempt to instil some order and meaning into the account.

'Oh, no,' said Peter, 'I don't live in Retfield.'

'You've said you've come home,' said Mr Askew, scratching his head.

178

'Yes, that's right.'

'But you just said you didn't live here.'

'I don't,' said Peter.

Mr Askew raised his voice. 'Then what the – I mean, what are you doing here?'

'I fell asleep,' said Peter as if that explained everything.

'You fell asleep ... that's very unfortunate. Now answer me two things. Where do you live and have you got a ticket?'

'Edwinton and no,' Peter replied.

'Now we're getting somewhere. Here's another question. Why haven't you got a ticket?'

'No money,' Peter said. 'You see, I went to Welham to work and there was no –'

Mr Askew held up a large red hand. 'Oh, no, we don't go through all that again. You'd better see the station-master and he can decide what to do with you. Leading me up the garden path – come along, let's see what Mr Crawford can make of it all.'

Obediently Peter trotted along with the ticket-collector to the stationmaster's office.

'You wait here while I get him,' Mr Askew said, 'and no running away, mind.' He knocked at the door and went inside.

Peter had no intention of running away. Apart from the fact that there was nowhere he could run to in Retfield, he had resolved to accept whatever Fate had in store for him. One thing was certain – it was simply not his day. The idea of running away had seemed so full of exciting possibilities in the morning but now its charm had withered completely. If only things had been differ-ent at Welham... He sighed and said aloud, 'If wishes were horses, beggars might ride...'

179

'Talking to himself now,' said Mr Askew, coming out of the office accompanied by the stationmaster. 'I wish you luck with him, sir, and I hope you can get more sense out of him than I could.'

'Right, Fred, leave him to me,' said the stationmaster. Peter looked up at the new arrival. He was very tall and broad, dressed in uniform with which he wore a cap with letters in gold announcing who he was. No top hat, Peter thought, vaguely disappointed. Not knowing what to expect, but prepared for the worst, Peter was amazed to see the man's face break into a huge smile which made his eyes go crinkly. He gave a deep chortle.

'Well, well, well,' he said in a voice that seemed to come from low down in his chest, 'from what Fred told me I expected someone quite different. Bless my soul, you're only as big as twopennorth of coppers! What's your name?'

Peter told him.

'Suppose you come inside and have a nice cup of tea and tell me all about it,' the stationmaster went on, 'and I think there's a piece of chocolate cake going begging. Would you like that?'

'Yes, please,' Peter said eagerly. The mention of food made his tummy rumble and he realised how hungry he was.

A few moments later and he was sitting in a big leather armchair in the stationmaster's office and nibbling his cake between sips of dark, sweet tea. Mr Crawford watched him, the smile still on his face. Then he said quietly, 'I suppose you wouldn't be running away from home?'

Peter almost choked on his cake. How did this man

know? He was sure he hadn't mentioned it to the other man. The sight of a sympathetic face made him decide to tell everything. After all, he was in such a mess already that things couldn't get much worse. 'Yes,' he said, 'as a matter of fact, I am – or was.'

Mr Crawford sighed. 'I thought so. Would you like to tell me all about it?'

'Yes,' Peter said, encouraged by the kindness in Mr Crawford's face. He drew a deep breath and began ... the fair, Lenny, Aunt Edna, his original plan, the journey to Welham, his rejection at the fair, the fat lady and Olliphant, and falling asleep in the train. 'So then Mr Askew brought me to you. I'm very sorry,' he finished.

Mr Crawford rose from his desk and put his hand on Peter's shoulder. 'You've had quite an adventure. Do you think it was worth it?'

'No,' said Peter without hesitation.

'And you won't think about running away again?'

'No. It's pretty rotten without Pauline and the others – and Mum and Dad.'

'And Aunt Edna?'

Peter grinned. 'Well...' he said.

'I think we can assume that you have learned your lesson,' Mr Crawford said. 'But how are we going to get you back to Edwinton? The last train has gone.' He thought for a moment. 'Do you know Albert Catchpole?'

'From Edwinton? Yes, I do. Billy Catchpole goes to my school.'

'Splendid,' said Mr Crawford. 'Wait here till I get back.' He opened a door at the other end of his office. 'In here – there's some scale models of engines you can be

181

looking at. I won't be long.' He picked up his hat and went out.

When he returned he found Peter absorbed in a working model of Stephenson's Rocket. 'Why didn't you tell us that your father keeps the Post Office in Edwinton, Peter?' he asked.

'I forgot,' said Peter.

'Hm. Perhaps that's not surprising. Albert Catchpole told me. I think I'd better telephone your father and tell him what's going to happen.' The stationmaster returned to the outer office, picked up the receiver and dialled. 'There's no reply,' he said after listening for a while.

'They can't have got home yet,' said Peter. 'They were going into Nottingham to meet Aunt Edna. It's funny Pauline didn't answer, though.'

'Never mind. Perhaps they'll be there by the time you get back. Now come with me and we'll find Mr Catchpole. He's going to take you back to Edwinton in about ten minutes. It so happens that he has to drive an engine back to the Nottingham sheds tonight, so he will see you safely back.'

'Thank you very much,' Peter said, glad that things were turning out so well. They left the office and walked towards the platform at the far end of the station.

'There's a snag though,' said Mr Crawford. 'The engine is going on its own and although it's strictly against the rules I'm afraid you'll have to travel on the footplate.' He gave Peter a sidelong glance. 'Do you mind?'

Peter stared into the stationmaster's face unbelievingly. 'On the footplate? Do you mean actually on the engine – with the driver and fireman?'

'I'm afraid so.'

Peter began to walk faster. This was too good to be true! In as steady a voice as he could muster he said, 'No, I don't mind at all.' Then he could not pretend any longer. 'On the footplate! Wow! That's *brilliant!*'

In the booking-hall at Welham Station five Greenwooders searched through their pockets and put an assortment of coins in Stephen's outstretched hand. When they had finished he counted up the money, the others looking on anxiously. 'We'll just do it,' he announced in relieved tones, 'with thirty pence over.' He went to the ticket-office and put down the money. 'Five singles to Edwinton, please,' he said. The man behind the grille looked suspiciously at the pile of small coins and counted them slowly. He grunted and pushed forward five tickets. 'Whose baby's money-box have you been rifling?' he asked.

Stephen ignored him loftily. 'Come on,' he said, 'the last train's due in about ten minutes.'

They reached the platform and sat on a seat, a line of drooping figures, each one busy with his or her own thoughts.

Suddenly Stephen sat up. 'There's a train coming in!' he said. 'That's funny – it's very early. I thought it wasn't due for another ten minutes.'

'Well, it's here,' said Sam. 'The sooner we get home the better.'

They stood up and waited for the train to come round the bend. With a roar and a hiss it slowed down and shuddered to a halt. Several carriage doors opened and

183

a crowd of people got out. Stephen frowned, 'What a lot of people,' he exclaimed. They climbed into a carriage from which half a dozen people had alighted. There were two passengers left, a middle-aged man and woman, both looking tired, red-faced and untidy. They were munching sandwiches and drinking tea from paper cups. They moved up hospitably as the Greenwooders crowded in. 'Plenty o' room for little 'uns,' said the man. His wife hunted in a large shopping basket and brought out a bag of fruit. 'Have an apple,' she said and offered them round. The Greenwooders thanked her politely and took an apple each, thankful for something to stay their hunger. The man winked at them in a friendly way. 'Been hot at Skegness,' he said.

'Has it?' said Tony. 'Er – is that where you've been?'

'Yes,' said the woman. 'We always go on this excursion after Easter. Just me and my husband. It's nice to get away from the kids for a day.'

'It must be,' agreed Tony, thinking privately that the kids might think it nice to get away from their parents too.

A sudden thought flashed into Stephen's mind. He drew in his breath sharply. 'Is this – is this an excursion train?' he asked. 'Is that why such a lot of people got off at Welham?'

'Aye,' the man agreed. 'Skegness to Retfield. It stopped at Welham to let a British Legion party get off. Next stop Retfield, home and bed.' He yawned hugely. 'The fresh air's made me feel right tired.'

'Me too,' said his wife.

The Greenwooders looked at each other in horror. Next stop Retfield. Then – then they had got into the wrong train...

184

Stephen gulped. 'Doesn't this train stop at Edwinton?'

'No, that it doesn't,' said the man. 'The regular train is about ten minutes after this. Why, did you want to get off there?'

'Yes,' said Stephen weakly. He looked at Tony and Sam and groaned. 'Now what are we going to do?'

They were too stunned to offer any suggestion. Felicity nudged Pauline, who blinked her eyes open. 'Do you hear that? We've got on the wrong train!'

Pauline said nothing, but the tears started to trickle from her red-rimmed eyes. She crouched in her corner as though she would like to have disappeared completely into the dingy upholstery.

'What's the matter?' said the man sympathetically. 'You'll be able to get back somehow – there'll be buses.'

'Don't take on so, love,' said his wife. 'It's easy done, I've done it myself.'

'It's not that,' Felicity explained, looking anxiously at Pauline. 'We're looking for her brother. He's lost. We thought we would find him in Welham, but we didn't, and it's most important to get back to Edwinton quickly.'

'We've properly made a mess of everything, haven't we?' said Tony.

There was a gloom-laden silence. Then Stephen looked at Sam and found Sam looking at him, the same thought in both their minds. Both pairs of eyes looked upward.

'What do you think?' said Stephen.

'Should we?' said Sam.

Tony followed their gaze. 'Five pounds for improper use,' he remarked.

Felicity's eyes opened wide with horrified excitement.

185

'You're not going to pull the communication cord, are you?' she gasped.

'Why not?' Stephen said.

'But – but we couldn't afford five pounds!'

'How do you know we'd have to pay it?' Stephen demanded.

'Well, look, it says so.'

'That's for improper use,' repeated Tony.

'How do you know our use is proper?'

'I should think it's just about as proper as it could be,' Stephen said. 'We've got into the wrong train and we're going miles further than we want to go. It's British Railways' silly fault if it runs a non-stopping train just before the proper one.'

'That stop at Welham wasn't a scheduled stop,' volunteered the man, who had been following their discussion with interest. 'It was only because of the British Legion party they did it.' He added, a trifle wistfully, 'I've never seen a communication cord being pulled...'

'Now, Joe,' his wife warned, 'don't you encourage them. You'd better not, my dears, you don't know what trouble you might get into. They're very strict on the railways nowadays, so I've heard.'

'You heard what the lady said,' Felicity put in anxiously. 'We don't want any trouble.'

'But I still don't see –' Stephen began stubbornly.

Tony had been infected by the general doubt. 'Perhaps we'd better not. I tell you what – as soon as we get to Retfield let's ring up Daddy and see what he suggests. Or the Post Office. Pauline's Mum and Dad might be back. I say, wouldn't it be funny if Peter answered the phone?'

186

'Hilarious,' Stephen said coldly. 'And don't forget we've got thirty pence between us.'

'Reverse the charges,' said Sam.

'Oh, all right.' Stephen subsided. 'But I still think the sensible thing would be to pull the cord.'

'Better luck next time,' said the man with a touch of regret in his voice.

Pauline, clutching a sodden handkerchief, had fallen asleep. The others made themselves as comfortable as their unquiet thoughts would allow. The man and his wife, having finished the remains of their picnic, and having exhausted their expressions of sympathy, divided an evening paper between them and read items of news aloud to each other, often at the same time. The time dragged by and the dark unfriendly countryside slithered past the windows.

Forty minutes later the train slowed down and ground to a halt. The man and his wife, their belongings gathered together, stepped briskly down from the carriage. 'Now, don't worry, young 'uns,' the man said in farewell. 'Remember it's a long lane that has no turning!'

'Yes, it's always darkest before the dawn,' his wife added brightly. 'Cheerio, nice to have met you...'

'I've heard *that* before,' Stephen muttered. 'Well, come on, let's see what's going to happen now.'

The train emptied quickly, the excursionists eager to get back to their homes and television sets. Soon only the five children were left on the platform. 'We'd better hang back a bit,' Stephen suggested, 'because there'll be a bit of explaining to do to the ticket-collector.'

He took the tickets from his pocket and advanced towards the ticket-collector. He held them out and said in

187

a voice higher than he had intended it to be, 'I'm awfully sorry about this. You see –'

The ticket-collector had taken the tickets automatically and was about to put them on the ledge beside him with all the others. At Stephen's over-emphatic voice he looked up, then at the tickets. 'Why –' he began.

'Yes, you see –' Stephen struggled to explain.

'These only took you to Edwinton.'

'Yes, that's where we were going –'

'And now you're at Retfield.'

'Yes.'

'I suppose you thought I wouldn't notice. Eh, is that it?'

'Not at all.' Stephen's voice grew sharper. 'We thought the train stopped at Edwinton.'

'That excursion was from Skegness to Retfield. Nobody said nowt about it stopping at Edwinton.'

'It stopped at Welham,' put in Sam.

'It wasn't due to.'

'Well it *did*,' Sam insisted. 'That's where we got on.'

'Then why didn't you get off at Edwinton?'

'Because it didn't *stop* there!' said Stephen.

'Oh, aye. I'd forgot for the moment it didn't stop at Edwinton, you're getting me so moithered.'

'We're not! You're getting yourself moithered.' Stephen took a deep breath and started again. 'Please listen to what I'm trying to say. We got on at Welham and bought tickets to Edwinton, thinking that the train stopped there. But we got on the wrong train, an excursion train, and it's brought us to Retfield. We're very sorry, but it was a genuine mistake...'

The ticket-collector took off his hat and scratched his head. 'Aye,' he said after some deep thought, 'well, that

188

sounds reasonable, I must say. Why didn't you tell me that in the first place?'

Stephen's jaw sagged. He tried to say something but no sound came. Sam took over. 'Could you advise us what we'd better do, please?'

The ticket-collector brightened up. 'Aye, that's easy. You just pay the excess.'

'Excess?'

'Aye, excess fare from Edwinton to Retfield. Let's see, now ... that's five pounds, fifteen pence, please.' He held out his hand.

Five Greenwooders looked at each other in consternation. 'Five pounds, fifteen pence? But – but we haven't got it – we haven't anything like that.'

'Thirty pence, to be exact,' said Sam.

The ticket-collector looked at them as though he had found them trying to steal the station. 'Ah, so that's it – trying to get by without paying – I thought there was something fishy about you lot.'

'Oh, *please* don't start all that again!' Stephen begged.

'Now, none of your impudence, *if* you please. I've had about enough of children for today. Looks to me as if the whole of Edwinton's taken it into their heads to get free rides. What with that other kid trying to mix me up with talk about an elephant's mother, and now you lot ... Do you think I'm daft?'

'Yes,' Stephen whispered under his breath, and Felicity hurriedly said, 'Of course we don't!' in a loud voice.

'Let's have less of your lip then,' said the ticket-collector, 'and hand over the money.'

Stephen began to wave his hands about in exasperation. 'But we haven't got it – don't you understand?'

189

'Half a minute,' said Tony, stepping forward. 'What was that about another kid? Do you mean there's been someone else from Edwinton here tonight?'

'Aye,' grumbled the ticket-collector, 'and a rare dance he led me. I had to take him to the stationmaster in the end.'

'Then take us there!' said Tony excitedly.

'And who, may I ask, are you giving orders to?'

'It wasn't meant to be an order,' said Tony. '*Please* take us to him.'

'All right,' said the ticket-collector, slightly mollified. 'I was going to, anyway. Just wait till I've put these tickets away.'

'Oh, please hurry!' Felicity had caught the infection. The idea had dawned on her too that the 'other kid' might be – could it possibly be? – Peter...

'Now, now, now,' said the ticket-collector with infuriating slowness, 'bide your time.' He stared at the group of impatient children. 'It's the first time I've ever known a lot of fare-bilkers eager to get what's coming to them. You're a rum lot, I must say. Well, on your own heads be it. Come on, we'll go and find Mr Crawford.' He set off at a leisurely pace, the children trailing after him. He knocked on the door of the stationmaster's office. 'More of 'em, sir,' he announced and, with a sigh, thankfully withdrew.

Mr Crawford got up from his desk and stared at them as though he had never seen children before. Their apprehension was slightly relieved by his look of patient resignation. 'More of 'em indeed!' he said. 'This is quite a night. I suppose you wouldn't have come from Welham too without tickets and fallen asleep and missed Edwinton?'

190

'Not quite, sir,' said Stephen. 'But – but how did you know we've come from Welham and that we missed Edwinton?'

'That's what the other one did. Still, never mind about him. What's your story? – and you'd better make it good!'

'Well, it was like this –' Stephen began, but he was interrupted by Felicity. 'Could you tell us the name of the other boy, please, before dealing with us? It's very important, really it is. We – we might know him.'

'I've no objection,' said Mr Crawford. 'It was Peter Christy.'

Felicity pointed dramatically at Pauline. 'Her brother!'

Pauline clasped her hands together. 'Then he's alive!'

'Very much so,' said the stationmaster, 'and back in Edwinton by now, if all's gone well. Now, let's hear about all your misadventures. I suppose you've been running away too?'

'Oh, no,' said Felicity, 'we've been running after Peter!'

'It was like this –' Stephen began again, and this time he was allowed to carry on with only minor interruptions.

Mr Crawford nodded his head thoughtfully when Stephen reached the end of his story. 'All very unfortunate,' he commented. 'But you still owe British Railways five pounds and fifteen pence, you know.'

'We'll send it tomorrow,' cried Felicity. 'We really will. Won't you trust us? We'll give you our names and addresses.'

'Well...' said the stationmaster, rubbing his chin.

'You're not –' her eyes grew large with fear – 'you're not going to send for the police, are you?'

Mr Crawford decided not to tease them any longer. 'Of

191

course not,' he said. 'As long as you send me the money all will be forgiven and forgotten. Now we'd better see about getting you home. I can't send you the same way that Master Christy went, unfortunately. But first, don't you think someone had better ring some of your parents and tell them what's happened and where you are? They might be getting worried. Parents do sometimes, you'd be surprised. What about it? Who will ring who?'

There was a pause. Then Tony said, 'Would you – do you think you would do it for us, please? It might be better –'

The stationmaster suddenly roared with laughter. 'You mean you want me to act as a buffer? Afraid of the reception you'd get, is that it? All right, I'll do it. What's your telephone number, young man?'

Tony told him the Vicarage number. The stationmaster picked up the receiver and dialled. It was quite a long conversation. The Greenwooders could not make out what was being said at the other end because, apart from his initial information, Mr Crawford spoke in mono-syllables or short phrases. They heard him say, at intervals, 'Don't worry about that ... I'll see to it ... no, I quite understand ... yes, I'll tell them ... certainly ... no, not at all ... I've got children of my own ...'

They gazed at each other. What was all that about? Who was being so long-winded at the other end? Their curiosity grew as the call went on.

At last it was over. Mr Crawford put the receiver down and turned to them. He was chuckling. 'That was the Vicar I was speaking to.'

Tony and Felicity paled.

192

'He suggested coming into Retfield by car to collect you, but I told him I would see to getting you home. There's no need to drag him out here at this time of night. He told me to tell you that the Doctor, Sam's parents and the Christys are all at the Vicarage. They were having a meeting to decide what to do when I phoned. So there'll be quite a reception committee waiting for you, won't there?'

There was a general shudder. 'And Peter?' Pauline asked anxiously. 'Did he say anything about Peter?'

'Your brother is fast asleep in bed,' the stationmaster said, 'worn out by all his adventures.'

'Lucky thing,' Pauline said. 'That's where I'd like to be.'

'And so you shall before long,' said Mr Crawford, 'because I'm going to put you on a train in a very few minutes.'

'Is there another train to Edwinton tonight?' asked Stephen.

'No!'

'Then how –'

'You just wait and see.'

Mr Crawford led them out of his office and down the platform to a siding. An engine was chuffing gently, almost ready to move off. There were only three closed wagons attached to it, and he opened the door of the first one. 'Hop in,' he said, 'and I'll tell the driver that he's got extra freight.'

Doubtfully the children climbed into the wagon, the interior of which was lit only by a couple of low-powered bulbs. Felicity gave a grimace and raised her nose in the air. She gave out a sudden wail. 'Fish!'

193

Mr Crawford laughed. 'That's right, you're in the fish train!'

Five horrified faces peered out at him. 'We shall smell –' Felicity began.

'Not more than all the other red herrings we've had tonight,' Mr Crawford assured her. He began to slide the big door of the wagon to. 'You'll be all right. You'll be home in half an hour. Oh, there's one thing I forgot to tell you.'

Felicity had gathered her frock round her and was standing like a timid paddler testing the water with one toe. 'What's that?'

'Your father said, "Tell Pauline that her parents arrived home without Aunt Edna".'

'They did?' yelled Pauline through the last few inches of space as the door was almost closed.

'Yes, she wasn't on the train she was expected by, nor the next two. When they got home they found a telegram that your assistant had taken, to say that she couldn't come after all. She's caught German measles! Goodbye!'

With great jerks and jangling of couplings the fish train started. In the dimly-lit wagon the children made themselves as comfortable as they could while avoiding the boxes of fish, and talked over the stationmaster's parting piece of news. 'I'm sorry she's got German measles,' said Pauline, 'but I'm jolly glad she's not coming now. If she comes when we're back at school it won't be too bad. Won't Peter be pleased!'

Felicity said something that nobody quite caught, and they turned and looked at her.

'What's that?' Tony asked. He saw the reason why her words had been indistinct and added, 'For goodness sake take that hanky away from your face, we can't hear a word.'

Felicity carefully adjusted the handkerchief so that, though her nose remained covered, her mouth was temporarily exposed. 'The smell,' she hissed through clenched teeth. 'Isn't it *awful*! What I said was, now that your aunt's not coming Peter's running away was all for nothing. And see where it's landed us! Wait till I see him tomorrow – I'll give him fish train!'

The next morning was tender with crisp greenness and the smell of new and growing things. The spring sunshine seeped through the trees and fell in golden patches on the grass of the forest clearing. Sam sat with his back to the hollow oak, whittling away at a piece of wood and humming tunelessly, thinking of nothing in particular. He was content to feel the sun on his face, to know that his friends would be arriving soon, to be conscious of troubles over and the hope of peace for the last few days of their holidays. The fact of school starting the next week was far enough away not to cast a shadow on the pleasantness of the present. Time enough to worry about that, and the fact that he still had to read the book set for holiday homework, the night before . . .

Tony and Felicity were the first to break through the gorse bush barrier and appear in the clearing. They greeted Sam and stretched themselves beside him on the grass. Tony lay full length, put his hands behind his head and turned his face to the sun. Felicity tucked her legs beneath her and arranged her skirt in a picturesque billow round her knees. She plucked a long blade of grass and stroked it over Tony's forehead.

'Stop it, sis,' he murmured in a friendly way. 'Sam,' he went on, 'we didn't really expect to see you here this morning. We thought you'd be confined to the cowsheds or something.'

'I thought so myself,' Sam replied, hacking away industriously at his stick, 'but Dad didn't make a murmur when I hinted I'd like the morning off. I thought there'd be a big row over yesterday but instead he gave me fifty pence. Funny, isn't it, how sometimes when you expect to get into trouble you don't, and when you don't, you do?'

'We're costing your father something, aren't we?' said Felicity. 'Fifty pence – and there was the five pounds for finding the Roman coin. We could have done with that yesterday, couldn't we?'

'What happened to you – about yesterday, I mean?' asked Sam.

'A bit of a lecture,' said Felicity. 'Daddy put on his stern face and looked over his spectacles and talked about thoughtlessness and giving trouble to people and not thinking before acting – you know, the usual sort of thing. We tried to explain that we thought we were doing the best we could in the circumstances, and he coughed a bit and said, "Yes, well," and then went on with his sermon because he'd prepared it and wanted to get it off his chest. We can always tell, though, when he's really angry. Tony, did you hear them *laughing* when they went up to bed?'

'Yes,' Tony answered, 'though I can't see what's funny about smelling of fish!' Felicity pulled a face. 'It's still in my hair – I can't decide whether it's haddock or cod!'

196

'I'm surprised it didn't turn you into a mermaid,' said Tony, 'considering the fuss you've made.'

Sounds of movements in the bushes made them turn their heads. Stephen appeared, his red hair tousled, his face alight with amusement. 'Hello!' he called. 'There's something fishy going on here!' He gave a shriek of laughter at the groans that greeted his remark, stepped on Tony's stomach, pulled Felicity's hair, sprang up to catch the lowest bough of the oak tree and hung there, long legs dangling, making hideous monkey faces.

'You're in a good mood this morning,' Sam remarked. 'Does that mean you got away with it too?'

Stephen released his hold and jumped down, landing on the grass at Tony's side. 'I did. I thought my father would lay it on hot and strong but all he did was slap me on the back and say, 'It's all experience, my lad,' and told me about being stranded in a boat on Lough Erne when he was a boy in Ireland.'

'Was he fishing?' Tony asked.

'Tony, will you shut up about *fish*,' Felicity moaned.

'But I've had it from Old Eva all right,' said Stephen. 'You should have heard her!' He put on a creditable accent, very like Old Eva's drawling country voice. 'Giving us a fright like that, you young monkey. We didn't know what had happened to you. Gallivanting all over the country looking for that daft Christy boy and us thinking all sorts of things. Proper worried, I was, and the sponge cake I was making went sad in the oven, and bringing that nasty smell in the house. Ah, well, you shan't have another jam turnover for a week, and that shall be true, as my old grandmother used to say.'

197

'I wonder what Old Eva's grandmother was like,' Tony said thoughtfully.

'Awfully boring, I should think. She was always saying, 'And that shall be true,' according to Old Eva. I believe she went to school with Mrs Haddock. I bet they made a fine pair!'

They were silent for a few moments, picturing Mrs Haddock and Old Eva's grandmother squeezed together at a desk in the village school.

'I shouldn't like to have been their teacher,' Stephen said at length. He lifted his head and cocked an ear towards the bushes. 'Ah, methinks I hear the twins – or is it a herd of buffalo?'

It was two or three minutes before the twins actually emerged from the thicket of gorse. During that time the others heard squeaks and cries from Pauline of 'Peter, you let that branch go on my leg on purpose!' and 'Peter, wait for me!' and just 'Peter!' From Peter came only 'Well . . .' When they finally appeared a line of Greenwooders had formed up to meet them. To Pauline they looked grim-faced and threatening and she cowered back, but Peter, oblivious to the atmosphere, advanced towards them with friendliness written all over his face.

'Hello,' he said brightly.

'And here,' said Sam, 'is the cause of all the trouble.'

'Hi, Sam.' Peter beamed at him.

Felicity folded her arms. 'Peter Christy, as members of the Greenwooders, we demand an explanation of yesterday's goings-on.'

'We also demand an apology,' added Tony.

'It was all your fault,' said Stephen.

Peter did not seem to take in the accusations and

198

demands. His thoughts were obviously elsewhere. 'Look what I've got,' he said excitedly. 'Mr Catchpole gave it to me.' He put his hand up his pullover and pulled down a dirty black object which he promptly put on his head. It was a waterproof cap of the sort worn by engine drivers and was much too big for him. It covered not only his head but most of his face as well. He made a noise like the whistle of an engine and pulled imaginary levers. 'Ooooooo – choo, choo, choo...' He chugged his way across the grass, round the oak tree a couple of times and back to his starting point, where he tripped over a little hillock and fell at Stephen's feet. Stephen hauled him up and stood him at arm's length. 'Peter Christy –' he began severely.

'Ooooooo!' Peter hooted.

'He's been like this all morning,' Pauline said. 'He's got trains on the brain.'

'It was great,' Peter gasped, taking time off from his train noises. 'We went at sixty miles an hour. Sixty! I've decided I'm not going to be an astronaut when I grow up – I'm going to be an engine driver! Ooooooo...'

'Be quiet!' said Stephen. 'Come on, boys, let's quieten him down.'

The three boys made a lunge towards Peter. He ducked under Stephen's arm and was away again. Eventually he was trapped and all four of them fell in a sprawling heap, Peter at the bottom. For a moment there was only heavy breathing, then came a sad little train whistle from Peter. Sam clapped his hand over Peter's mouth and order was restored.

Good humour returned to the Greenwooders. They sorted themselves out and sat down in a friendly group.

'Now, Peter, tell us all about it,' Felicity urged. Peter was only too ready to oblige and his story came out in a rush, finishing up with 'Mr Askew – I thought he was Mr Fred the stationmaster, he was smashing ... did I know Billy Catchpole's dad ... there weren't any carriages ... did I mind travelling on the footplate...'

'No!' said Stephen enviously.

'*Yes!*' said Peter. 'And it was brilliant. Mr Catchpole gave me some overalls that were too big, but I tucked

'*Now, Peter, tell us all about it...*'

them up and off we went. He let me sound the whistle and the fireman – that's Mr Twigg – he let me stoke the fire. Mr Twigg was nice too. He joined Nottingham Forest in 1936 but he broke his leg and never played for them. He saw every home match in 1950 and 1951. It was their best scoring season – 110 goals in 46 matches – but he hasn't been regular since – and there was only one lot of signals against us all the way. Mr Catchpole gave me a sandwich – sardine –'

'Fish again,' Felicity muttered under her breath.

'– and the sparks were flying out of the funnel. Doesn't coal smell funny? We went through a tunnel and it was terrific – and Mr Catchpole gave me this hat and said not to tell Billy so I can't wear it at school and –' suddenly the flow of words dried up, '– and that's all.'

'Quite enough to be going on with,' said Tony. 'Now, what happened before that? How did you get to Retfield in the first place? What happened at the fair?'

'Oh, that,' said Peter with maddening indifference. 'I didn't like the fair, and I fell asleep in the train. Do you want to know the number of the engine, I've got it somewhere?'

'No,' said Stephen. 'Next time you run away will you tell us before you go?'

'Just so that we can say goodbye,' said Tony.

'Run away?' Peter sounded surprised. 'I'm not going to do that again – why should I?'

'That's what we'd like to know,' said Sam. 'If your Aunt Edna comes to stay when she's better will you be off again?'

'Of course not,' Peter said with a sniff. 'Mr Catchpole

201

said I must put up with things like a man. He says he sympathises because he's got a mother-in-law.'

'Never mind,' said Felicity, 'it all turned out all right in the end – for you, anyway. You didn't have to ride in a fish train. Which reminds me, you haven't apologised yet. Don't you think he ought to, Pauline?'

'Yes, you ought, Peter. You know we all set out to rescue you as soon as we knew you had run away. You gave us a lot of trouble.'

Peter lifted a shining and unconcerned face to his friends. 'OK. I'm sorry. Hey, Stephen, I've got a lump of coal here – a real one from the engine.' He plunged his hand into his trousers pocket and pulled out, not a piece of coal, but an extremely dirty envelope. 'Oh, gosh, Pauline, look what I've got. I forgot to post it when we came out!'

'Peter!' Pauline said despairingly. 'I knew I should have taken charge of it. Fancy forgetting it – and the pillar box is right outside the shop.'

'What on earth is it?' asked Felicity, intrigued by the crumpled envelope which was liberally blackened by the lump of coal with which it had shared Peter's pocket.

'It's a card,' said Peter. 'A get well card – for Aunt Edna . . .'

FAMINE FUND

Peter sat alone in the kitchen at the back of the Post Office, finishing his breakfast. Pauline had finished hers and had gone out shopping for her mother. Peter and Pauline had always had certain jobs to do before they were free to join the other Greenwooders, and now that the new baby, Robin, had arrived, Mrs Christy had to rely more and more on the help she got from them, and Pauline, in particular, enjoyed the added responsibility.

Peter had peeled the potatoes and collected vegetables from the garden, but it was not those things that had made him late for breakfast. The blame lay with Mr Puff, a white rabbit with the silkiest ears Peter had ever seen. He was not usually a very adventurous rabbit and spent most of his time lying half asleep in the summer sunshine, waking occasionally to nibble at the lettuce leaves with which Peter kept him generously supplied. This morning, however, Peter had decided that the partitioned-off part of the garden where Mr Puff lived could do with a tidy-up. As the rabbit was lying peacefully in one corner, reluctant even to stir himself to eat his own breakfast, Peter had not bothered to fasten the gate. As a result, the moment his back was turned, Mr Puff had decided to see a bit more of the world and had lolloped out of the compound, his whiskers twitching at the unfamiliar smells that greeted him.

When Peter noticed the rabbit's absence Mr Puff was out of sight. It was several minutes before he spotted the fluffy white figure hiding among the tall rhubarb stalks. On Peter's approach Mr Puff ran off and hid among the bean poles. With the aid of a broom handle, a fresh cabbage leaf and a serious lecture on the dangers of wandering, Peter managed to grab him and get him safely back home. After all that there was no time to give more than a brief greeting to his white mice in the wire-topped box in the tool shed.

Peter gathered up the yellow fragments of scrambled egg on his fork and popped them in his mouth. He drank deeply from a glass of milk, and looked with distaste at the burnt toast crusts on the edge of his plate. To him they were dark brown and unappetising, though, he admitted to himself, grown-ups would probably deny that they were burnt at all. He wondered how to get rid of them. There was no room in his pocket, and in any case they would make it greasy, and he couldn't put them on the fire because there wasn't one. He knew his mother hated waste, and if she saw them she would give him a good telling off.

There was a gruff little bark from George, the twins' spaniel, who was apparently having doggish fantasies about the old slipper that was his constant plaything. Of course, thought Peter, that's the solution! 'George,' he called. 'George, good dog, come here.'

The dog pricked up his ears and padded over to Peter at the table. 'Lovely toast for you, George, nice eaties,'

Peter said. He picked up a crust and tried to put it into George's mouth. But George snapped his mouth shut and then sniffed at the toast suspiciously. It was obvious that the smell did not recommend itself because he averted his head and would have returned to his slipper if Peter had not grabbed his collar.

'George, you are very naughty! Eat this up ... look, I'll eat some...' Peter pretended to take a bite and chew. 'Ooh! Yum-yum! George have some?' Peter tried to get the toast into the dog's mouth again; more sniffing, again a turning away of the head. 'George, there's no need to *smell* it! Toast is very good for you – it'll make your hair curl and stop you getting – er – hard pad. Eat it up before Mum comes. Lovely toast with good farm butter!'

'Peter!' His mother's voice breaking in unexpectedly forced him to release George who, unconcerned, trotted back to the slipper. 'How many times have I told you not to feed the dog at the table, not to mention giving him some of your breakfast?'

'I don't know, Mum, I've never counted.'

'Peter!' his mother said warningly.

'Anyway, it's burnt.'

Mrs Christy looked at the crusts. 'Nonsense,' she said. 'It's toasted rather more than usual, perhaps, but it is not burnt. If you had been in time for your breakfast –'

'Sorry, Mum, it was Mr Puff's fault. He got out.'

'Fancy blaming that poor rabbit! Peter, I don't like to see you wasting food. All over the world there are thousands and thousands of starving children who would be very glad of those crusts.'

'Then why don't we pack them up and send them to

205

Africa?' said Peter, convinced that a lot of fuss was being made over nothing.

'Don't be cheeky, Peter,' said Mrs Christy, 'or I shall have to find you some more jobs to do.'

'Sorry, Mum,' said Peter, who knew when he had gone too far.

'Just you remember the saying "Waste not, want not",' his mother went on. 'Remember what a lucky boy you are, well fed and well clothed. And while we're on the subject, I want you to look out some of those clothes that have got too small for you. There's a couple of pullovers, that pair of grey corduroy trousers and the gabardine raincoat. I want to make up a parcel for the Oxford Committee for Famine Relief.'

Peter was not sure that he had heard properly. 'Oxford Famine?' he asked. 'Why has Oxford got a famine? I thought they were all rich and clever and things in Oxford.'

'Of course there isn't a famine in Oxford,' said Mrs Christy. 'It's the headquarters of Oxfam, an organisation that helps towards famine relief in other places all over the world.'

'I see,' said Peter.

'They need money and good clothes and suchlike, and those things of yours are hardly worn out at all. I did think of keeping them for when Robin is bigger, but they'd do more good going to less fortunate children now.'

'I know,' Peter said, suddenly enthusiastic, 'you could send that horrid cissy jersey with the silly sailors on it that Aunt Edna gave me.' What a good idea, he thought, to get rid of the embarrassing present from his unfavourite aunt.

206

'Er – we'd better not do that,' his mother said. 'You don't have to wear it though – until Aunt Edna pays us a visit.'

Peter crossed his fingers under the table and silently hoped that such a thing might not come to pass.

His mother turned to go out, but paused as she remembered what had started the conversation. 'What about those crusts?'

Peter thought of the way out. 'George has been sniffing them, Mum.'

Mrs Christy sighed. 'All right, you can leave them, but don't let it happen again. I don't suppose the rest of your Greenwood friends leave their crusts,' she said as she went out.

'Greenwood*ers*,' he corrected her and, putting out his tongue at George, he slipped out of the back door.

As Peter approached the clearing in the forest he was puzzled by the silence. The rest of the Greenwooders ought to be there by this time, he thought, yet he could not hear any voices. Perhaps they had gone off somewhere without him – if so, Mr Puff had a lot to answer for! He reached the gorse bush barrier that screened the clearing from prying eyes and ducked through the secret passage between the prickly branches.

As he came out the other side he saw, to his relief, that they were all there, including Pauline, who, he thought, might have told him before she left home that she was off to the meeting place. He saw why there had been no sound. They were all busy chewing, and obviously enjoying, chocolates from a large ornate box which Felicity was holding and which Pauline was carefully studying.

The boys waved at Peter, their mouths too full to greet him any other way. Felicity looked up. 'Hello, Peter,' she said, 'you can have one in a minute. Hurry up, Pauline.'

'Not that squiggly one,' said Pauline, 'because that's Turkish Delight, and the round one with the comma is –' she consulted the lid of the box – 'coffee cream. No, not that – I'll have a – yes – a strawberry cream...' She took the chocolate and bit into it, her eyes shining with pleasure as the pink filling ran into her mouth. 'They're lovely. Thank you, Felicity.'

'Let's have another,' said Tony, perched on the lowest branch of the hollow oak.

'In a minute,' said Felicity. 'You've had two and Peter hasn't had one yet. Help yourself, Peter.'

Peter did not reply. Nobody but he knew the struggle that was being waged inside him. Nutty crunch, caramel cream, almond praline, cherry nougat – all the marvellous and mouth-watering names of chocolates flashed in front of his mind's eye. He tried to recapture the lovely smooth taste of chocolate melting in the mouth and the sticky sweetness of the fillings. There was nothing in the world he would have liked better at that moment than a chocolate... The pause got longer and longer, and the others were looking at him curiously. Then, 'No, thank you,' said Peter smugly.

The effect on the Greenwooders was electric. Tony nearly tumbled out of the tree. Felicity almost dropped the box. Pauline stopped in mid-bite and Stephen swallowed his the wrong way and had a burst of coughing which Sam tried to stop by slapping his back.

'I beg your *pardon!*' Felicity said weakly.

'No, thank you,' Peter repeated.

208

'But why?' asked Tony. 'Are you ill?'

'I'm very well, thank you,' Peter said with dignity. 'I am very well looked after at home and given the best of everything.'

'He's gone mad,' said Stephen, eyes goggling.

'But you're usually the chocolate-guzzler-in-chief,' said Tony. 'There *must* be something wrong when you refuse one.'

'There's nothing wrong with me. It's just that I don't think it's right to fill yourself up with chocolates when there are millions of people starving in Africa and Asia. Not to mention Oxford,' Peter added.

'Oxford?' said Tony. 'Do you mean Oxfam?'

'I expect so,' Peter said. 'My Mum told me about it this morning and she said they would be glad of my burnt toast. Anyway, I'm never going to waste anything again and I'm not going to eat sweets either – well, not so many.'

'Wonders never cease,' said Stephen.

'Don't make fun of him,' said Felicity. 'I think it's very decent of him and if you ask me he shows the rest of us up.' Peter beamed happily. It was rare for him to be held up as an example. 'But I still think you could have a chocolate, Peter,' Felicity went on. 'After all, they've been opened and it only means that someone else would have your share.'

'You won't help anyone by refusing a chocolate,' said Stephen. 'In fact, you'd be helping the starving children if you did have one.'

'How?' asked Peter, ready to grasp at any straw to justify a change of mind.

'By the fact that you've told us about them – stirred our consciences,' said Stephen.

'That's right,' said Sam. 'You have made us feel guilty

and if you don't have a chocolate we shall feel even worse.' He exchanged a wink with Stephen.

'Will you really?' said Peter.

'Of course we shall,' said Tony. 'Go on, have one for our sakes.'

'Please do,' said Felicity, joining in the entreaties.

'*Please!*' said Pauline.

Peter thought they had argued their case well. 'All right,' he said, 'perhaps just one...' Felicity held out the box and with a swift and sure movement he took the largest and most exciting-looking chocolate from the very centre. He popped it in his mouth, and with a look of ecstasy on his face announced, 'Vanilla fudge...' Soon afterwards, when the chocolates had been handed round again and Peter had made up for lost time, the subject of starving children came up again. 'I wish we could do something to help,' Felicity said.

'Like what?' asked Stephen.

'Like sending clothes you've grown out of,' said Peter. 'That's what my Mum's doing, but she won't send the awful pullover Aunt Edna sent me.'

'I wouldn't have much to give,' said Sam. 'I use all my old things for working on the farm and it doesn't matter if they're a bit too small. What else do they want?'

'Jewellery,' said Felicity.

'Huh!' said the boys in chorus.

'My father's got some pamphlets about Oxfam,' Felicity went on hurriedly, 'and they'll tell us. There's going to be a lot of activities connected with the church soon, and we might get some ideas from them.'

'The best thing is to raise money,' said Tony. 'Let's think up some ways of doing that.'

'A concert!' said Felicity, out of the blue. 'I could recite Shakespeare.'

'You mean people would pay money to shut you up?' said Tony, quickly clambering out of her reach.

But Felicity had decided that a dignified silence was the best answer, and she addressed her next remark pointedly to the others. 'We could persuade Miss Pope-Cunningham to play the piano.'

'I can play a bit,' said Peter.

'Yes, I know,' said Felicity, 'but people would get rather tired of hearing Chopsticks over and over again. Sam could do lassooing and rope tricks, and Tony conjuring with the magic set he got last Christmas...'

'I could tear paper into funny patterns,' said Peter.

'Hilarious,' said Stephen.

Felicity was warming to her subject. 'And Pauline,' she continued, anxious to air the theatrical knowledge she had gained during her brief appearance with the Retfield Repertory Company during the previous year, 'Pauline can be wardrobe mistress.'

'Can I?' said Pauline, slightly alarmed. 'What would I have to do?'

'Make our costumes,' Felicity explained. 'You're ever so good at sewing.'

'What about me?' said Stephen. 'Can I pull the curtain?'

'No! You can – you can – I know, you can do some caricatures. You're awfully good at that sort of thing.'

'No, thank you!' Stephen said emphatically. 'Not after the Christmas Fair, when I had a table in the Church Hall and was doing caricatures at tenpence a time. Well, a caricature is supposed to exaggerate, but when I gave Mr Bunbury a big nose he got all upset and complained to your father and he said it might be a good thing if I didn't do any more.'

'But Mr Bunbury has got a big nose,' said Tony.

'Yes, but he thinks nobody nose,' Peter suddenly screeched with laughter. 'See? Nose – knows – I've made a joke!'

'Don't you dare make another,' Sam growled. He turned to Felicity. 'Anyway, who's going to come to a concert at this time of the year? Suppose it's blazing hot that day. Where are we going to have it, and where do we practise?'

'He's right,' said Stephen. 'It wouldn't work.'

'Very well. I give up. You think of something.' Felicity lay on her back with her face to the sky. 'I have retired from the discussion.'

'Let's have a Baby Show,' said Pauline, who had always longed to attend one but had never had the chance.

'There aren't enough babies in the village,' Tony objected. 'I can only think of about half a dozen under two years of age.'

'Our Robin would stand a good chance of a prize then,' said Peter. 'He's not bad as babies go.'

'He's *marvellous*,' Pauline said indignantly.

'What about a Dog Show?' Stephen offered.

'Yes, and what would happen when Prince, Beauty, George and Chummy got together?' said Tony. 'To say nothing of their mother. There'd be an almighty scrap.'

'Then we could charge tenpence to call them off,' said Stephen.

'We're not being very serious about it,' said Sam. 'Let's have a pause for really practical ideas.'

212

They fell silent. Stephen rolled over on to his stomach and put his head on his arms. Sam chewed a blade of grass thoughtfully. Peter climbed into the tree and straddled one of the branches. Pauline sat decorously by Felicity's side. Tony yawned, the heat making him drowsy.

Then Felicity sat up suddenly. 'Toffee!' she said.

'Thank you – where?' said Peter, peering down from his perch.

'We make it – Pauline and I. Treacle toffee, or something like that, and we sell it in twenty-pence bags. Pauline's a very good cook, aren't you?'

'Not bad,' Pauline admitted modestly.

'She makes smashing coconut ice,' said Peter.

'We could have a table outside our gate and sell it from there,' went on Felicity, her enthusiasm mounting.

'You could sell other things too,' said Sam, 'such as toys and books that we've finished with.'

'Like my scooter,' said Peter.

'Peter, your scooter hasn't got any handlebars,' said Pauline. 'Who'd want to buy that?'

'Somebody who's got handlebars and no scooter,' Peter replied.

'They mustn't be too old or broken,' said Tony. 'We should be able to raise a fair amount of stuff between us.'

'We'll have to decide what ingredients to get for the toffee and where we're going to make it,' Felicity said to Pauline, all brisk and business-like again. 'We shall want –'

Tony interrupted her. 'Details can wait till later. So far we've only decided what you two are going to do. Any ideas for the rest of us?'

213

While they had been talking Stephen had been idly sketching one of the trees on the edge of the clearing, using the back of an envelope and a ball point pen. Felicity leaned over to see what he had drawn and suddenly had an idea. 'I've got it,' she said. 'An art exhibition! Do you remember that time we went to London at Easter and Daddy took us to the fair on Hampstead Heath?'

'Yes,' said Tony, 'I see what you're getting at. There were all those paintings on show by the side of the road – hundreds of them.'

'That's right,' said Felicity. 'Both you and Stephen paint, so why can't you have a show of your own paintings hanging on the railings outside the school?'

'You mean sell them?' Stephen asked. He looked doubtful. 'Who'd want to buy them? They're not all that good.'

'They are,' Felicity assured him. 'Everybody says so. In any case, you needn't charge much.'

'A lot of mine are at school,' said Tony, 'and I couldn't get hold of them.'

'Then you can paint some more, can't you? You can have a week to do them in. Please, Tony, I think it's a wonderful idea.'

It would certainly be new to Edwinton,' Tony said. 'What do you think, Stephen?'

Stephen shrugged. 'I'm game, though I doubt whether we'll sell many.'

'Good, that makes four of us fixed,' Felicity put her hand to her brow and looked thoughtful. 'What about Sam and Peter?'

'I can't paint!' Sam said hastily.

'But you can *make* things,' said Felicity. 'You're always

214

whittling away at bits of wood. Haven't you got any models we could sell on our toy and toffee stall?'

'Sorry,' said Sam. 'I don't actually make things – I only whittle. I can mend things though, and there might be some engineering work I could do on some of the toys.'

'That's a jolly good idea, but you must have an official money-making job too. Perhaps we will get some sort of guide from those pamphlets in the church.'

'That's it!' Peter shouted, scrambling down from the tree in a hurry and landing in a heap on the grass. 'Sam and me – we can be guides – take people round the forest – you know. There's always visitors going round, and we can show them all the famous places.'

The Greenwooders looked at Peter's flushed and earnest face. 'What do you think, Sam?' Tony asked.

'I suppose we could try something like that,' Sam said slowly. 'But exactly what sort of a tour, Peter? It would take hours to show them round the whole forest.'

'Only special places,' said Peter, 'like Major Oak and Robin Hood's Larder.'

'There aren't many real Robin Hood places now,' said Felicity.

'Well –' said Peter, 'we could make some up...'

'That's dishonest.' Pauline was shocked.

'No, it isn't,' Peter protested, 'not really. I mean, nobody knows for sure where the Robin Hood places are, so it would be all right to guess a few.'

'Like Robin Hood's Garage,' said Sam with a grin.

'Or his telephone box,' added Tony.

'I do wish you'd be sensible,' said Felicity, exasperated. 'I think it's clever of Peter to think of tours of Sherwood Forest, so let's all help to work things out.'

215

In the end they decided that each trip would take about half an hour and that they would charge fifty pence per person. It would be made quite clear what the proceeds were in aid of, and Sam and Peter would wear armbands with GUIDE on them. Each boy would take it in turn to escort their customers while the other one would collect the money and make bookings.

'We must all have large cards announcing who and what we are,' said Felicity, her organising passion having a field day. 'I suggest they have GREENWOODERS' FAMINE FUND on them in big letters.'

'We ought to find some way of advertising what we're going to do,' said Tony, caught up in the general excitement. 'Do you think Dad would let us use the church photocopier for some leaflets that we could distribute in the village?'

'I'm sure he would,' his sister replied.

'Let's go now. There's no time like the present and we don't want to waste a minute.' Tony left no time for argument as he led the way through the bushes. As they walked home through arches of green leaves they split up into pairs, Felicity and Pauline discussing ways and means of toffee-making, Stephen and Tony suitable subjects for watercolours, and Sam and Peter interesting routes through the forest.

Preparations for the GREENWOODERS' FAMINE FUND were soon in full swing. The attic was renamed Campaign Headquarters and two meetings a day were held there so that progress could be reported and help and advice given. The Vicar had readily given permission for his

216

photocopier to be used and had even provided the paper for the leaflets. The children agreed that only the bare facts of their activities need be mentioned on the leaflet. As Stephen pointed out, the fewer the words, the more likely people were to read them.

Stephen and Tony selected their subjects for fresh paintings, and the greater part of their days was spent at their easels. The view from the attic window was popular with both boys, especially as it meant they did not have to go further afield. While Stephen worked at the window Tony painted a still life, and vice versa. 'Portraits are definitely *out*,' Stephen had said, remembering the reaction of Mr Bunbury to his caricature. Besides, it was difficult to do portraits from memory, and the other Greenwooders were much too busy to pose for them.

After one of the progress meetings Felicity took Pauline on one side. 'I've borrowed my mother's Mrs Beeton,' she told her. 'I thought that if we're going to make old English treacle toffee we ought to use an old English recipe.' She opened the heavy book, looked in the index and then found the page she wanted. 'Here we are...' They pored over the book. 'It sounds a bit odd,' Felicity said. 'Treacle and sugar and butter are all right – but vinegar!'

'Half a gill of vinegar,' Pauline read. 'How nasty! How much is a gill?'

'I'm not sure – half a pint, I think. Or is it a quarter of a pint? I don't think we should use vinegar at all – surely it would make it taste awfully funny.' Felicity returned to the book. 'And it says half a teaspoonful of bicarbonate of soda. Essence of almonds too. I didn't think we should need all those things.' Pauline was reading the method of cooking. 'What does this mean? "Boil to the 'large ball' degree", and then later on, "Boil to the 'little crack' degree".'

'Blessed if I know,' said Felicity. 'It sounds very strange. Do you think we should make chocolate toffee instead? Then if it goes wrong we can call it chocolate fudge.'

'It might be a good idea,' said Pauline, 'but let's try to find another treacle toffee recipe first, just in case the vinegar mightn't be necessary.'

'Miss Grymsdyke in the library must have some cookery books,' said Felicity. 'Come on, let's go there now.'

The Edwinton branch of the County Library was next door to the Police Station. 'It has to be there,' Stephen had once explained to Peter, 'so that people who are maddened by reading can be put away quickly after they run amok.' Miss Grymsdyke, who came in three times a week to open the library, was a small grey mouse of a lady who got very enthusiastic over children who liked books. When Felicity told her they wanted a cookery book she scurried to a shelf and returned with an armful of books which she dumped on a table. 'There you are!' she said. 'Recipes from all over the world. Invalid cookery, Jewish, French, Italian, Chinese; cooking for bachelor girls and hostesses who want to cut a dash; recipes for slimmers and gourmets –'

'Actually,' Felicity said, 'we only want to know how to make treacle toffee –'

'Without vinegar,' Pauline added.

Miss Grymsdyke was slightly disappointed, but soon

218

'Here's the very thing.'

rallied. 'Here's the very thing,' she declared, diving to the bottom of the pile. ' "Sweets that grandmother made". Be sure to clean your teeth well afterwards,' she warned them.

'We will,' Felicity promised. 'Thank you, Miss Grymsdyke. 'We'll bring you some of the toffee...'

Peter and Sam had agreed to take on the jobs of collecting toys and books and storing them in the toolshed at the bottom of the Vicarage garden, delivering the leaflets in the village and making posters and armbands. The delivery of the leaflets presented certain minor problems which were overcome by Peter's brilliant logic. They were not deterred by notices on gates which said NO HAWKERS OR CIRCULARS because, according to Peter, they were not selling anything, and the leaflets were oblong, not circular. He had provided himself with a pocketful of dog biscuits in case they should meet any dog of which a notice warned them to BEWARE. When they saw such a sign outside Miss Plumb's bungalow Peter laughed outright. 'Fancy having to beware of Miss Plumb's Sooty,' he said. 'I bet he'd even run away from Mr Puff!' Their visit to Peat's Farm to collect Sam's cast-off toys was particularly rewarding as Mrs Peat gave them buttermilk and apple tart. She also told them to tell the girls to go to the farmhouse to make their toffee. 'Your mother has quite enough on her hands with the baby, Peter, and Mrs Brooks surely can't be doing with them. Tell them I'll provide the sugar.'

By the time Saturday arrived the Greenwooders were in a fever of impatience. The toffee, made to a recipe that did not require vinegar, had been weighed in quarter pounds and put into bags. Mrs Peat had given a batch of shortbread, and Old Eva had baked some date scones and vanilla slices. Mrs Brooks had come forward with ginger nuts and Mrs Christy had taken time off from washing baby clothes to dash together some rolled oat cookies. Set out on the stall outside the Vicarage gate

220

the things looked delicious and appetising. 'Thank goodness Peter isn't helping to serve,' said Pauline.

The other half of the stall was taken up with toys, games and books. Peter's scooter had been refused, much to his disgust, but delving into toy cupboards had produced a wide variety of objects – motor-cars and fire-engines, snakes and ladders, jigsaw puzzles, water pistols, boxes of bricks, a cowboy uniform, a nurse's outfit that Felicity had looked at long and wistfully before deciding that it was much too small for her, an assortment of dolls, quoits, draughts and miscellaneous smaller items. The book department was not very well stocked. Tony, Felicity and Stephen were hoarders, and unwilling to give up any book from their shelves in case they might want to read it again at some unspecified time in the future, but they had managed to find a number of out-of-date annuals. All in all, the display looked impressive. They had decided not to put price tickets on anything in case there should be customers willing to pay generously for the cause.

Felicity looked up at the sky. It was blue and white and benign, but there were one or two little clouds like purple bruises lurking in the west. 'I hope it doesn't rain,' she said anxiously.

Pauline refused to consider the possibility. 'It just couldn't!' she declared. 'I wish somebody would come along and *buy...*'

Further down the road, nearer to the crossroads, Tony and Stephen were putting the finishing touches to their exhibition. They had hung most of the paintings on the railings of the playground of the village school, and had provided themselves with a couple of orange boxes to sit on. It was a colourful display, though there was a sameness about the subjects that caused Stephen, seeing all the pictures together, to give only a doubtful approval to the final arrangement. 'Do you think we used that fruit too often?' he asked.

Tony put his head on one side. 'I don't think people will notice,' he said. 'We rang the changes pretty well, and with different backgrounds and in different positions they should be all right. Anyway, there are the landscapes.'

'There's an awful lot of trees in them,' Stephen objected.

'We're both good at trees,' said Tony, 'and it *is* Sherwood Forest, after all.'

'Well, it's too late to make any alterations now,' said Stephen, still critically examining a peach and a banana in front of a bunch of roses. 'I don't suppose we shall sell anything, anyway.'

'I bet we shall! Don't be so pessimistic. You're a good artist – didn't you know that?' said Tony.

'Pooh,' Stephen said, secretly pleased with Tony's opinion. He wondered whether it would be worthwhile sending something to the Royal Academy next year...

Sam had set up an old card table on the patch of grass at the corner of the forest between the main road to Worksop and the cricket pitch. The stump of a cut-down fir tree made a convenient seat. He opened a haversack and took out a couple of arm bands. 'There's yours,' he said, handing one to Peter.

Peter proudly pulled it up his arm and fixed it to his shirt sleeve with a safety-pin. 'Official Guide,' he read. 'Sam, who's made us official?'

'We have,' said Sam. 'The organising committee of the Greenwooders' Famine Fund.'

Peter wrinkled his brow. 'Who's on that?'

'All of us, dope,' said Sam.

'Oh,' said Peter, satisfied. He unrolled a large sheet of cartridge paper he had been carrying and prepared to pin it to the edge of the card table. Then he stood back and looked at his handiwork. 'It's a bit crooked, I know,' he admitted, 'but you try printing capital letters on a big bit of paper on the bedroom floor.'

Sam looked at the poster. GUIDED TOURS IN ADE OF THE GREENWOODERS' FAMINE FUND. 'Oh, Peter,' he said with a sigh, 'why didn't you ask somebody? That's not how to spell it.'

'It *is*,' Peter said indignantly. 'I looked it up specially. I was going to put GIDE, but the dictionary said GUIDE. And if you think you know better than a dictionary –'

'Not GUIDE,' Sam said. 'It's the ADE that's wrong. It should be a-i-d. Did you look that up?'

'No need to,' said Peter. 'I know how to spell lemonade.'

'What's that got to do with it?'

'Well, a-d-e comes at the end of lemonade, doesn't it?'

Sam drew a deep breath. 'Look, Peter, I'm not arguing with you, I'm just telling you. It's a-i-d, and you can jolly well alter it, quick!'

'Oh, all right.' Peter pushed his lower lip out, but he got out a pencil and laboriously began to correct his error.

'Hurry up,' Sam said, 'there's some people coming.'

A car had pulled on to some bare ground that was used as a car park, and three people got out. Peter tugged at his arm band to make sure the words could be seen. But the driver and his two women companions

223

passed the stall without a glance, concentrating their attention on an ice-cream van further along the road.

'Huh!' muttered Peter. 'Anybody would think we're invisible.'

Another car rounded the corner. The boys looked at it eagerly. Nobody emerged. The occupants pulled up the windows, switched on a radio and buried their heads in newspapers. 'They could do that in their garage and save petrol,' Sam said bitterly.

A couple of pedestrians approached. The man, stout and sweating, was carrying his jacket and showing red braces. His knotted handkerchief fitted his bald head like a skull cap. His wife, even stouter, wore a frock emblazoned with what seemed to be purple cabbages and scarlet parrots. Her cardigan was yellow and her sandals pink, and she fanned herself with a mauve handkerchief. They waddled to a stop in front of the card table and silently mouthed the words of the poster.

'Well, did you ever!' said the man. 'What will they think of next!'

'What Famine Fund, young man?' the woman asked suspiciously.

'We're collecting for all the children in the world who haven't got enough to eat,' said Sam.

'Oh.' The woman's voice softened. 'That's nice. Eh, it's a pity about my feet – I'd be no good for walking round. You'd have to carry me back.' She began to heave with laughter.

'Oh, no!' Peter involuntarily gasped, looking at her vast bulk. 'No, you'd better not go, had you?'

The woman dug her husband in the ribs. 'What about you, Perce?' she said. 'Why don't you have a go?'

224

'Yes, Perce, please do,' Peter murmured under his breath.

'You have a walk round the forest with these two lads,' the woman went on, 'while I have a rest on that seat over yonder. Go on, it'll do you good. Get some of your fat down!' She seemed near to collapse with mirth.

The man read the poster again. 'Well, if it don't take too long. We've got to get back for us teas at the caff down the road. We've got to keep our strength up, you know! How much?'

'Fifty pence, payable in advance,' Peter said.

'In advance, eh? I suppose you think I'll not get back, do you? All right, young man, here's your money.' He presented a pound coin to Peter, who handed it to Sam, who put it with a flourish in a tin on the table. 'Well, come on, let's get started.'

'Who's going to take him?' Peter whispered. 'We can't very well toss for it in front of him.'

'I will,' Sam said bravely. 'I'll cut down the route a bit so that he doesn't get too tired. Look after the money while I've gone – never mind about the ice-cream van!'

'As if I would,' Peter said in a virtuous tone.

The stout gentleman began to follow Sam along the sandy path to the Major Oak. 'So long, Millie,' he called to his wife, who was powdering down the flush on her cheeks.

'Goodbye, Perce,' she called back. 'Mind you don't run that lad off his feet!' Her shoulders began to heave again and a cloud of powder floated round her head.

'Good luck, Sam,' Peter said. 'I'll keep the queue in order while you're away...'

Although at first business was not terribly brisk as far

225

as taking money was concerned, Felicity and Pauline could hardly complain of lack of attention. Very soon after they had taken up their positions behind the trestle table a trickle of village children had arrived, and they stayed there in relays throughout the afternoon. The girls had great difficulty in keeping them confined to the toy end of the table in order to have the confectionery department clear for the transaction of genuine business. The children, used to the free-for-all of jumble sales, could not understand the girls' insistence on keeping the two departments separate, and once or twice nearly succeeded in pushing the whole lot over. Only one child stood still, a small girl with button-black eyes set in a bun-round face, who, thumb in mouth, stared with yearning intentness at a very pink doll with long eyelashes. At one point Felicity relapsed from the ladylike attitude she had adopted as a stallholder and gave a wriggling and persistent boy a hefty swipe on his back, muttering as she did so, 'Keep back!' Fortunately she was able to put on a sweet smile when the boy's mother, whom she had not realised was present, bought a bag of treacle toffee.

'Come along, Christopher,' the boy's mother said, 'they're all too rough for you here.'

The toffee and cakes sold steadily, mainly to grown-ups. The invaders of the toy department generally bought one bag of toffee between half a dozen, and munched and dribbled as they inspected the toys.

'If you do not wish to buy,' Pauline said haughtily to Hugh and Harold Mottershead who were riotously immersed in a game of blow-football, 'kindly do not handle the goods.'

226

'Coo,' said Hugh, the blowing tube sticking from his mouth like a cigar, 'listen to old toffee nose.'

'I am not!' said Pauline. 'But whoever does buy it will not want your blow all over it, thank you very much.'

Harold, who sat behind Pauline in school and was a secret admirer, replaced his blow tube, and after a moment trying to think of a reasonable but not too withering remark, said, 'Oh, go and lick stamps!'

'I'll tell your Amy of you,' Pauline threatened, whipping away the box from under their noses and turning her back on Hugh and Harold.

Impervious to the pushing and shouting around her, the small girl continued to stare at the simpering pink doll, a podgy, thumb-sucking statue.

'I wish you wouldn't breathe on the shortbread,' said Felicity to a tiny boy with massive steel-rimmed spectacles.

'How much?' he asked in a piping voice.

'Tenpence a slice.'

The boy turned away from the stall and concentrated for a moment on the contents of his pocket. 'I've only got fivepence,' he said at last. He looked challengingly at Felicity.

It would be worth losing on the deal to get rid of him, Felicity thought. 'Very well,' she said, holding out her hand for the money. 'I'll make an exception for you.' The boy held out two hands, one containing fivepence, the other to receive the shortbread. The transaction completed, he moved further along the stall to inspect the toys.

Felicity soon realised that it had been a mistake to make a concession for one customer. Within a minute there were several children round her, holding out five pence, demanding shortbread. It was useless to protest. 'Larry Warburton only paid fivepence,' they cried. 'Why not us?' Felicity gave up and sold the remaining pieces at cut price, wondering whether to put up the price of the toffee in compensation.

Billy Catchpole spent ten minutes mouthing the words of a story in the 'Bumper Adventure Book for Boys'. Pauline became aware of it when she noticed him squatting on the pavement a few yards from the stall with the book in his hands. 'This isn't a lending library, Billy Catchpole,' she called. 'Aren't you going to buy it?'

Billy wandered back to her. 'How much?'

'Twenty pence,' said Pauline.

'Think I'm a millionaire?' Billy asked scornfully.

'It's worth it,' said Pauline. 'It's ever such a big book.'

'So you sell them by weight, do you?' Billy said. 'I'll give you tenpence.'

'Tenpence!' Pauline repeated, shocked.

Felicity overheard and added her comment. '*Tenpence!*'

'All right,' said Billy, his conscience pricking him. 'Fifteen pence.'

The girls looked at each other. Then Pauline said, with a resigned sigh, 'Very well then,' and held out her hand.

'Fancy having to sell things at cut prices so soon,' Felicity complained. 'What is Edwinton coming to...'

The pudding-faced little girl, still glued to her position, had begun to breathe heavily. Not only had the doll hypnotised her, but she was having the same effect on Pauline, who had to blink rapidly to prevent herself from going into a trance. In desperation she picked up the doll, thrust it into the child's hand and said, 'Here – have it for nothing, but please go away!'

The little girl accepted the present calmly. Without a word or a look at Pauline she walked away, only the furious sucking of her thumb betraying her emotions.

A well-known voice suddenly broke in over the chatter of the children. 'Well, well, well, and what have we here?' It was Miss Pope-Cunningham, dressed for a summer's day, but with a fox fur round her shoulders. Felicity and Pauline had often seen it before and the glazed dead eyes of the unfortunate animal never failed to haunt them. Miss Pope-Cunningham looked at the stall and the poster attached to the railings. 'How very enterprising of you. I passed the boys on my way but I didn't have time to stop – I'm going to the Vicarage. What a wonderful display you have. How is business?'

'Not too bad,' said Felicity. 'We've taken seventy-five pence so far.'

'Very good,' said Miss Pope-Cunningham. 'What a go-ahead group you are. Where is your brother?' she said to Pauline. 'Is he helping?'

'He's guiding,' said Pauline.

'Guiding? Surely you mean scouting?'

Pauline giggled. 'No – he and Sam are taking people on guided tours round the forest at fifty pence a time.'

Miss Pope-Cunningham gave a laugh that went down the scale and up again. 'Silly me! Really, the things you Greenwooders think of! Now, what have we here?' She inspected the confectionery department. 'Mmm – delicious. I'll have a bag of your treacle toffee. Home-made, I see.' She produced a fifty-pence piece from her purse.

'If only more people would think of others as you are doing, the world would be a happier place. I'll tell you what I will do – I will double whatever you take. There! Come and see me when you close your stall and I will add my mite. Now I must be off.' She twitched her fur so that the fox's head looked over her shoulder at the girls as she turned in at the Vicarage gate. Pauline could have sworn that it winked at her.

'She's funny, but she's nice,' Felicity said approvingly. 'Now, back to business.'

Sam emerged from the trees and cut across the grass to where Peter was waiting impatiently. The stout man, breathing heavily, rolled alongside him. His face seemed to have swollen up like a red balloon, and his eyes had almost disappeared in the folds of flesh. 'Ee, I'm that peckish,' Peter heard him saying, 'that walk's given me a real appetite.' He called across to his wife on the seat. 'Coming, Millie. It's been grand, I can tell you.' He turned to Sam. 'Thank you, young fellow. Here's another fifty pence for your fund.' Sam's hand was out in a flash. 'I hope you do well. Good luck to you both.' As he made his way slowly back to his wife they heard him begin a description of the tour. 'We went to that there tree first – you know, the Major Oak. A right whopper it is too, I nearly got stuck trying to get inside it . . .'

'He did too,' Sam said. 'I had to tug like mad. Well, what's been happening to you?'

'There's somebody coming back,' Peter announced. 'I told them you wouldn't be long and then it'd be my turn, so they said they'd stroll around for a few minutes.'

'I hope they're not fat,' said Sam. 'I've never walked so slowly in all my life.'

'No, they're not, they're American.'

'Are they?' Sam brightened up. 'All Americans are rich – I wonder if we ought to put the charges up.'

'I've already told them it's fifty pence,' said Peter.

'Oh, well, never mind. Are these the ones – this man with the camera and the lady with the funny hat?'

'Yes. There's somebody else following them. I wonder who he is, he wasn't with them before.'

'Hello, there,' the American said to Peter. 'We're back, you see.' He adjusted the camera slung over his shoulder. 'I hope there'll be some good subjects for pictures.'

'Oh, yes, lots,' said Peter. 'By the way, this is my partner – his name's Sam. Mine's Peter.'

'Glad to know you, Peter. And you, Sam. I'm Jed Kaliski, and this is my wife, Claudia.'

'Hi,' said Mrs Kaliski, beaming through spectacles that seemed to be on the verge of flying off her face. Her hat was a confection of flowers perched on blue hair, and Peter wondered vaguely if she had to water the hat every night. She was carrying an enormous handbag. Her husband had spectacles too, but his had thick, dark frames. He wore a tan suit, silk shirt and a dazzling tie that competed with his wife's hat. They both looked very kind and friendly. Behind them another man was reading the poster. He was about forty, with greying hair, and was dressed in dark flannels and a grey sports coat. His face was serious and his eyes were shrewd. Peter was reminded of Hawk Collingwood, the private eye of his favourite comic. He did not seem to be with the Americans.

231

'I'm Jed Kaliski, and this is my wife, Claudia.'

'I'm ready now,' Peter said to the Kaliskis. He glanced at the other man. 'Er – are you coming on the tour?' he said.

The stranger gave him a quizzical look. 'I might as well. It will be interesting to see Sherwood Forest through the eyes of a native of the village.'

Peter turned on him indignantly. 'I'm not a native – I'm English. Now, ladies and gentlemen, that is, lady and gentlemen, the tour is about to begin. Follow me, please. We'll be about twenty minutes, Sam.'

'Isn't he cute?' Mrs Kaliski murmured.

They proceeded up the centre path, and soon the trees had closed in on them and speckled the ground with diamonds of light. Flies buzzed about them in noisy swarms and rooks called harshly above their heads.

'Gee, so this is Sherwood Forest,' Mrs Kaliski said appreciatively. 'Everything's so old – and gnarled.'

'It is old,' Peter assured her, 'thousands of years old. The tree we're going to see first was there when Robin Hood was alive.'

'Isn't that something!' exclaimed Mr Kaliski. 'Robin Hood now – I guess you know a whole lot about him?'

'Everything,' said Peter casually. 'Guides have to, you know. He was married in Edwinton Church, and every Sunday I sit in the pew that Maid Marian's parents sat in at the wedding. The forest is full of places connected with him. Over there, for instance –' he waved a hand at a giant oak that lay sprawling by the side of the path '– he used to sit on that trunk when he was waiting for Maid Marian to come back from Edwinton with the groceries – only they called them provisions.'

'Why didn't he help her to carry them from the village?' said the grey man.

'Well – er – he couldn't, you see, because the man who kept the shop was a spy for the Sheriff of Nottingham, so of course Robin couldn't let himself be seen too often.'

'I see,' said the man.

'We shall soon be at the Major Oak,' Peter went on, 'and then I'll show you where Robin Hood and his Merry Men used to hide. The tree has got a hollow trunk, and they used to crowd in there when danger was nigh. It's closed up a lot since then but –' He looked at the three grown-ups speculatively '– I expect you could all get in, you're not fat like the man that Sam took round. There's sometimes an ice-cream stall near the Oak.' They rounded a bend and the squat, massive tree came into sight. 'But there isn't today,' Peter added wistfully.

'I must take a picture of this!' Mr Kaliski exclaimed. 'Gee, it's tremendous. There's nothing like this back in Oklahoma.'

'Can I be in it?' Peter darted away from them and perched himself on one of the huge boles that stuck up like the hump of a prehistoric sea monster. 'Did you know that it's twenty-two yards round the bottom of the tree – the length of a cricket pitch?'

'Cricket,' said Mr Kaliski, 'now there's a game I shall never understand. Hold it, son –' He raised his camera and clicked.

Peter leaped down and rejoined his party. 'Now I'll take you to Robin Hood's Larder. That's where they used to keep the venison, you know. There's not much of the tree left now – it got on fire once.'

They were now on a grassy path that wound its way through silver birch trees whose delicate branches almost met overhead in a tracery of green. 'If you see an adder, don't panic,' Peter warned them, 'it might only be a grass snake.'

'We have snakes in America –' began Mr Kaliski.

'We have all sorts of things in this forest,' Peter inter-

rupted, 'foxes, rabbits, stoats, weasels, deer, squirrels and
– and things. There used to be bears and wolves and
wild boar too, but they've died out. Robin used to hunt
them, though.'

'Did Robin Hood hunt the mammoth too?' asked the
grey man.

'I expect so,' said Peter. 'Look.' He pointed to the
charred stump of a tree standing among a number of
saplings. 'That's Robin Hood's Larder.'

Mr Kaliski got out his camera again. 'I suppose I might
as well be in this one too,' said Peter. 'Then you'll
remember you took it in Sherwood Forest.'

'Are there any other places round here that are asso-
ciated with Robin Hood?' asked Mrs Kaliski, looking
round her. 'It's all so quiet, almost eerie. One might
almost see an outlaw in Lincoln green peeping round a
tree.'

'I've often –' Peter began, then realised that it might
be as well not to boast of the number of times he had
actually seen the Merry Men disporting themselves in the
greenwood. 'Er – oh, yes, there's lots of places yet. Some
of them are too far away, though, for this tour. It would
cost a lot extra to show you them, and I really haven't
got the time. But –' he racked his brains to think of
something to please his audience '– on the way back I'll
show you a tree that got pierced by an arrow that was
meant for Robin Hood, only it just missed him and hit
the tree. And there's another one they used as a gallows
to hang the Sheriff's men from – at least, they used to
threaten to hang them from it, but they were kindhearted
really, and they didn't actually do it. There's a tree they
used to bury jewels and money under that they took from

rich monks when they caught them travelling through the forest. There's nothing there now, of course, it got dug up long ago. Over there there's a special place where me and my friends play –'

'My friends and I,' said the grey man, half to himself.

Peter looked startled. 'Oh,' he said, 'I've never seen you there.' He turned back to the Kaliskis. 'It's a big patch of grass hidden away and there's gorse bushes all round it, so I can't take you because they would knock the lady's hat off, and anyway, it's very private and we don't show it to anybody. At one end there's a big oak tree and you can climb down into it because the trunk's hollow, but you have to know the way to climb up first, and I expect you're all too old. We'd better start going back now because it's Sam's turn and you've nearly had your fifty penceworth.'

'More than fifty penceworth, I should think,' said the grey man.

'Oh, do you think so?' Peter wondered for a moment whether to suggest that they paid him extra then and there, but decided against it. 'We believe in giving value for money, you know.' He fell silent, needing his breath to climb an incline.

'Tell us some more,' Mrs Kaliski urged. 'It's been fascinating.'

Peter thought hard. Well, Robin Hood they wanted, and Robin Hood they should have. 'I don't expect you know,' he went on, 'but I'm a descendant of Robin Hood myself . . .'

'You are!' Mrs Kaliski gasped. 'But that's wonderful!' She shot a quick glance at her husband.

'Oh, it's nothing,' Peter shrugged nonchalantly. 'It was

236

a long time ago since he was one of my ancestors. I was going to be christened Robin but my Aunt Edna – she's awful – persuaded my mum to call me Peter. But my baby brother's called Robin, so it's still in the family.'

They were on their way back. The sky had clouded over and the air became oppressive. The smell of the earth and of rotting vegetation came strongly to their nostrils. Mrs Kaliski had picked a piece of bracken to wave the flies away. Her husband had lit a cigar and his head was surrounded by a cloud of pungent smoke. The grey man was glancing round him, his keen eyes taking in the ancient trees, the thick undergrowth buzzing with life, the flapping birds winging from one tree to another, and the silvery green moss growing by the side of the path. He *is* like a detective, Peter thought. His eyes seemed to take everything in. Perhaps there are criminals hiding in the forest, and he's been sent to look for them. But if so, why go on a conducted tour? Peter began to feel slightly uneasy, though he could not think of anything he had done recently that would warrant the attentions of a detective. Of course, he had said all that about Robin Hood, and a lot of it wasn't strictly true, but he didn't think you could go to prison for exaggerating. He thought he had better get the grown-ups interested in something else, but before he could decide what, Mrs Kaliski asked a question that gave him the opportunity he needed.

'I suppose you go to school in the village?' she said.

'Oh, yes, it's round the corner from the church,' he said, grasping at the straw eagerly. 'Of course I shall be leaving there next year because it's only a Primary School.'

237

'Where will you go then?' asked Hawk Collingwood.

Peter wished he would keep quiet. 'I'm not sure, but they're just finishing a new comprehensible school at Ollerthorp, and I'll probably go there.'

'What's a – what did you say? Comprehensible school?' said Mr Kaliski, puzzled. 'I don't think we have those in the States.'

'It's a school where you all go,' Peter explained. 'Boys and girls together and whether you're clever or dull – or medium, like me. You can leave at sixteen or you can go on till you're eighteen, and there's all sorts of courses, like metalwork and printing and cookery and bricklaying, as well as the usual subjects.'

'It sounds very comprehensive,' Mrs Kaliski remarked.

The grey man allowed a thin smile to appear on his lips. 'As a matter of fact, it's called a comprehensive school,' he said.

Know-all! thought Peter. Just because he was a detective he needn't think he was an expert on schools too. 'That's what I said,' he said witheringly. 'Anyway, Edwinton School's a jolly good school, and I don't want to leave. I'll be in the top class after the holidays, and we'll have a lot of fun. I'm in the football team, and I came top in History.'

'In History!' Hawk Collingwood's screwed-up eyes opened wide.

'Why not?' asked Peter. 'Our teacher – his name's Battersby but we call him Bats because he can't see very well – bats don't, you know,' he explained kindly to the Kaliskis, 'well, old Bats doesn't know half of what goes on. I read comics behind my atlas, and things like that. It's different when the Head takes us, of course. He sees

238

everything, but he makes a lot of jokes and we like him. He left at the end of the term because he's old and he's had to retire and we saved up to buy him a transistor radio. When he told us he was going to leave he said he was going to breed mice because they'd be nice and restful after forty years of children, so the next day I took him one of my white mice as a present, and do you know what happened?'

'He thanked you, I suppose,' said Mrs Kaliski.

'He did not!' said Peter. 'His face went white and he had to sit down and have a glass of water. And the mouse went through a hole and I haven't seen it since. Seems a bit silly to me to start breeding mice if they make you feel faint but grown-ups are funny, aren't they?'

'They certainly are,' Mr Kaliski agreed with a chuckle.

'Our school is very old,' Peter went on blithely. 'I shouldn't be surprised if Maid Marian didn't go there.' He caught the grey man's eye. 'I don't suppose she actually *did*,' he went on hurriedly. 'Anyway, there's a big hole in the floor just near where I sit, and we push things down it. I bet if you took up the floorboards you'd find millions of rulers and pencils and things. I've pushed a few down myself,' he swaggered.

'It must be a very expensive school to run!' said Mr Kaliski. 'What else do you do?'

'Oh, lots of things. We have a board to put the hymn numbers on, and one morning I changed all the numbers before Assembly, and when old Hambone – that's Miss Hamilton – started playing "Glad that I live am I" we all started to sing "We plough the fields and scatter". We didn't half laugh!'

Mr Kaliski gave a guffaw. 'Some kid!'

239

Peter preened himself in the American's approval. 'I could tell you all sorts of things – about the time I played truant for two days and nobody found out, and how Billy Catchpole gets an extra bottle of milk every day because he's the milk monitor and he always adds one on to the number he gives to old Bats, and where old Bats' spectacle case got hidden, and how to stop the school bell from ringing and – oh, lots.' He paused at length, rather breathless from his recital.

'Fascinating!' breathed Mrs Kaliski. 'I do admire children with spirit.' She turned to the grey man. 'What do you think?'

'It's all been very illuminating,' he said gravely.

Peter looked sharply at him. Surely he hadn't said anything incriminating? But the grey man seemed to be interested only in the forest and Peter relaxed.

Soon they were back at their starting-point, where Sam was hopping about fretfully, trying to prevent two middle-aged ladies from deciding that they couldn't wait any longer. 'Oh, here you are,' he said. 'You've been ages. We shan't make much money if you take all afternoon for one trip.'

'You have to be *thorough*,' said Peter.

'The very word,' muttered Hawk Collingwood. 'Thank you, Peter, for a very instructive tour. I've learned a lot of History – among other things. I wish your fund well – here's something to add to it.' He gave Peter a searching look and strolled away.

'Coo – a pound!' Peter looked at the retreating figure. 'For a detective he's not bad at all.'

'A detective, did you say?' Sam frowned. 'How do you know he's a detective?'

240

'Well, I don't exactly *know* – it's just that he reminded me of Hawk Collingwood, that's all.'

'Ass!' Sam turned to his next customers.

Mr and Mrs Kaliski were still hovering round, enthusing about the wonderful time they had had. 'This'll be something to tell the folks back home,' Mrs Kaliski was saying. 'Fancy meeting a real live descendant of Robin Hood!' Peter coughed loudly so that Sam should not hear any more dangerous utterances. 'Jed, you must take another picture of Peter before we go – just him alone.'

Peter arranged himself in front of the table, with one hand across his front like Napoleon. 'Pity I haven't got a bow and arrow with me,' he said. 'Will you send me a copy when you've developed them? Peter Christy, Edwinton, will find me because I live at the Post Office.'

'We sure will,' Mr Kaliski promised. 'Now we'd better get back to the village, we want to see over the church. Maybe somebody will point out Maid Marian's pew for us.'

'Oh – I think it's been taken away – to be mended,' Peter said hastily. 'Look, why not visit our art exhibition? Tony and Stephen have got it outside the school – just turn up Manford Road – there's some jolly good views of the forest.'

'What a dandy idea,' said Mrs Kaliski. 'We'll go there now, shall we, Jed? Here, Peter.' She opened her enormous handbag and produced a handful of coins. 'Take a couple of those big silver ones, will you? I can never remember what they're called – and add them to your fund. Goodbye, you've given us a great time.'

'Simply great,' Mr Kaliski echoed. 'So long, son.'

* * *

241

Tony thrust his hands deep into his pockets and stamped furiously from one end of the railing to the other. 'Not one sale,' he said savagely. He threw a glance at the pictures displayed on the railings. 'What's the matter with them? You'd think anybody would be proud to have one of these hanging on the wall. Why isn't anybody buying?'

'Well, this is Edwinton,' Stephen said philosophically, 'not Hampstead Heath, you know.'

But Tony was not to be placated. 'We're in the wrong position, for one thing. We ought to have been round the corner in Church Street so that people going to the forest would have passed us.'

'Be patient,' Stephen advised. 'We haven't been here very long. Old Mr Marples liked them, he said so.'

'Yes, but he didn't *buy* one. And Miss Pope-Cunningham was in too much of a hurry to stop. And everybody else who's been past has either treated the exhibition as a huge joke or looked the other way.' Tony cocked an eye skywards. 'Now it's going to rain any minute. What a day! Who thought of this brilliant idea, anyway?'

'Felicity, of course.'

'She would.' As Tony spoke a few large drops plopped heavily on the pavement. 'That's torn it. What do you say to giving up?'

'I say it's a rotten idea,' Stephen said firmly. 'Look, you dash home and get some macs for us and some polythene or something for the pictures. I don't think it'll rain long. Then if we haven't sold anything in about half an hour we'll pack up.'

'Oh, all right.' Tony reluctantly started off towards the Vicarage. The rain grew heavier. Stephen gazed anxiously at the still lifes and landscapes. He stood in front of as

242

many as he could, hoping to shield them with his body. Then he dodged up and down the line, covering first one and then another. But his efforts were in vain. Slowly, inevitably, the colours began to run... Green trickled into blue, red into yellow. Purple infiltrated into green, and little tongues of orange ate into areas of white and grey. Outlines became blurred and misty, and shapes lost their reality. Stephen threw up his arms. 'I give up!' he said aloud.

Just as Tony came rushing back with protective covers the rain stopped. One moment the huge drops were splashing on the ground like liquid coins, the next the sun was shining out of a blue sky as innocently as though it had been there all the time. Tony stopped dead in his tracks. 'Well...' was all he could find to say. Stephen gestured towards the paintings. 'Look at them,' he exclaimed bitterly, 'spoiled, all of them.'

Tony examined them curiously. 'Gosh, don't they look funny!' He dabbed at one with his finger. 'They look as though we'd painted them like that.' He gave a chuckle. 'Well, it's no good crying over spilt paint, I suppose!'

'We'd better pack them up quickly,' Stephen said, 'before anybody sees them and won't believe that the rain was to blame. Hurry, there's someone coming now.' He had noticed two people who had obviously come down Church Street to the crossroads and had turned up Manford Road.

Tony glanced their way. 'Cor, look at that hat! I'd like to paint that!'

Mr and Mrs Kaliski approached, beaming widely. 'I guess you're the two boys Peter told us we'd find here,' said Mr Kaliski jovially.

243

'Peter told you –' Tony began.

'Yeah, that cute little kid who showed us round the forest,' Mr Kaliski went on. 'He said you were having an art show. Is this it?'

'This was it,' Tony said, but Mr Kaliski was not listening. He and his wife had bent down and were scanning the ruined watercolours with great interest. Tony looked stonily at Stephen. 'Just our luck to have somebody look at them properly when it's too late,' he whispered. He began to explain, 'I'm afraid the rain –' when he was interrupted by a little scream from Mrs Kaliski.

'Gee, why, they're gorgeous! Aren't they just cute, honey?'

Mr Kaliski grunted. 'Now, Claudia, you know I don't know anything about art –'

'But I do!' She passed along the line, looking at each one closely. 'My, what a superb sense of design. Who painted them?'

'We both did,' said Stephen, wondering if he had heard aright.

'It's amazing how alike your styles are,' she went on. 'Such brilliant colours – don't you just love the way the sky and the grass seem to merge, Jed?'

Mr Kaliski nodded. 'Fine, fine.'

Stephen decided they could not sail under false colours. 'They merged because the rain fell on them,' he said.

But Mrs Kaliski, bubbling over with enthusiasm, seemed determined not to listen. 'They remind me of Turner – it's simply remarkable how two such young boys can have such technical brilliance. Those still lifes too – they have the same dream-like quality.' She straightened up. 'Jed, I must have some of these – they'll be perfect

244

in the parlour back home. And won't they make the neighbours' eyes pop out! They are for sale, aren't they?'

'They were –' said Tony. He was beginning to despair that they would ever make clear the fact that the paintings had been ruined by the rain.

'You mean you've sold them all?' Mrs Kaliski looked horrified.

'No – but – you see –' Suddenly Tony gave up. 'Yes,' he said loudly, 'they're for sale, and you can buy as many as you like.'

'Yippee!' Mrs Kaliski clapped her hands. 'Jed, I'm going to be greedy!' She pointed to a view of the forest that looked as though a kitten had rolled in the wet paint. 'I want that – and that – and that – and that – and that! How many is that?'

'Five,' said Tony, his mind awhirl.

'Sure that's enough, honey?' Mr Kaliski was drawing out a thick wallet. 'Well, young man, how much do you want for that lot?'

Tony gulped. He looked at Stephen, who shook his head helplessly. 'Do you mind if I discuss this with my partner?' Tony said.

'Go right ahead,' said Mr Kaliski. 'Try to let me down as lightly as possible, though.'

Tony and Stephen withdrew a few yards and held a whispered colloquy. 'We were going to charge a pound each,' Tony said doubtfully, 'but we can't now, can we?'

'Better make it fifty pence,' Stephen said, 'and if they think that's too much, then bring it down to thirty pence. Anything to make something for the fund.'

'All right.' Tony returned to the Americans. Mrs Kaliski was still rhapsodising over the 'post-impressionist quality'

245

of the pictures, and her husband was listening good-humouredly. 'We think – er – f-f-f –' he stammered.

Mr Kaliski cut him short. 'Very reasonable – I'm going to close on that before you change your mind!'

The boys sighed with relief. At least they wouldn't be empty-handed when it came to counting the receipts. Fifty pence a picture wasn't a fortune, but it was better than nothing.

Mr Kaliski drew a note from his wallet, flicked it between finger and thumb, and handed it to Tony.

'I'm afraid we haven't any change,' said Tony. 'I suppose you haven't got the right money?'

'But this is the right money, isn't it? Didn't you say five pounds? I don't mind telling you we've got a bargain – it'd be worth more than five pounds to see my wife's friends' faces when they see them hanging up in our parlour!'

'It sure will,' his wife agreed with a giggle.

Tony's hand was trembling so much that he could hardly hold the five-pound note. He felt the colour leave his face with a rush, and he wanted to sit down quickly before his legs gave way. He tried to speak, but only a faint mew came out. He staggered rather than walked over to the railings, took down the five paintings, and handed them over in a daze.

Mrs Kaliski hugged them to her. 'What a day this has been,' she said. 'First we meet a real live descendant of Robin Hood and now these – these undiscovered geniuses! I'll take these along to the car, Jed, in case it rains again. I wouldn't want them spoilt by the rain...'

Mr Kaliski shook both boys by the hand with great force and said goodbye. 'It's been a great pleasure meet-

246

ing you,' he said, 'and you've given my wife a good deal of pleasure. If you'll just stand by your exhibition for a moment I'll take a picture of you that we'll hang up next to the paintings.'

The churning in Tony's inside began to settle and he managed a sickly grin at the camera. Then Mr Kaliski followed his wife, and the boys saw them go towards a gleaming Cadillac which was parked on the roadside beyond the Vicarage.

'Whew!' Tony whistled when the Americans were out of earshot.

And Stephen could only nod weakly in agreement.

The Kaliskis walked in silence until they were out of the boys' hearing. Mr Kaliski waved goodbye again, turned back to his wife and said with a chuckle, 'Now, let's get one thing straight, honey. You weren't on the level, were you?'

'Why, Jed,' said Mrs Kaliski, 'whatever do you mean?'

'All that talk about Turner, superb sense of design, undiscovered geniuses, and so on...'

'What about you with your 'bargain at five pounds' – were you on the level?' Mr Kaliski coughed uncomfortably. 'Well, not exactly. They weren't bad pictures, except that they looked like they'd been given a bath. I guess I just said that because you were so crazy about them.'

Mrs Kaliski laughed. 'Don't look so grieved, Jed. Of course I didn't think they were as good as all that. It was just those kids! Think of all the work they must have put in to make money for their fund. It was the same with the little fella in the forest – all that about Robin Hood!'

Mr Kaliski joined in the laughter. 'He certainly had a nerve! When he grows up he'll make a fortune in public

247

relations – I bet he could sell oil to a Texan! Hey, you didn't think *I* was taken in by that young Peter, did you?'

Mrs Kaliski put her arm through her husband's, and gave him a knowing smile. 'I did just wonder, honey!' She pointed to the stall outside the Vicarage gate. 'Seems to me we haven't finished yet, Jed Kaliski – these Greenwooders are everywhere!'

Tony and Stephen, carrying the remains of their exhibition, arrived at the girls' stall. 'Aren't you packing up?' Tony asked.

'When I've got rid of Georgie Gedge,' said Felicity, who was engaged in an argument with a serious-looking boy with a black fringe. 'He wants to swap his crane for a fire-engine. I've told him we're here to sell, not to barter.'

'You can sell my crane, can't you?' said Georgie. 'And it's worth more than the fire-engine, so you'll be gaining.'

'That's not the point,' said Felicity. 'Besides, who says the crane is worth more?'

'I do,' said Georgie, 'because I know how much they both cost when new. The fire-engine is more use to me for my model village.'

Stephen was getting impatient. 'For goodness sake, let him swap,' he said.

'Please don't interrupt, Stephen,' Felicity said sharply. 'This is a matter of principle.' She heard the boys sigh. 'Oh, very well, but I shouldn't, Georgie. It's not good for business.'

'It is for me,' said Georgie, picking up the fire-engine. 'Thank you very much.'

248

'Well, at least he's got good manners,' said Felicity as Georgie walked away, his fringe flapping on his forehead.

'Where's Pauline?' asked Tony.

'Gone to take the umbrellas back that we fetched when the rain came on. It didn't last long, did it? What happened to you – did the pictures get wet?'

'I'll say they did, thank goodness,' Stephen said, grinning at Tony.

'How did you do?' Felicity asked.

'Quite well,' Stephen said. 'And you?'

'There's some toys left, but none of the cakes and toffee. There would have been but – it's a funny thing – I sold the last lot just before you came. We had several bags left, then a lady and gentleman came up and bought the lot.'

'They did?' said Tony.

'Yes,' Felicity went on. 'They were ever so funny. They kept on laughing and the lady said she remembered her mother telling her about Old English Treacle Toffee and she just must take some back.'

'Fancy that!' said Tony. 'Were they Americans?'

'How did you know?'

Tony produced the five-pound note and waved it in front of Felicity's nose. 'It's a well-known fact that Americans are very partial to treacle toffee, and very good judges of paintings too!'

Felicity gazed at the note with awe. 'Tony!' she said, her voice an octave higher than usual. 'Where did you get *that*?'

Before he could answer, familiar voices hailed them from the crossroads. Peter and Sam were hurrying towards them.

'Good, here are the others,' said Stephen. 'Now we can get everything cleared away and then have the grand counting.'

Felicity clasped her hands. 'Oh, I wonder how *much*,' she said.

Five tired Greenwooders were slumped in various ungainly attitudes around the attic playroom. Only Sam was upright. They had agreed that the counting would be done quicker if it were left to one person, and Sam had been elected because he was the least likely to make mistakes. He sat at the table by the window counting the combined takings, and the only sounds in the room were the chink of coins and Sam's mutterings.

At last he scribbled some figures on a piece of paper and drew two lines underneath them with a flourish. 'I've finished,' he announced. The children were immediately awake and alert. 'How much?' they asked, almost in unison.

'The total,' said Sam, 'is –'

'Yes?' Felicity bounded to her feet eagerly.

'– is,' Sam repeated, 'nine pounds, thirty pence, and one coin like a five pence but with foreign writing on it.'

'Over nine pounds,' said Tony. 'Not bad, is it, for an afternoon's work?'

They agreed that it certainly was not bad. 'I didn't think we'd get anything like that,' said Felicity. 'It's marvellous! Congratulations to all of us!'

'It's been well worth it,' said Stephen with quiet satisfaction.

Peter, who had been reading a stencilled sheet of

foolscap, said, very loudly, 'Hooray!' He waved the paper at them. 'That means we can give nine cups of milk to nine children in Angola for a week, plus a hot meal a day for a fortnight to an Arab child in Jordan.'

'Let's have a look at that,' said Felicity. They crowded round Peter and looked over his shoulder at the list of the things that contributions to Oxfam could provide, and were busy discussing some of the things their takings might be used for when a knock at the door announced that the Vicar had come to see them.

'All back safe and sound, I see, and no doubt rolling in money!' When he heard what the amount was he whistled. 'You must have very persuasive ways,' he said. 'I can see that I shall have to enlist your aid for the Organ Fund! Let me see how much I have in my pocket...' He took out a handful of change and counted seventy pence. 'There you are,' he said, handing the money to Sam, 'now you have the nice round sum of ten pounds.' He cut short their thanks. 'What I really came up for is to deliver a message to Peter and Pauline. I mustn't stay long – we are having what is known as a social tea downstairs. I have just had a telephone message to say that your Uncle Gordon is due to arrive tonight, so will you please not be late home.'

The thought of being late to welcome Uncle Gordon was unthinkable to the twins. They considered him the most wonderful person in the world after their parents.

'Three million cheers!' said Peter, his eyes shining with delight. 'Wait till we tell him about the adventures with the dinghy, Tony. He won't half laugh...'

When the Vicar had gone Tony announced, 'Ten pounds now. That means we can pay for ten thousand multi-vitamin tablets. I wish we had eight pounds more, then we could send a water buffalo to a Chinese refugee family in Burma.'

'We have!' Felicity said excitedly. 'Pauline, I've just remembered – Miss Pope-Cunningham!'

'You're not going to send her to Burma, are you?' said Stephen.

'I don't suppose she'd go,' said Felicity. 'But she told us that she'd double everything we made, didn't she, Pauline?'

Pauline nodded solemnly. 'Yes, those were her very words'

'That's brilliant,' said Tony. 'Think of it – twenty pounds!'

'There's nothing on the list for twenty pounds,' said Peter.

'Well, there's the water buffalo and milk for Angola as well. I wonder if you can say which you prefer.'

'I doubt it,' said Sam, 'but it doesn't really matter as long as the money does good to somebody somewhere.'

'When do we get Miss Pope-Cunningham's money?' Tony asked.

'I don't know,' said Felicity. 'She's downstairs at the social tea, but we can't very well butt in there, can we?'

They agreed that the best thing would be to catch her as she left the Vicarage, or approach her after morning service the next day. In the meantime, they decided, they would relax on the Vicarage lawn and make plans for the following week. They clattered downstairs, chattering noisily. Before they reached the front door Mrs Brooks appeared from the sitting-room.

'Children – before you go,' she called, 'will you come in here a minute?'

Tony groaned inwardly and looked agonised. There was nothing he disliked more than being plunged into adult social activities, held, he considered, far too frequently in the Vicarage.

'Tony,' said his mother, 'don't look so sour. Miss Pope-Cunningham wants to see Felicity, and there is someone else here who is anxious to meet you all.'

They trooped into the room. A dozen or so people were sitting about, holding tea cups and balancing small plates on their knees. There was Miss Pope-Cunningham, of course; the choirmaster, Miss Plumb, Lady Blogg, and other well-known faces from the congregation.

'Ah, Felicity,' said Miss Pope-Cunningham, 'I have been telling everyone about your Famine Fund. We all think you are very clever, and now I can reveal my promise to double your takings. How much do I owe you?'

'Sam is the treasurer,' Felicity said, pushing him forward. 'Go on,' she whispered, 'announce the figure.'

'We took exactly ten pounds,' said Sam. There were surprised gasps from the guests, and a little burst of applause. The Greenwooders smiled proudly. Then they became aware of Miss Pope-Cunningham's face, open-mouthed and bewildered.

'Ten p –' she said, and stopped.

'– ounds,' Peter finished the word for her.

'– ounds?' she repeated. 'From treacle toffee and cakes?'

'Not only from that,' said Pauline. 'From picture selling and forest guiding too.'

253

'Sam is the treasurer.'

Miss Pope-Cunningham's cheeks wobbled. She seemed at a loss for words. Her tongue popped in and out of her mouth several times, and when at last she spoke the words sounded as though they had been in a mincing-machine. 'F – forest selling and – and picture guiding ... I see ... I didn't realise ... that is to say, I thought it was only the treacle toffee double I promised to stall ... good gracious me, I'm all mixed up!' She took a minute lace handkerchief from her handbag and dabbed at her forehead. 'I mean, it hadn't occurred to me that I had

undertaken to double the *grand total* ... how embarrassing!' She looked at the Greenwooders' expectant
faces and then at the other people in the room. They
seemed to be waiting for her to continue with bated
breaths.

Miss Pope-Cunningham came to a decision. She drew
a deep breath. 'No!' she said with a force that made
Pauline jump. 'A promise is a promise. Ten pounds it
shall be. Well – well done, children.'

The Vicar thought it was time to intervene. 'My dear
Miss Pope-Cunningham, I feel sure the children would not
expect you to contribute such a large sum...'

Tony took the hint and shook his head. Reluctantly the
others shook theirs too.

'It was a clear misunderstanding,' the Vicar went on,
'and I'm sure they all appreciate that.' He turned away
as though to indicate that the matter was settled, but
another blast from Miss Pope-Cunningham made all eyes
turn to her again.

'No!' she said. 'No and no again! This will teach you
to be more precise in future, Angela, my girl,' she
reproached herself theatrically. 'It was my own fault if my
offer was misunderstood. I absolutely insist on keeping my
word. It is the least I can do after their valiant efforts. I
will write out a cheque here and now.' She delved into
her handbag again, took out a cheque book and pen and
began to write. There was dead silence as she did so.
Then she handed the cheque to Sam, and went pink with
pleasure at the surprised and grateful applause that
greeted her action.

'Before you go,' said the Vicar when Miss Pope-
Cunningham had retired to her chair, still blushing, 'there

is someone I would like you all to meet.' He gestured towards a man sitting in a low chair by the fireplace who had, up to that moment, been partially hidden by the Vicar. 'Mr Ridge is the new headmaster of the village school. He is taking over at the beginning of next term. This will be of special interest to you, Peter and Pauline.' He turned to Mr Ridge. 'The Christy twins – two of your future pupils...'

Peter felt the blood drain from his face. He did not know where to look or what to say. It couldn't be – but it was – without any doubt – the grey man... Hawk Collingwood.

Pauline smiled at Mr Ridge demurely. He looks very nice, she thought – a bit severe but quite understanding. Peter thought of the many deadly school secrets he had given away and of all the tall stories he had told. His throat was tight and his eyes glazed over. He heard dimly the voice of Mr Ridge cutting through the tingling in his ears.

'I am delighted to meet you all. But I think I've already met this young man –' His eyes seemed to bore into Peter, isolated in the semi-circle of Greenwooders. 'He showed me round the forest most efficiently, and I learned quite a lot about the school. I am looking forward very much to next term.' He moved a step towards Peter with an expression on his face that Peter had seen on Hawk Collingwood's every time he unmasked a villain. 'We have a lot to teach each other, I'm sure, so I mustn't forget your name. Peter – Christy, is it? Or Hood?' He extended a hand for Peter to shake.

Peter clapped one hand to his mouth and looked blindly at his fellow Greenwooders for support. If only he

256

were thousands of miles away – in Angola, perhaps, with the water buffalo! Then he took the outstretched hand limply.

'Gosh!' he croaked.